"Do you have to do this?" Rolf asked

"Do what?" Julie asked in return.

"Leave. How can I convince you that you belong in this house, with my children? With me?"

"Don't you see, Rolf? This would never work."

"Why?"

"There are too many obstacles in the way."

"Nothing we can't overcome."

"Our age difference," she persisted.

"It's not that much."

"You have children who are old enough to be my kid brothers and sister," she pointed out. "They deserve a mother, not a baby-sitter."

"They respect you for the mature adult you are, Julie. They look up to you. They need you."

"You're set in your ways," she persisted. "I'm still finding mine."

He shut his eyes. "I had hoped we might find a way together. I guess I've made a mistake." He turned his broad back on her.

The gesture made her feel small. Biting her lip, she went to the door, turned the knob and walked out.

Dear Reader,

Those of us who've been out of school for a while know
that tests don't end on graduation day. Life is full of pop
quizzes and final exams. At least, we hope they're final—
like finding our one, true love. The characters in this story
are faced with a new battery of multiple-choice tests. How
they answer them will determine whether they find
happiness.

This is the fourth book in the continuing saga of
THE FIRST FAMILY OF TEXAS. Julie is the youngest
daughter of Adam First, former owner of one of the
biggest spreads in the Lone Star State. She's just received
her master's degree in education. Now come the real
challenges—a corrupt school administration and a man
almost a dozen years her senior, who also happens to
be the divorced father of four. Oh, yes. Make no mistake.
This is definitely a test. Pass or fail. Her happiness
depends on it.

Most of our public schools are quality places of learning,
staffed by dedicated people. The Coyote Springs
Independent School District is a figment of my imagination.
As are the people I've created. I've also taken a liberty or
two with the Texas educational system. That's one of the
wonderful things about writing. I can make things up.

I enjoy hearing from readers. You can write me at
Box 4062. San Angelo, TX 769092, or through my Web sites
at www.superauthors.com or www.outreachrwa.com.

K.N. *Casper*

A Mother to His Children
K.N. Casper

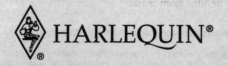

HARLEQUIN®

TORONTO • NEW YORK • LONDON
AMSTERDAM • PARIS • SYDNEY • HAMBURG
STOCKHOLM • ATHENS • TOKYO • MILAN • MADRID
PRAGUE • WARSAW • BUDAPEST • AUCKLAND

ISBN 0-373-71041-0

A MOTHER TO HIS CHILDREN

Copyright © 2002 by K. Casper.

My thanks to Jan Daugherty and Marcia Lindsay.
For their invaluable insights.
And to Mary, who reads faster than a speeding bullet
And always comes through.

PROLOGUE

"No." Julie's raised voice trembled because her heart was pounding. "I won't marry you."

Jerome Benton's dark-brown eyes narrowed as he rolled off the side of the bed and stood naked in front of her, tall, self-possessed and Greek-god handsome. The firm muscles he cultivated at the local health club were well-defined in the slanting light from the bedside lamp. He stared down at her, his cheeks hollow.

"Why?" He raised one brow. His voice was mild, as if he were merely confused, but she knew him well enough to recognize seething anger. Apparently the possibility that she'd reject his proposal had never crossed his mind.

"Because my function in life isn't to bear *your* children, to keep *your* house and spend my days trying to figure out how to make *you* happy."

She and Jerry had been dating for almost a year. They seemed so compatible—physically, emotionally and spiritually. Why hadn't she seen they were so far apart on the things that really mattered, like life roles? Had she been blinded by his good looks? His charm? His intelligence? Probably. Or maybe she'd been in love with a desire to have her own family. But a family at any cost wasn't what she wanted.

He'd just offered her a modest but tastefully elegant diamond engagement ring. She'd been ready to accept his proposal, until he proudly informed her—no, boasted—that she could recall all those resumés she'd just sent out because he didn't believe in a wife working outside the home. Not when she didn't have to, he explained, and Julie First definitely didn't need to work for a living. Besides, he bragged, she wouldn't have time. There'd be plenty to keep her busy giving dinner parties and attending social functions to enhance his career as a rising bank executive. Until the children came along, of course. Taking care of them would then be her sole concern.

Her mouth had literally dropped open. She'd been pleased by his espousal of traditional family values. It had never occurred to her that they harked back to a caveman mentality. Well, Julie First would work if she wanted. She'd welcome being pregnant, too, but not barefoot. She wouldn't be a kept woman, a housekeeper or a governess for *his* progeny…or a stepping-stone for her master's ambitions. What a fool she'd been to think this "pretty boy" cared about her instead of himself.

"When I marry—" she climbed off the bed and slipped into the silk dressing gown she'd earlier tossed on the steamer trunk at its foot "—it'll be a partnership, fifty-fifty. My husband will respect me as an independent person, not a servant."

After closing his eyes and taking a fortifying breath, Jerome circled the four-poster and stretched out his arms to her. "I respect you as a woman, Julie," he declared with quiet dignity. "A beautiful, talented, caring woman."

The patronizing son of a—

She dodged his embrace, then stood with her back

to the shaded window, facing him. "My station in life is not to be subordinate to you or any man."

Shaking his head, he picked up his pale-blue bikini briefs, held them in front of him and gazed at her with half-closed eyes. "Don't be melodramatic."

His arrogant condescension riled her even more than his outlandishly archaic attitude about *her* place in *his* home. She crossed her arms over her chest and held up her chin, impatient now for him to get out of her bedroom and out of her life.

"I don't think we have anything more to say to each other, Jerry. It's over between us. Time for you to leave."

He studied her a moment, and she could see conflicting emotions warring in his gaze. Erupt or concede? Naked or not, dignity won out. Adroitly balancing himself on one foot, he put on his underwear and donned the perfectly creased khaki trousers he'd carefully draped over the back of a chair.

"I worked hard to earn my master's degree in education," she felt compelled to remind him. Her pulse had calmed a little, but the tension in her neck hadn't abated. "I don't see why all my training should go to waste."

Snorting, he interrupted buttoning the boldly striped gray-and-maroon button-down shirt to wave her comment away. "There aren't many education jobs here in Coyote Springs, sweetheart, unless you want to be a first-grade teacher and wipe the snotty noses of a bunch of kids for a living."

She'd prepared herself for elementary education because she believed strongly it was where character was formed and basic ideas implanted. It galled her when she discovered during her teaching internship that, as much as she loved education intellectually, she found the day-to-day repetition tedious and unsatisfying. Jerry knew that.

He sat now in the upholstered chair to put on his navy-blue socks and shiny brown loafers. "Funny," he noted without looking up, "you have no problem baby-sitting other people's brats, but the idea of staying home with your own children is somehow demeaning."

Anger flared, hot and intense. She should have known he'd twist what she said. To think she used to admire his ability to use words.

"There's nothing demeaning about wiping sniveling noses," she countered lightly, "regardless of who those noses belong to. Someone had to wipe yours, after all." His eyes darkened from milk chocolate to bittersweet, giving her a small measure of satisfaction.

"What will you do now?" His tone suggested her life was doomed without him.

"Don't you worry about me, Jerry. I'll find a job in education—and a good one."

She strolled to the bed, leaned over and retrieved the velvet ring case that still lay on the rumpled sheets. The diamond winked at her. Holding it out to him, she murmured, "Goodbye, Jerry."

He tightened his jaw and scowled at her, as if she were a foolish little girl, and accepted the box. Closing it with a crisp snap, he slipped it into his pants pocket and sauntered to the door. "Good luck on your job search."

I'll need it, she thought, as she heard her apartment door close behind him.

CHAPTER ONE

"TIME FOR THE inevitable paperwork." Alyson Shaddick escorted Julie down a carpeted hallway of the brightly lit Coyote Springs Independent School District administration building. "We're so glad to have you join us, Julie," the woman said with a kind of professional enthusiasm that might or might not have been sincere. In her late thirties, she wore a pink straight skirt that topped her knees, emphasizing her long legs and slender hips. Julie felt underdressed in her simple bleached-sand blouse and spruce-colored tailored pants.

"This is sort of a dream come true," she admitted.

And a godsend. A full-time teaching position had been open in one of the high schools, but she knew of the pitfalls there—student distractions like the opposite sex and extracurricular activities. Then she'd learned of an opening for a curriculum writer and jumped at it. This was exactly the kind of challenge she was seeking.

"It's going to be different," she mused, "being on the other side of the blackboard, so to speak."

Alyson emitted a pleasant chuckle. "I'm sure it is, but you'll find the job very rewarding. I don't think I have to tell you how important it is."

While each school district in Texas had independent authority to raise funds through local taxation, it was the state that established uniform academic requirements. These standards were evaluated each year through the Texas Assessment of Academic Skills, the TAAS test. Meeting the eighty-percent passing grade meant prestige and rewards. Marginal performance provoked state inspections and increased interference. Failure would prompt complete takeover of the district by the Texas Education Agency from the local school board.

Alyson led Julie past small offices on either side of the hallway. Through open doors, Julie glimpsed personalized work spaces with pictures, awards, mementos and state-of-the-art computer terminals. The carpets smelled new and were quite thick. Easy on the feet. They entered a large room at the end of the corridor opposite the school superintendent's office.

"This shouldn't take long." Alyson went to the long counter just inside the doorway.

"Everything's all ready," an older woman in a dowdy brown dress handed a manila folder to the administrator.

"Thank you, Nancy." Alyson motioned Julie to a small writing table in a corner. Her pearly-pink fingernails riffled through the forms approvingly before she passed them over to Julie. "Everything seems to be in order. You'll like our medical plan. It's one of the most comprehensive in the state." She smiled with satisfaction. Health coverage was a major concern in any employment contract. "Sign on the lines marked by the Xs," Alyson prompted.

The paperwork was standard. A tax withholding form. A locator card, giving her address and tele-

phone number and the person to call in case of an
emergency.

Julie sensed a fluttering of impatience on Alyson's
part as she perused the small print on forms and doc-
uments, but her father had taught her to read everything she signed. A personal history questionnaire
was prefaced with a stern warning that her police records would be checked for any criminal offenses,
even traffic tickets, and that if she was not completely
truthful, her employment could be immediately terminated. She would rather forget the citation she'd
received for speeding six years ago, but she marked
it down and acknowledged receipt in writing of her
official job description, then signed up for the coveted
health insurance. She came to the form for her
bumper sticker and reserved parking space, filled in
her license plate number but had to go back down to
her car to retrieve her proof of insurance so they could
photocopy it for the files.

Pleased with herself, she came to the last piece of
paper, the only document that had to be witnessed.
She read it over carefully:

> I have been advised that direct or indirect unau-
> thorized disclosure of school district information
> can cause irreparable damage to the administra-
> tion's ability to perform its duties. I pledge that
> I will never divulge such information, in any
> form or manner, to anyone who is not specifi-
> cally authorized to receive it. I understand that a
> violation of this agreement may result in termi-
> nation of my employment. I make this agreement
> without any mental reservation or purpose of
> evasion.

Being told to shut up and do as she was told had never worked with Julie. Her father had learned a long time ago that if he wanted compliance with rules he had to explain why, even justify them. And Adam, God bless him, had done so.

Then there was the matter of civil rights.

She pursed her lips. "This sounds like a gag order."

Alyson began gathering the other papers into the folder. "It's quite standard." She quirked her mouth, but the smile didn't reach her eyes.

"I've never heard of anything like this," Julie commented. "Do teachers sign these, too?"

"It applies to everyone in the school district," Alyson assured her.

Julie didn't want to sound argumentative to the woman who was about to become her boss, but she had to ask the obvious question. "Why?"

The paper-straightening gesture intensified. "It's important that school matters stay in school, Julie. We have regular board meetings that are public, in which policies can be openly discussed. Details of implementation, however, are often very confusing to people who aren't familiar with how schools are run on a daily basis. We don't want to be impeded by Monday-morning quarterbacks who think they know better than the experts how to handle routine matters."

"The public does have a right to know," Julie pointed out.

"No one's trying to hide anything." Alyson's tone betrayed the first signs of real annoyance, then she seemed to catch herself. "But I understand your concern." She combed her fingers thoughtfully through her shiny blond hair. "A couple of years ago, we changed our lunch period for administrative personnel from an hour to forty-five minutes. One of our employees didn't like it and made a big stink in a letter to the editor. In actuality, the change was to accommodate employees who use public transportation. By moving up the end of the workday fifteen minutes, they were able to get an earlier bus home and save nearly an hour a day. It took us weeks to sort things out. We don't need public debate on such petty complaints, Julie. It wastes a lot of time and energy and distracts us from our real work, which is educating children.''

Julie couldn't argue with that.

Alyson folded her hands calmly on the edge of the table. ''We've had a few problems with former employees, who frankly were troublemakers. They questioned everything. How often we paint the walls. The color of the carpet. You name it. We have people who're paid to make those decisions. You wouldn't want to be challenged on every test question you write.''

Again Julie had to agree.

''We need team players, Julie. I hope you're going to be one.''

''Of course I am. But wouldn't issuing a policy letter be adequate?''

Alyson shook her head, making the soft curls of her blond hair jiggle. ''We tried that, but our lawyer said it was unenforceable. He insisted we needed something that went beyond employees knowing and understanding the policy. They have to agree to abide by it.''

''Do I have to sign this?'' Julie still didn't like it.

''You do if you want the job,'' Alyson replied firmly. ''It was approved unanimously by the school

board last year.'' She eyed her new subordinate
sternly. ''It's a condition of employment.''

Julie reread the paper, still not picking up the pen
a few inches away.

''I hope you're not going to make an issue of this,''
Alyson said with concern. ''I think you'll be a valuable asset to our system. Everyone in the school district has signed it. It hasn't been a problem for them.''

Julie caught the glance of the woman Alyson had
called Nancy, who was standing on the other side of
the counter, but Julie couldn't read her expression
well enough to determine if the older woman was
supporting her challenge or amused by her nit-
picking.

Still, Julie wasn't completely comfortable with
what seemed to her an abridgement of her civil right
to free speech. Then Jerry's sneering remarks blos-
somed in her mind. Damn it, she wanted this job.
Taking up the pen, she scribbled her name on the line.

''Good.'' Alyson collected the paper with obvious
relief and signed the witness block. Nancy averted her
eyes and busied herself with other tasks. ''Now, let's
go see your new office.''

The room on the first floor turned out to be rather
small and cramped, with a single window overlooking
the parking lot. The furniture wasn't very new, but
that was all right. With time, she'd earn a better location with nicer accommodations.

The loyalty statement was relegated to the back of
her mind.

ROLF MURDOCK SLAMMED down the phone harder
than he'd intended, not that he wasn't angry, but because he tried hard not to let emotions intrude on the

job. His assistant, Jake Tarns, wouldn't be able to make it this afternoon. His mother was ailing, and he'd had to take her to the hospital emergency room. Mrs. Tarns was a hypochondriac, but she also had enough genuine medical problems to warrant Jake's concern. Given a choice between family and job, Rolf couldn't argue with Jake's decision.

Unfortunately, it meant Rolf would have to work late again, the third day in a row. The other times hadn't been Jake's fault, either, but it added to Rolf's already heavy workload as the owner and operator of the Coyote Lumberyard and Builders Supply Company.

He was already putting in more hours than he wanted to. He ought to hire additional help. Another employee, though, would seriously cut into already narrow profits. Coyote Springs was growing and diversifying. Adding new products and services would eventually pay big dividends. In the meantime, it meant lean earnings and long workdays.

Now came the hard part. He picked up the phone and poked out a number he knew too well. Several rings went by before someone answered.

"Hello." The female voice was out of breath.

"Bryn, it's Rolf."

"Hi, guy." She had a familiar lilt in her voice. "What's up?"

"I'm afraid I'll be late again this evening. I'm awfully sorry. Is it going to be a problem for you?"

"Nah." She sounded too chipper. On the other hand, he should feel grateful that she was so accommodating. She'd moved in next door about four years ago after her husband's sudden death of complications following what should have been a simple appendectomy. Rolf hadn't really gotten to know her, though, until two years ago after Sheryl left.

He'd thought he knew exactly what he wanted: wife, children, business, community involvement. They all added up to what he defined as success. He'd had it all, and somehow it hadn't been enough. Or maybe he just hadn't loved well enough. His wife had left him, not just for another guy, but for a career, as well. That was really hitting below the belt.

He still had a business and the children, and he was involved in the community. As satisfying as those things were, something vital was missing. A woman in his life. A helpmate, a partner, a wife.

But he was too committed to change directions now. The rational part of him knew that even if he remarried, he might not get his dreams—he hadn't with Sheryl. But he could survive.

No use kidding himself. As a divorced father of four, he wasn't likely to attract the kind of woman who would round all the sharp edges. Maybe he should settle for less, find someone who would merely alleviate the pressure, gratify his animal needs.

"We're outside digging rocks from one of the flower beds so I can put in a fall garden," Bryn explained. "I planned to throw a couple of hot dogs on the grill for Daniella and me. I'll just add a few more."

"I owe you a mountain of hot dogs already," he reminded her. She and her daughter seemed to live on hot dogs and pizza.

"Hamburgers, too, but you can make up for it another time."

Bryn hadn't exactly hidden her willingness to become more involved, and she was an attractive brunette with big brown eyes and generous curves. But she was the clinging type. She wouldn't be satisfied with a physical relationship. She'd want commitment, devotion…adoration. Was that the price he'd have to pay?

"I really appreciate this, Bryn. I should be home around seven-thirty."

"No problem. Oh, wait a minute, Leah wants to talk to you."

The phone made shuffling noises and his twelve-year-old daughter came on the line. "Are you going to be late again, Daddy?" She ended the question with a dramatic sigh of long-suffering impatience.

"Afraid so, sweetheart. Jake's mother's in the hospital and he has to stay—"

"Again? She's always in the hospital."

Rolf knew his daughter wasn't nearly as insensitive as she sounded, but she was going through a difficult stage. It was hard for an adolescent to remember she wasn't the center of the universe. "I don't think she likes being sick any more than you do when you come down with the flu or strep throat."

"Yeah, I know," the girl muttered contritely. "But…"

Anew, he resented Sheryl's decision. He could forgive her for leaving him, even if he couldn't accept her being unfaithful to him. But he couldn't excuse her abandoning their children. Even more than the boys right now, Leah needed a positive female influence in her life, a woman who could understand the changes she was experiencing, who could guide and encourage her. Rolf did his best, but he wasn't a substitute for a mother's affection.

"I'll try to make it up to you and the others," he told his daughter.

"How?" The question was a challenge as much as a genuine inquiry.

Think quick, he told himself. "How about Saturday afternoon we go fishing out to the lake. If we catch anything, we can have a fry-up. If not, we'll go to Catfish Heaven for all you can eat."

"Jeff doesn't like catfish." Her nine-year-old brother was remarkably fussy, while his twin, Foster, consumed everything in sight. Yet, despite their totally different tastes and appetites, they were exactly the same size and weight.

"Maybe we can convince him he's Foster and that he loves catfish," Rolf suggested.

"Not likely." Her chuckle lightened the mood. "We could hold him down and force-feed him."

"Only if you clean up the mess," Rolf told her.

"Hmm. Maybe it's not such a good idea after all. So we're going to the lake this Saturday. You promise?" But she didn't wait for his reply, possibly because she knew he wouldn't promise what he wasn't absolutely certain he could deliver. "Okay, I'll tell the others."

He hung up a minute later, his conscience eased by the thought of time spent with his kids. Fishing was one of their favorite pastimes. Even Jeff, who refused to eat fish, enjoyed catching them. Rolf felt a subtle pang of guilt, too. Bryn hated fishing, so did her daughter, Daniella, who tended to be a whiner. He could invite them with full confidence they'd turn him down.

Rolf closed the lumberyard on Wednesday evenings at six. It was church night, so many hobbyists put their pet projects on hold for the evening. Years ago fix-it chores and minor construction had been almost exclusively a male domain. These days at least as many women wielded hammers and power tools.

At a quarter to six a young lady strolled in the door. From the way she surveyed the place, Rolf deduced this was her first visit. He definitely hadn't seen her before. Medium height, small-boned with fine features, she had a creamy complexion and honey-blond hair.

"May I help you?"

She turned to face him, an air of confidence behind an inquisitive expression—a very alluring combination. "I want to put up shelves in my bedroom."

Rolf had a sudden mental image of her soft voice close to his ear on a pillow. Damn. True, he hadn't had a female in his bed since Sheryl left, but still, it wasn't like him to react this strongly to a woman fifteen seconds after meeting her.

"Do you want them to be freestanding or attached to the wall?" She had the most beautiful blue eyes Rolf had ever seen. It was hard to keep from staring.

"Attached to the wall…and adjustable."

"Come this way." With a tilt of his head, he half turned and invited her to follow. "I'll show you what we have in stock."

He was supposed to lead her but walked beside her, instead, catching a whiff of her cologne.

"What color is the wall you want to hang the shelves on?" he asked, in an attempt to keep his mind off the way her silky lavender blouse curved over her breasts. She wasn't buxom, but she was definitely a female.

Her glance acknowledged awareness that he'd been

looking—and approving. She scanned the row of assorted shelves and brackets. "Forest green."

"Pretty dark," he noted. "You'll probably want something light. What color is the woodwork?"

"White."

He smiled and watched her eyes smile back. "Very dramatic," he noted, unsure himself if he was referring now to the color scheme of her walls and woodwork or how the dark-blue outer circle of her irises emphasized the warmth within them.

"I thought maybe a natural wood."

Natural. Was it natural for a man to want to be swallowed up by a woman's eyes? "Another option worth exploring," he agreed. "Depending on the accessories in your room, you might consider a dark walnut, but a blond—" like your hair, he almost blurted "—oak is also an option."

She fingered the pierced aluminum runners. "How strong are these brackets?"

"I don't recommend them for the entire *Encyclopaedia Britannica,* but they'll hold most other books."

"That's what they'll be used for, books," she commented.

"Do you enjoy reading in bed?" Where the devil had that question come from? To hide his embarrassment, he started to rearrange hardware that had been hung on the wrong hooks. In doing so, unfortunately, he missed whatever expression had crossed her face.

"In bed, at the dinner table," she responded with a chuckle. "In the bathtub."

She was laughing at him. She must be. She had to know he was going crazy trying not to stare. And now she was taunting him with images of her naked body

hidden under a billowy cloud of warm bubbly bath-
water.

Their eyes collided. "How many shelves do you
want and over how long an expanse?"

"Floor to ceiling, but I'm not sure how wide." She
shot out her arms to estimate the width and slammed
her hand into a tower of spray paint cans he'd been
stacking for display. They went tumbling with a clatter.

"Oh, I'm sorry," she jabbered. "I…I should have
watched what I was doing."

"Are you all right?" He seemed more worried
about her than the cans rolling noisily across the aisle.

She gazed at the chaos. "I'm fine, but…" This
could have been avoided if she hadn't been checking
out how long the lashes were above his luscious hazel
eyes. Realization that she'd been flirting brought heat
to her face.

"No harm done." That she was blushing both
amused and further distracted him. "I don't know
what I was thinking when I stacked them here. Much
too crowded."

He squatted down and started rebuilding the pyramid in exactly the same spot, his movements jerky,
his breath catching in his throat when he realized his
face was mere inches from her perfectly shaped legs.

She crouched beside him and began uprighting
fallen cans. "My name's Julie First, by the way."

"Rolf Murdock." Sweat broke out on his forehead
as he took her extended small, soft hand in his. Not
a good idea when he was balanced on the balls of his
feet. He almost tumbled like his paint cans.

"Aren't you on the school board?" She put the
plastic cap on one of the cans.

"Its newest member," he agreed.

She had an impulse to brush her hand along the curly hairs of his forearm. "There's a matter I'd like to talk to you about when you have a few minutes."

"Anytime." Anyplace, he wanted to add. "If I'm not here, you can find me at home. I live on Coyote Avenue. One-nineteen."

They worked in silence for the next few minutes, rebuilding the display. Their movements assumed an easy coordination, like two people who'd grown up playing together.

For the last piece of the pyramid, he pulled over a ladder and was about to climb it, when she clasped his forearm. Her touch was like warm liquid rushing through him.

"Let me," she requested. "I knocked it down. It's only fair I put it back up."

"Be careful," he said, and held her hand as she mounted the first step. "I don't want you to get hurt."

His breathing stalled and his blood raced as she ascended the rungs, her smooth, perfectly toned legs directly in front of him. She reached back for the last spray can. He handed it to her and watched as she stretched forward and balanced the shiny red cylinder in place.

In the background, one of Rolf's people was pulling down the overhead doors to the fenced-in stacks of lumber behind the building. All but one cash register in front had been closed out.

She worked her way down the wooden steps and glanced at the big clock on the wall over the main entrance. "What time do you close?"

"At six on weeknights."

It was quarter past. "I've delayed you. I'm really sorry. About the mess and everything."

"No harm done." *Except to my libido.*

"I'll pay for those two cans that got so badly dented.

"Not necessary. I'll just write them off as damaged goods. Thanks for your help restacking them."

She grinned. "My pleasure."

Julie left the lumberyard with its owner very much on her mind. Rolf Murdock was a nice man. She ran her tongue across her teeth. Well, nice was a bit of an understatement. He was a cross between Crocodile Dundee and Tim the tool man. Snug jeans and a rugged starched khaki shirt. Cute buns and a smile that looked sincere and dangerous—with just a touch of little-boy mischief. A couple of inches taller than Jerry, he had the kind of taut-muscled build that made her think of hard work in the bright sun rather than calculated workouts in an air-conditioned health club. She could almost feel the sun kissing his skin. And the smell of him—musk and piney woods—was oddly intoxicating.

A bit old for her, maybe. She didn't usually pay much attention to men ten or more years her senior. But Rolf Murdock was not an ordinary thirty-something-year-old.

A smile swept across her face at the recollection of how his neck had darkened when she mentioned reading in the bathtub. It didn't take much imagination to figure out what was on his mind. Well, turnaround was fair play. She could fantasize about him in the shower.

The man was definitely fantasy material. Unsettling, too. Enough for her to have checked out his left hand. No ring, not that that meant anything. A lot of married men didn't wear wedding bands. And she'd detected a kind of shyness in his glances, as if he were doing something wrong. Maybe he was married and uncomfortable with what he was thinking.

She pulled into the parking space at her apartment complex. What would Rolf Murdock look like on a horse? Tall, straight, broad-shouldered, his long legs wishboning a saddle. Oh, yes, definitely an image worth contemplating. One that would stay with her all evening and late into the night.

"HOW HAS YOUR FIRST WEEK on the job been so far?" Julie's sister-in-law, Clare, asked over the phone.

"Hectic." Julie kicked off her shoes and started unbuttoning her floral-print empire-waist dress. Alyson had quietly informed her on Monday that the women working in administration were expected to wear dresses, rather than slacks or pantsuits. The superintendent felt it conveyed a more professional image. Julie didn't agree, but she decided to comply, at least until her probationary period was over.

"Are you coming out here tomorrow night?" Clare asked. This was Thursday.

"Probably not until Saturday. Now that I'm a working woman I don't have much time during the week to do laundry, wash the truck, grocery-shop."

"Poor baby," Clare moaned without an ounce of sympathy in her voice. Theoretically, she didn't work outside the home, but when home was the Number One Ranch, keeping busy wasn't hard, especially with four kids. "Can you add one more item to your list of must-do things?"

"Absolutely." Julie stepped out of her dress and tossed it into the hamper. "That doesn't mean I'll get it done, of course."

"Seneca's pups are ready to be weaned. Would you pick up a sack of puppy chow at the feed store? Put it on our tab."

"Sure."

"We'll get it when we see you at the Home Place on Sunday."

Sunday dinner at the Home Place, the sixty-thousand-acre ranch that Julie's father, Adam First, had carved out of the Number One two years ago when the bank took it over, was a weekly family ritual. Michael, Clare and their brood would be there, as well as Julie's brother, Gideon, and his new wife, Lupe, and her two children. Julie's elder sister, Kerry, and her husband, Craig, lived in Dallas, but they could make an appearance via his Lear jet with little or no warning.

"We want to hear all about your new job adventures," Clare reminded her.

On Friday afternoon, Julie drove directly from work to the feed store, parked near the loading platform and entered the building. Bill Marcus, the chairman of the school board, was standing at the counter.

She'd met him at various charity events her father had dragged her to, as well as social affairs, ranging from symphony concerts to the rodeo. Less than six feet tall, he was the widest human being she'd ever encountered—a massive frame, immensely broad shoulders, a nearly bald head and thick meaty limbs. He moved with the slow silence and dignity of an elephant.

"Hello, Julie." His gravelly bass voice suited him.

"How's your dad? Fully recovered from his heart attack?"

"He's doing fine, Mr. Marcus, thanks. As active as ever." His hand, the size of a catcher's mitt, swallowed hers when they shook. "He smiles a lot. Claims he cheated the grim reaper."

Marcus gave a rumbling laugh. "Well, I suppose he did. How's your new job? All settled in?"

She chuckled. "Hardly. There's a lot to learn."

"A smart little lady like you? I'm sure you'll do fine."

She didn't particularly like being called "a little lady," but there was no point in making an issue of it. He had no idea the sobriquet was offensive and probably wouldn't have understood if she'd tried to explain it. She almost smirked. Neither would Jerry, and he was half this man's age.

"Thanks." She ordered a fifty-pound sack of puppy chow from the strapping young man behind the counter.

"I need a twenty-pound bag of birdseed," Bill added. "For my wife's feeders," he seemed compelled to explain. "I understand you had a few questions about the loyalty oath," he remarked after the clerk had left to fill their orders.

The comment took her completely by surprise. How would he know about that? Who'd even have mentioned it? And why?

"What's the problem?" His manner was a shade less friendly than a moment earlier. "Why would you have reservations about being loyal to your employer?"

"It's not that at all, Mr. Marcus." She didn't appreciate his putting her on the defensive, either. "I'm a professional, and I expect to be treated like one. I don't understand—''

''Is it asking so much to require employees to work within the system?''

''Not if problems can be resolved within the system. Of course not.''

He leaned against the counter and braced one hand on the edge behind him. ''Let me give you a few words of advice, Julie.'' He spoke very softly, as if it were in confidence. ''Do your job and don't rock the boat. I know being a member of the First family you're used to privilege and deference. But you've entered the workaday world now. If you want to succeed, don't make waves. Everyone else in the school district has accepted that piece of paper. It was gone over with a fine-tooth comb by our legal adviser. So I suggest you either decide to abide by it, or seek other employment. You're not exempt because of your last name.''

If Bill Marcus thought he was dealing with some coddled rich girl, he didn't know her or her father. Being a member of the First family and growing up on the Number One had given her certain advantages, but coddling was definitely not in Adam First's nature, and she was damn glad of it. She'd been living on her own for the past six years, ever since she started college. At twenty-four, she knew how to take care of herself.

Nevertheless, there was nothing to gain by arguing with this man. ''I'll keep that in mind, Mr. Marcus.''

It could have been the ice in her reply and the realization that he'd offended her, or it could have been the sound of the clerk returning with two bags of feed hoisted on his shoulder that caused the old man to break eye contact.

"Here we are, folks," the brawny teenager announced. "Those birds and pups ought to be real happy." He skirted the end of the counter and went outside to load their vehicles.

"Sorry if I came on a little strong," Marcus apologized after the clerk was out of earshot. "I'm afraid you caught me late in the day when I'm not at my best. No offense intended."

"None taken," she lied with a smile. "I'm glad we had a chance to have this talk."

If this oath was so widely accepted, if their attorney had been so thorough in drafting it, why was the head of the school board so het up about it?

By the time she arrived home, her mind had taken another turn. Rolf Murdock hadn't been a member of the school board when the oath had been unanimously approved. She wondered if he even knew about it. Maybe she ought to approach him and see exactly what his reaction was. She smiled to herself. His reaction to the oath, that is.

CHAPTER TWO

ROLF CLOSED THE LUMBERYARD at four o'clock on
Saturday. He'd considered expanding hours to accommodate weekend do-it-yourselfers, but on a two-
month trial run last summer, it hadn't brought in
enough revenue to justify the overtime he had to pay
his limited crew. By five, he was home. The kids
didn't stay with Bryn on Saturdays. She had her own
chores to attend to. Asking her to drag his four kids
around town with her and her daughter was pushing
the limits of neighborliness. Mrs. Tremain was a retired widow living on social security who earned a
few extra dollars minding people's children. She was
straitlaced, didn't have much of a sense of humor and
tended to be overly protective, but she took her job
very seriously. Rolf had absolute confidence they
were safe with her.

"Can we go now, Daddy?" Leah begged. The second child and only girl, she was apt to be pushy.

Her elder brother snorted. "Will you at least give
him a chance to change his clothes?"

At thirteen, Derek was assuming an authoritative
and occasionally condescending tone. At least his
voice had ceased cracking and had settled into a rich
deep baritone. He, too, was passing through a stage
Rolf could only recollect by seeing it reenacted in his
son. Impatience, rebellion, confusion. The juices were

flowing and the boy didn't know how to handle them. Rolf's father had taken an active interest in his life at that age—involving him in sports, pushing him academically to make the National Honor Society, teaching him to stand up for what was right and to respect women. Rolf hoped he was the same kind of positive role model for his sons.

"Thank you, Mrs. Tremain." Rolf escorted her to her car and handed her a fold of bills. "I hope they weren't any trouble."

"They're good children, Mr. Murdock. I wish a few of the others I sit for had their good manners. Enjoy your fishing trip." She crawled behind the wheel of her shiny ten-year-old sedan. "Oh, a woman called. Asked if you'd be home this afternoon. I told her for a while. She said she might stop by."

"A woman? Did she leave her name?"

Mrs. Tremain turned the key in the ignition. "First. Julie First."

He pictured her crouched on the floor beside him, an arm reaching out for a fallen spray can, her blouse hugging the tantalizing swell of her breast.

He closed the car door. "Next Saturday?"

"That's fine. Leah tells me you're putting in a lot of overtime. If you need help during the week, let me know."

Rolf nodded. "Thanks. I'll keep that in mind."

He stood for a moment and watched the older woman back cautiously out of his driveway, but his mind wasn't on her.

Back inside, he noted the children had already gathered the fishing gear by the back door. The front doorbell chimed.

"I'll get it," Leah sang out from the living room. "Dad, there's a lady here to see you."

He knew who it was and felt a stirring that was totally inappropriate to the occasion.

The porch of the old two-story house cast the entrance in cool shade, but there was nothing cooling about the sight of Julie standing in its shadowy light, wearing snug jeans and a baggy T-shirt. He had to catch his breath before he spoke.

"Hi, Julie." They gazed at each other, her incredible blue eyes, as depthless as the summer sky on a cloudless day, capturing him anew. The grandmother clock by the telephone table ticked.

"D-a-d," Leah called out from the other end of the hall. "Are you going to make her stand on the porch with the door open?"

He snorted and grinned, then shook his head in self-deprecation. "Sorry." Julie smiled, too. "Come on in." He stepped aside. As she glided by him, he inhaled the clean scent of flowers and immediately fell under the spell of the warm radiance of the afternoon light glowing in her golden hair. His blood heating, he closed the door behind her.

The twins came charging down the stairs, sounding like a herd of buffalo instead of two young boys. As one, they skidded to a standstill at the sight of the visitor.

"My sons Foster and Jeff," Rolf announced. "This is Miss First." He grinned with amusement. She eyed one, then the other.

"Okay, guys. Are you willing to let me in on the secret of telling you two apart, or do I have to figure it out for myself?"

They gave her identical impish grins. "I'm Jeff,"

the one on the right informed her. "He's Foster. But next time you're on your own." Their eyes twinkled merrily.

Julie grinned right back. "I love a challenge. At least you don't dress alike." They were both wearing jeans, but Jeff had on a yellow T-shirt, while his brother's was turquoise.

"Sometimes we do," Foster told her with a sly smile.

"Are you coming fishing with us?" Jeff inquired.

"Fishing? No, I—"

"Miss First is here to discuss business," Rolf explained.

"But it's getting late. We have to go," Foster complained. "Dad, you promised."

"I'm interfering with family plans." Julie retreated toward the door. "I'll come back another time. I should have checked with you personally before dropping by, anyway."

She had to wonder about her motives in coming to his home like this, the way a schoolgirl acted when she was interested in a guy—making an excuse to see him. He was so undeniably attractive. Being near him made her feel pretty, very different somehow from the way she felt with Jerry, even though she hardly knew Rolf.

"Is it something we can clear up quickly?" Rolf asked, feeling a bit panicked at the thought of her leaving so soon.

"It's about the school board. I don't know how long it will take, probably more than you want to spend right now."

Leah had moved up to them. "Are you a teacher?"

"I work in the administration office."

Rolf's curiosity was piqued. "What do you do there?"

"Curriculum writer." Julie took another step toward the front door. "I'll call you next week."

Rolf had an impulse to reach out and hold her back from leaving. He remembered all too well the feel of her skin when they shook hands.

"Are we ready to go?" Derek asked from the top of the stairs.

"Have a good time, guys." Julie put her hand on the doorknob, but instead of twisting it, she turned. "Catfish or crappy?"

Leah brightened. "Cats."

"My favorite. Well, good luck."

"You want to come with us?" Foster blurted out.

Julie pursed her lips. "Thanks, but this is your time to be with your dad."

"He doesn't mind," Jeff assured her.

She quirked a grin at Rolf. "As I said, thanks, but…"

Derek bounded down the stairs two at a time. "She probably doesn't like fishing, anyhow," he intoned disparagingly.

Julie raised her chin. "Actually, I love fishing."

"Can we go now? Please? If you want," Leah said to Julie, "you can follow us out to the lake and talk to Dad there."

"I don't know." She eyed him skeptically.

Joining him and his children probably wouldn't be wise, but the man intrigued her. Thursday morning, when she and Nancy had been unpacking the latest editions of the *Texas Essential Knowledge and Skill* booklets, she'd recounted the incident at the lumberyard with the spray cans.

The older woman tittered. "If I were twenty years younger—and single," she emphasized, "I'd really have the hots for that guy."

"He is sort of good-looking," Julie agreed.

Nancy pressed her hand on Julie's, merriment dancing in her soft brown eyes. "Honey, that's like saying Arnold Schwarzenegger's in decent shape."

The two women laughed, then continued dusting shelves and lining up binders. Nancy was about the age her mother would have been had she lived. Maybe that was why Julie found her so easy to talk to.

"I would have expected him to get upset when I knocked down that big display," Julie added, trying not to think about how the man's body affected her. "But he just shrugged it off as if it was really his fault."

"Four kids teaches patience and forgiveness. My five were a real trial, I can tell you—"

"Four kids?" The lightness in Julie's chest at the thought of the lumberman fell like a leaden weight into her belly. She should have realized he was married. Married or a Casanova, and the way he'd blushed when she caught him staring at her legs didn't suggest the latter.

Nancy smirked. "Divorced," she added, easily reading the younger woman's thoughts. "Must be over two years now. Sheryl, his ex, decided she didn't like the mother role anymore. She taught anthropology at the university, decided an archaeologist in another department was more fun and ran off with him to dig around in South America somewhere. Can you imagine?"

Rolf's wife had been a professional woman. Julie

couldn't help feel a little jealous. She liked to think she was capable of great things, too, if only she could figure out what they were. In her mind, she was a successful businesswoman with a loving family. But there was something disquieting about what Nancy was telling her. Apparently Sheryl Murdock had had it all and walked away from it.

Julie shook her head. "No, I can't," she mumbled.

What unseen flaw could Rolf have that would drive the mother of his children to abandon them? And if he did have some terrible imperfection, what kind of woman could leave her children with him? There was one possible consolation. If Nancy's assessment was correct, the fault was Sheryl's, not Rolf's.

"That's not a bad idea," Rolf agreed, enormously pleased with his meddlesome offspring. "Give us a minute to load up the van. It's less than a twenty-minute drive. We can talk while the kids are setting up."

"You don't mind? I mean—"

"D-a-d," Leah whined impatiently. "At this rate it'll be dark by the time we get there."

Rolf cocked his head, encouraging Julie to join them.

"Okay." Her hesitation vanished. "Can I help you? I have room in my pickup, if that will make things faster and easier."

"Way out." Derek shot down the hall to the kitchen.

Julie wasn't averse to a fishing outing, but, she reminded herself, she was only going to the lake to talk to Rolf about the oath. After that, she'd be on her way.

She helped the children put their tackle and bait box into the back of her truck.

"Can I ride with you?" Leah asked her.

The girl was at the awkward age, Julie noted. Not graceful and not quite pretty, though the elements of both were present. Her features hadn't yet matured and her body was in that gawky transition between child and woman. Her long hair was decidedly brown, without a hint of red, but it wasn't dark. Her most striking asset was definitely her eyes—amber with dark aureoles that lent them a golden quality. Before too long, boys would find them fascinating.

"Sure, if it's all right with your dad," she replied.

"I already asked him."

Without thinking, Julie glanced over to Rolf, who gave her a high sign. Leah grimaced at the implied insult of having her word doubted.

"Hop in. Glad for the company."

Determinedly swallowing her annoyance, the girl climbed into the cab of the pickup and slammed the door.

"I'm so tired of being around boys all the time," she complained as she secured her seat belt.

"Especially brothers," Julie agreed with a chuckle. "I had three of them around when I was growing up, too, so I know what they can be like."

Leah's expression brightened. A kindred spirit. Someone who understood. "Any twins?"

Julie shook her head.

"They're the worst," the girl complained.

"Probably because they're younger."

"Are your brothers all younger than you?"

"One was." Julie wished she hadn't brought up the subject or had phrased it differently.

"What do they do?" Leah asked, apparently not picking up on her use of the past tense.

"Michael's a rancher on the Number One, and Gideon's a physical therapist."

"What's that?"

"He helps people recover from injuries, or if they have a condition they can't recover from, he teaches them how to compensate for their handicaps."

"You mean people confined to wheelchairs or who've lost an arm or a leg."

"Exactly."

"I'd like to help people like that someday, too." Compassion rang in the girl's voice. "I'm thinking of becoming a nurse, maybe even a doctor."

"I hope you do. The most satisfying jobs in the world are the ones that help people. But they can also be the toughest. People don't always appreciate being helped."

Leah stared out the side window. "Yeah, well, at least they're alive. It's better than digging up a bunch of bones."

Julie recognized bitterness in the girl's words. A reference to her mother, no doubt. She wondered if it was an invitation to ask questions.

Leah swiveled as far as the seat belt would allow to face Julie. "What about your other brother, the one younger than you?"

"He was killed in a car accident a few years ago," Julie explained quietly.

Leah blinked and lapsed into silence. Julie could almost feel her thinking, trying to imagine what it would be like if one of her brothers died.

"I'm sorry," the girl finally muttered.

"Thanks," Julie responded simply.

"Do you have any sisters?"

"Yep, one, and she's older, too. She lives in Dallas."

"I wish I had a sister instead of all brothers."

Julie could have told her that at times she wished she didn't have a sister, but there was no point in disillusioning the girl. Besides, in the past year or so, Julie had grown to like Kerry. To escape the subject of siblings, she asked, "Do you enjoy fishing?"

"Yeah, it's fun. Mostly I like to do things outdoors."

"Does your dad take you very often?"

The girl shrugged philosophically. "Not as often as we'd like. He has to work a lot."

"Who takes care of you when he's not home?"

"After school we stay with Bryn. She lives next door." Julie didn't detect any affection in the statement. "It's only for an hour or so. On Saturdays, Mrs. Tremain comes over."

"So he doesn't leave y'all alone?"

Leah snorted. "Not Dad. One time he couldn't get anyone to stay with us when he had to go into the lumberyard because one of his employees was out sick, so he dragged us all there with him. Made us sweep the floor and stack shelves." She paused. "Actually, it was sort of fun."

A conscientious father, Julie thought approvingly, but somehow she wasn't surprised. One meeting was hardly sufficient to reach any definitive conclusions. But Julie had always had good instincts about first impressions—except for Jerry, of course. She was still trying to figure out how she could have so completely misjudged him.

Rolf led them to a public park at the lake. Since it

was Saturday, the place was abuzz with fishermen, boaters and campers taking advantage of one of the last warm days before fall weather became unpredictable.

"Derek, see if you can find us a spot." Rolf climbed out from behind the wheel of his Chevy Express. "The rest of you help unload this stuff."

With practiced ease, everyone lent a hand, collecting poles and tackle boxes, worms and folding chairs from the back of Julie's truck.

"The kids seem to enjoy coming out here," she remarked, as she trailed behind the exuberant youngsters.

"I wish we could do it more often. I guess the good side is that it's a real treat when we do."

"They get along pretty well together."

He laughed. "They're on good behavior in front of a stranger. Wait till they warm up to you. Then you'll see the true Murdocks appear."

Julie wondered if she'd be around them long enough. She wasn't here because she was invited as much as because she'd invaded. Confirmation came with Rolf's next question.

"So what was it you wanted to talk to me about?"

She recounted being hired by the school district and filling out all the paperwork. "The last thing I had to sign was a statement promising not to discuss district affairs with anyone."

Rolf unfolded their chairs under a sprawling mesquite that was probably a hundred years old. Its feathery leaves didn't afford dense shade, but it gave a semblance of protection against the still-broiling late-afternoon sun. She'd grabbed a gimme cap from her truck and had it set at a jaunty angle on her head.

Unfortunately, she'd also put on sunglasses. He was disappointed, but maybe it was just as well he couldn't see into her eyes. The woman was distracting enough without him losing himself in those beguiling blue pools.

"Is that a problem?" he asked.

She screwed up her mouth with annoyance. "When my employers tells me who I can talk to about what, I think it is."

"Seems like a stretch." He bent over the cooler they'd brought, his jeans outlining hard thigh muscles. "Name your beverage. We have Coke, orange juice, Gatorade and H2O."

She shifted her gaze to the shiny lake. "I'll pick up something at the concession stand later. Those are for you and your family."

He looked over from his crouched position. "There's plenty, Julie. I assure you. What'll it be?"

She conceded gracefully. "Juice, thanks."

He pulled a plastic bottle of orange juice from the icy water, held it out to her, snagged a Gatorade for himself and straightened. Simultaneously, they unscrewed the caps and took long drafts of the cold beverages.

"Come on, Dad," Derek called. "They're biting. You want dinner, don't you?"

"Up to dangling a line?" Rolf asked Julie.

Did he realize he already was? That there was something about him that made her feel safe and insecure at the same time.

"I didn't bring a pole."

Rolf snickered. "I wouldn't be a good Boy Scout if I didn't come prepared. I have an extra rig in the back of the van."

"One condition, though. Anything I latch on to goes to the common cause." His smile sent goose bumps up her spine.

"All contributions gratefully accepted, and I don't even make guests clean their own catch."

He returned to the van and retrieved the pole. Side by side, they walked toward the dock, where his kids were busy shoving one another for elbowroom.

"I'll be with you in a minute."

Rolf watched her saunter to the refreshment stand, mesmerized by the way the worn denim clinging to her hips rocked rhythmically. Forcing himself to stop staring, he turned toward his brood and was amused to see his eldest son observing her, too. Suppressing a grin, he joined his other kids on the narrow wooden dock.

"Watch what you're doing," he cautioned. "I don't want anyone getting hurt. Jeff, you don't have to hog the entire end of the dock. Take one corner and give Leah the other."

"Okay, guys, clear the way for a real angler." Julie strode past Rolf onto the wooden pier. "I'll show you how cats are caught. Anybody else need bread?"

"Bread?" Foster asked. "We use worms."

"You guys really are novices. I guess you don't know catfish are particularly fond of worm sandwiches."

"Yuck." Leah curled her upper lip in disgust.

Ignoring the commentary, Julie opened the cellophane-wrapped tuna sandwich she'd bought. "Now watch this." She baited a worm, then took a piece of the crust, compressed it and added it to the hook. "Give me five minutes," she intoned solemnly, "and I'll have you one of those whiskered critters."

She extended the pole over the water and, with a flip of her wrist, tossed the line into the lake. Everyone eyed her, including Rolf. Whether she caught anything or not, he decided, she'd captivated his kids. And him.

Four minutes later, she gave a triumphant cry. "Yes!"

The line jiggled. Dramatically she reeled it in. Rolf enjoyed watching the theatrics, though there wasn't much arc in the rod.

Everyone was staring now, including people on shore.

Then Derek started laughing. It took a moment for the others to figure out why. Sure enough, she had a catfish on the line. It couldn't have been more than six inches long.

"Hey—" Foster guffawed "—is that one bite or two?"

"Maybe it's an appetizer," Jeff added sarcastically.

"Send it back to its mommy," someone on shore called out.

"Cradle robber," another voice yelled.

"Gentlemen, please," Julie admonished, though she had a difficult time keeping a straight face. "You weren't listening. I didn't say how big a catfish I'd catch. I merely stated I'd snag one within five minutes. Voilà." She pulled it up and dangled the ugly creature from the end of the line.

"Duck everyone—the game warden," came a stage whisper from Derek.

Foster and Jeff actually cringed, making their elder brother and the others laugh.

Julie threw the fish back and gave the remains of

the sandwich to the kids. After washing her hands at a water tap, she rejoined Rolf on dry land in the lawn chairs.

"Do you normally use bread to entice catfish?" he asked.

"That and anything else I might have around. I've caught them with everything from bubble gum to popcorn. I don't really think it makes much difference. But experimenting is fun."

They drank their beverages for a minute in silence.

"Let's get back to that paper you're so concerned about," he said. "If you found it so objectionable, why did you sign it?"

"Because I wanted the job," she replied bluntly.

"But if it bothers you—"

"It restricts my freedom," she explained. "It makes my silence a condition of employment, and that smacks of censorship and conspiracy to me."

He drew back, not quite sure if he was amused or discomfited by her statement.

"Don't hold back, Julie. Tell me what you really think." When she merely scowled, he went on. "Conspiracy, huh?" He raised an eyebrow. "What do you think is being conspired? To raise the level of education in our schools?"

He watched a muscle in her jaw flex with annoyance.

"Our educational system is public," she reminded him. "It's supposed to be open to scrutiny, not hidden in secrecy behind closed doors."

He couldn't help but chuckle, though he realized she didn't appreciate the humor of it. "Do you realize how paranoid that sounds?"

She stood up and tossed her empty bottle into a

nearby receptacle. "I see I'm wasting my time." Was this the chink that had driven his wife away? A self-righteousness that tolerated no opposition, no criticism? "Say goodbye to the children for me. Sorry to have disturbed your free time."

He jumped from his seat. "Whoa! Julie, hang on." He reached out and grabbed her arm, then released his hold the moment he realized what he'd done.

"Julie, hold on a minute." Gently he guided her around to face him. "I'm sorry if I offended you. Obviously, this is important to you. Let's talk about it."

"So you can call me crazy? No, thanks."

Rather than argue with her, he decided a direct question might be more productive and divert her from leaving.

"Did you ask anyone at the admin office about this?"

"My supervisor, Alyson Shaddick. She gave me a very plausible explanation—that under the previous administration, employees had broadcast policies they disagreed with and blabbed about all kinds of problems."

"Didn't you believe her?"

"Yes," she admitted. "I understand that disgruntled employees can be very disruptive. But that doesn't justify silencing anyone who doesn't agree totally. It doesn't excuse not allowing a discussion or spinning things in favor of the administration." She repeated the example Alyson had used.

With an inviting wave of his hand, he coaxed her back into the chaise she'd vacated. "Who else have you talked to about this?"

"I haven't talked to anyone about it. But I ran into

Bill Marcus yesterday, and he made a point of bringing it up. Alyson or one of the people in her office
must have told him about me asking questions. Now,
why do you think they'd do that? He gave me a lec-
ture on owing loyalty to the people who hired me.''

"Is that unreasonable?'' Rolf asked. "Loyalty, I
mean.''

"Depends on what you mean by loyalty. If it keeps
people from expressing opinions that don't mimic the
company line, then it is too much.'' She'd calmed
down, but she still wasn't relaxed. "On the surface,
this pledge makes perfect sense. But I have to ask
myself why, if this is all so honest and forthright, is
everyone so sensitive about it?''

A valid question. "How long has this policy been
in effect?''

"So you're unfamiliar with it?''

He nodded. "This is my first term on the board.
I've attended one meeting. I suspect there are a number of school policies I'm not aware of yet.''

"Which is why I came to you with it. I'm told the
board unanimously adopted this oath last year.''

"And you figure I don't have a vested interest in
it and might be able to look at it objectively.''

"Can you?''

He liked the fire in her eyes, the willingness to
challenge, to fight. "I can certainly ask a few questions,'' he agreed. "But I have to tell you up front, I
don't see a black-cloaked villain lurking in a corner
here. This policy might appear a little extreme, but I
doubt its purpose is to stifle legitimate criticism. Until
I read it for myself, I'm giving the administration the
benefit of the doubt. From what you've told me,
you're being asked—told, if you prefer—that your

first recourse regarding school policies is the people responsible for them. What's wrong with that?''

She threw up her hands in frustration. ''Does the expression fox guarding the henhouse mean anything to you?''

A shout from the dock diverted their attention. They'd reached an impasse and any further discussion was likely to exacerbate the situation rather than resolve it.

Both Foster and Jeff had caught good-size cats.

''Fish fry,'' Derek announced. He turned to Julie. ''You eat them, too?''

''You can have my share,'' Jeff declared. ''I hate fish.''

''Thanks, but I really have to leave.''

Among a group of frowns, Rolf noted, ''There'll be plenty. You sure you can't stay?''

''I appreciate the offer, but I'm due out at the ranch this evening.''

''You own a ranch?'' Jeff asked, intrigued, as were the others.

''My father does.'' Impulse and hazel eyes had her asking, ''Do y'all like riding horses?''

Four young heads nodded enthusiastically. She turned to Rolf. ''You?''

''Yep.''

''How would y'all like to spend next weekend on the ranch? It'll give me a chance to return the courtesy of your inviting me on your fishing trip.''

All eyes turned to Rolf.

''Seriously?'' he asked.

''Ranchers' daughters don't joke about horses, partner. Of course I'm serious. You interested?''

Rolf surveyed his children. ''What do you think?''

He didn't have to ask. Their unanimous and enthusiastic decision was written all over their faces.

"This is very generous of you," Rolf told to Julie. "But shouldn't you check with your father first?"

"Trust me. He'll be fine with it. Besides, I have an ulterior motive." She gazed at him with humor in her eyes. "I want you to see I'm not crazy."

CHAPTER THREE

ARRANGING FOR ROLF and his four children to come out to the Home Place for a weekend stay was no problem.

"Bring them over to our house," Clare suggested when Julie raised the subject at Sunday dinner. "They can go swimming with our kids."

So everything was set. They'd stay in the guest house on the Home Place. Had it not been available, there would have been other options. The big two-story house her sister, Kerry, used to live in on the Number One, or the bunkhouse.

Julie arrived at the Murdocks' on Saturday morning at eight o'clock—an ungodly hour for a weekend, but she'd awakened to the sound of the alarm clock at seven with a smile on her face and eagerness in her heart. Rolf greeted her at the back door with a coffee mug.

"The kids have been up for over an hour, waiting for you," he announced. "But as soon as you drove up they remembered all the things they'd forgotten. You probably have time to finish that cup and have a second before they get their acts together. Otherwise you can bring it with you."

Stepping inside the country kitchen, she inhaled the comforting aroma of cinnamon and caramel. "Somebody baking?"

"Leah decided the trip to the ranch required sweet buns."

"I won't turn them down." Julie chuckled. "But we'll be there in less than an hour."

"With sticky fingers," he added with a smile.

She liked it when he smiled at her that way, but it distracted her enough that a long moment of silence elapsed before she said, "Take some wet paper towels in a plastic bag."

Enlightened, he held up a finger. "Good idea."

While he was tearing towels from the roll suspended under the overhead cabinet beside the stainless steel sink, Derek charged into the room. "Dad, Leah's changing her clothes again."

Julie laughed. "Everybody be sure to bring swimsuits. And sunscreen," she added as he darted out through the swinging door to the dining room. He called out a happy "Yes" to the others, as he clambered up the stairs.

She sipped her coffee and smiled over the rim. "Haven't they ever been to a ranch before?"

He refilled his cup from the pot on the stove. "We were set to go to a dude ranch last summer, but my assistant manager's mother had a stroke and we had to cancel."

"Too bad. But this isn't a dude ranch. It's a working ranch, so it might not be as much fun."

"I doubt it." He took a slug of the steaming brew. "At least a dozen times this morning I heard them talking about going to a *real* ranch, with *real* cattle and *real* cowboys." The way his eyes danced with hers the statement might as easily have been: *I'm a man and you're a woman.*

"No six-guns or shootouts, though."

He nodded. "Good. About their riding... They're not very experienced—"

"Safe horses, I promise. Dad has several laid-back critters they'll be able to handle just fine. Everyone will have a good time, but there's not much danger of anybody being run away with."

"Does that include me?"

Humor bubbled into a smile. "Depends on how fast you want to ride and how hard you want to fall."

The twinkle matured into a gleam. He was about to reply, when Leah appeared at the back door, hands on hips, the picture of impatience. "Can we go now?"

Rolf shook his head, laughed and deposited his half-empty cup in the sink. "We're on our way," he said without breaking eye contact with Julie.

It was another twenty minutes before they pulled out of the driveway. Julie left her pickup in Rolf's garage and climbed into the front seat of the Chevy Express beside him. Sticky buns were passed around and a spirit of adventure filled the noisy van. The kids asked all sorts of questions about the ranch. How big was it? Did they have cowboys working there? How many cattle did they have? Julie answered all of them.

"Why don't you live there?" Derek wanted to know. "I mean, why would you live in town when you could be on a ranch?"

The grass was always greener on the other side of the fence, Julie reminded herself. "When you live on a big spread, going to town is a special treat. Besides, I like meeting new people, and that's hard to do out in the middle of nowhere."

"But you meet cowboys," Leah pointed out.

"I hate to disillusion you, but the kind of cowboy

you're probably thinking of is only a part-time job. The day-to-day work is done by ranch hands who live on the place, and most of them are married.''

"Married?" Leah's jaw fell. It apparently hadn't occurred to her that cowboys married, settled down and raised families. The ones who didn't were drifters who couldn't stay put long enough to fall in love—though they could break hearts.

"It's that or love 'em and leave 'em." Julie didn't receive a response to her observation.

They were wiping their hands on wet towels when they arrived at the gate leading to the Home Place. Julie got out, opened it, waved Rolf through, then climbed back in beside him. "It's another three miles," she told him.

"Your father owns all this land?" Derek asked.

"Almost ninety-four sections of it," she confirmed.

"Do any of you know how big a section is?" Rolf asked.

His children shrugged. "An acre?" Foster speculated.

Rolf slanted a grin at Julie. "A section is a square mile. Six hundred and forty acres."

"Wow! That's bigger than Coyote Springs," Derek exclaimed.

Julie had grown up taking for granted that her family's property extended as far as the eye could see and beyond. The Number One, out of which the Home Place had been carved, had been eight hundred sections, eight hundred square miles. She could drive for hours and hours and never leave home.

As they passed a mesa, she told them about the house at the top, where she'd grown up.

"Can we go and see it?" Foster asked.

She shook her head. "It's not there anymore. It was destroyed in the big tornado we had two years ago. The twister picked it up and tossed it off the side of the butte."

Derek was wide-eyed. "For real?"

She nodded. His expression told her he wished he'd seen it happen. She was grateful she hadn't. Dealing with the aftermath had been difficult enough.

Rolf reached over and covered her hand with his. She didn't think she'd let the sadness of the memory show. His sensitivity took her by surprise and made her uncomfortable, until she realized her response wasn't completely unpleasant.

"Was anyone hurt?" he asked, his other hand curled around the steering wheel.

"My dad broke his leg, but otherwise no one was seriously injured. Bear right here," she instructed.

He turned off the wide caliche road onto a narrower but equally well-maintained dirt lane that led down into a lush valley. As they descended into the box canyon, the live oak trees became bigger and more plentiful.

"This is beautiful."

"We call it the Home Place because it was part of the original land grant my great-great-grandfather received from the Spanish government in 1820." She turned to the children in the back seat, who seemed equally amazed by the very different landscape. This was well shaded and much cooler. "Have you ever seen where a river begins?"

"They start as little streams in mountains," Jeff explained.

"That's one way. The Coyote's source is springs that come up from underground. Which is where we're headed.'' She pointed to the silvery glint of a metal roof ahead of them. ''My dad restored the house a couple of years ago.''

''Impressive,'' Rolf commented. ''Everything is.'' He grinned over at her. ''Your dad can be very proud.''

''Was it built by the Spanish?'' Leah asked. ''Mom would be interested in it if it was. She always gets excited about things other people do.''

Julie noticed that no one else picked up on the comment. She glanced over at Rolf, who was occupied with driving the big vehicle.

''This house was built in the 1890s,'' Julie explained, ''and was nearly destroyed in a fire in 1952. It was nothing but a burned-out ruin until my dad rebuilt it.''

Rolf pulled up in front of the log-and-stone house. Her father stood on the porch, his wife, Sheila, at his side.

The kids tumbled from the van, then froze, awed by the surroundings, unsure of themselves. Rolf turned off the engine and climbed out. He was filling his lungs with the pine-scented air when Julie came up beside him.

Adam and Sheila had already descended the wide steps and were approaching with welcoming smiles. Julie made the formal introductions. Rolf shook hands with his hosts and thanked them for their generous invitation. Then he presented his children.

Sensing their shyness, Adam invited everyone to the stables, where they could pick their horses.

''Leon Cordero and his wife asked that y'all drop by their place for lunch,'' Adam told Julie. ''About then, everyone will have developed their first blisters.''

She chuckled. ''Yeah, but I bet they don't admit it.''

Her father laughed. ''Not unless kids have changed.''

By the time they selected their mounts, saddled them and had received their introductory lessons on starting, stopping and turning, barely an hour and half remained before they were expected at the Cordero place.

Lucinda Cordero had raised six children of her own and at forty-five already had four grandchildren, so a house full of excited young people was no strain and very welcome. The visitors chattered on about the merits of their particular horses, the enormous skills they'd mastered, razzed one another about mess-ups and gloried in the knowledge that they'd be the envy of their schoolmates come Monday morning.

While the children were busy helping Leon build the fire for the fajitas he was about to grill or trying their hand at throwing horseshoes, Julie and Rolf had time to sit quietly under a sprawling mulberry tree and take huge mouthfuls of minted iced tea.

''You've been on a horse before,'' she remarked. He'd sat tall, his back straight, his long legs in the correct position, while his hips moved comfortably in the western saddle. He wasn't at all hard on the eyes in his cowboy hat, western shirt and tight-fitting jeans.

''Not in many years. My folks had a small ranch north of town. Nothing glamorous. Dad ran a few head of cattle, then sheep and finally goats. Never made much money, but it was a good life. Bought and sold horses, too, so they were always around for me to ride.''

''Do your folks still have it?''

He shook his head. ''Pop fell over dead of a heart attack when I was in college. Mom tried to hang on to the place for a couple of years, but it was too much for her. As I said, it never paid well, and she couldn't afford to hire help to run it. Besides, the city was starting to encroach. It wasn't as rural as it had been. The nights weren't as dark, the stars not nearly as bright.'' He leaned against the back of the rustic wooden bench. ''As a kid I remember sneaking outside on hot summer nights, stretching out on the cool grass of the lawn and feeling as if I could reach up and touch those little white pinpoints. They were always just out of reach.''

Julie wondered what it would be like to share a star-studded black velvet night with him.

''Mom finally sold the place and moved into an apartment in town,'' Rolf continued. ''Three months later, she went to bed one night and didn't wake up in the morning.''

''I'm sorry,'' Julie murmured. ''They both died so young.''

''But they lived good and for the most part happy lives,'' he assured her. ''I have wonderful memories of them. In the end, I guess that's about all any of us can hope for.''

She wanted to console him but didn't know how. Her mother had succumbed to breast cancer when Julie was still in elementary school. Telling Rolf right now wouldn't lessen his pain. Sometimes, she remembered her father saying once, silence is the best gift we have to offer.

It didn't last, though. The call to lunch brought activity and renewed enthusiasm, relegating the quiet moment of poignancy to the past. The meal was lively, spicy and filling. Afterward, Rolf offered his kids' services to clean up, but Lucinda wouldn't hear of it, nor would she allow Julie to help. Leon invited the children on a tour of his barn, his tractor and the various pieces of equipment he used on it. Rolf and Julie found themselves left alone on the patio of the Spanish hacienda.

"Care to take a walk?" Julie asked.

"I'd love it. The food was delicious. I ate too much."

"Lucy's a good cook."

Julie led him through an ornate wrought-iron gate to a pecan orchard Leon had planted more than thirty years earlier. This time of year, the boughs were heavy with nuts, several of them supported with two-by-four braces so they wouldn't snap under the weight.

"Everything is so peaceful here," Rolf commented. "Your folks' home. This place. Living in the country is definitely the good life. Don't you miss it?"

"I've never really left it," she explained. "I don't live here full-time anymore, but I come out often— to be with the family, to recharge my batteries, to put things in perspective."

"But you don't want to be a rancher's wife, is that it?" He sounded as disappointed as his son had earlier.

"Is that your way of asking if I plan to get married?" She grinned. "Someday. But not yet." She'd thought she wanted to marry Jerry Benton—until he'd

asked her and she'd found out what his idea of wed-
ded bliss was. "I know this seems ideal, and in many
respects, it is. But it can be a lonely life, too. My
sister stayed here longer than she should have. My
brother, Gideon, has found his niche in town. For me
now, that's where I belong, too."

"I guess I can understand that."

They came to a simple concrete slab supported by
two rough stone pillars in one corner of the orchard.
The house was on the other side of a small rise, out
of sight. They sat down, next to each other, alone in
the dim green light cast by the old trees.

"Thank you for letting us come out here today."
He was only inches away from her, or had been until
he reached over and covered her hand with his. His
long fingers were tough skinned from handling lumber. Warm from the sun they'd shared.

"I'm happy you could make it," she responded in
almost a whisper.

He shifted enough to face her, their bodies closer
now. Raising his hand, he caressed her cheek. A soft
gentle touch. Slowly he brought his mouth closer to
hers. She could have backed away. She could have
jumped up from the seat. She could even have said,
"Don't."

But she didn't.

Instead, her eyes closed at the very moment his lips
met hers. She didn't need light to feel his kiss. She
didn't need sunshine to return it.

"Your lips are impossible to resist," he murmured
when he drew away enough to put words between
them. "And I've resisted long enough."

Should she tell him she felt the same way? That
the wait for his kiss had been worth it?

"Unfortunately," he said with a smile in his voice, "we have to go back before they send out a search party for us."

She rose to her feet a little unsteadily. "You're right." She didn't have to repeat *unfortunately*. It was understood.

He took her hand in his as they walked back under the pecans. His touch was undemanding, yet oddly possessive. She was free to have pulled away, but she didn't want to—until they reached the edge of the orchard. Then, by some mysterious nonverbal signal, they released each other and walked side by side to the house.

A little while later, Julie led them from the Cordero place in a circuitous route through a rocky ravine, along the edges of fields of cotton, across open prairie where cattle grazed, to her brother's home. During the easygoing procession, she kept an eye on her companions. Rolf was quiet, lost in reverie. Was he thinking about her and the kiss she'd returned? Or did this open terrain remind him of his long-dead parents and the way of living they'd treasured? He'd obviously loved them dearly, and he must miss them even now. They hadn't survived long enough to be grandparents. Her mother hadn't, either. Did Rolf ever wonder what they would have thought of how he'd handled the life they'd given him? No doubt they'd be disappointed at his failed marriage, but Julie was equally certain they'd be proud of the man he was and the father he'd become.

She had to chuckle as she observed the kids now. Sagging in their saddles. Eyes half-closed, heads hung, their young bodies swaying effortlessly to the rocking motions of their mounts. They perked up, though, when she announced they were getting close to the swimming hole.

Michael wasn't home, but his wife, Clare, and their four offspring were. Lethargy quickly slipped away, forgotten by the Murdock children, as introductions were made.

At the house they changed into the bathing suits they'd stuffed in their saddlebags, then ran up the path to the swimming hole.

Julie found it difficult to concentrate on the children or the setting, though, when Rolf emerged from the house wearing snug swim trunks. Manual labor in a lumberyard had a lot to recommend it, she decided. His broad shoulders appeared even broader without a shirt covering them. His chest and arms, sprinkled with dark hair, were heavily muscled, his belly narrow and flat. She'd noticed the sharp V of his build on more than one occasion, but awareness wasn't nearly as unsettling as beholding the naked flesh.

They trailed behind the kids more leisurely, wearing shower clogs and toting big fluffy towels.

The swimming hole, as its name suggested, wasn't fancy, just a manmade pond over a small rise from the house. Originally it had been a stock tank, but through the years the family had reserved it exclusively for human use. Dense, sprawling live oaks offered shade on the south side. Michael had constructed a wooden raft at the west end that was joined to the bank by a narrow floating dock. At the east end of the wide oval pond a windmill pumped a steady stream of water over a picturesque ladder of rocks.

The kids were already splashing around by the time she and Rolf tossed their towels on the chaise lounges on the sunny side of the pond.

"Beat you in," he called out as he charged onto the dock and jumped into the sparkling water.

Julie laughed when he came up to the surface sputtering. "Did I forget to tell you well water is cold?" she asked innocently.

"Forget?" He blew in and out through trumpeted lips while he frantically treaded water, not to stay afloat, but to keep his blood from congealing. "Neglected is more like it. You're a sadist, Julie First."

Or maybe a masochist, she told herself as she plunged in to join him. The chill took her breath away, but not nearly as much as the sight of Rolf Murdock's wet body when he pulled himself onto the dock. He turned around, winked at her mischievously, then dove in again to surface a few feet from her.

A water fight ensued. Rolf teamed up with his kids, Julie with her nieces and nephews. Each got as well as gave, and after about twenty minutes, Rolf cried uncle.

"Or blue," he corrected himself. "I think I'm turning blue."

"But such a pretty shade," Julie agreed.

"I like the color of your eyes better," he said, and for a moment her heart lurched.

They climbed out and dried off in the lowering sun.

Even with goose bumps from the cold, she was beautiful, enticing enough to make him grateful for the frigid temperature of the pond. She ought not to wear a bikini, he decided, not with other people around. It was a picture he would very much like to keep all to himself. Her slender arms and legs, her small waist and flat belly, just enough filling the skimpy top to drive him pure crazy, especially with the icy water puckering her nipples. His pulse was playing ragtime, yet not staring was damn near impossible.

They stretched out on the lounges for a few minutes while the kids continued their games. His eyes kept wandering over to her legs, to the smooth curve of her thighs, the satiny skin around her navel. A man could have a coronary gazing at Julie First.

Rolf was almost relieved when her brother showed up and distracted him from fantasies he had no right having in broad daylight.

Michael First was a big man, several inches over six feet, with a ready smile and a friendly manner. He pushed back his straw hat and crossed thick-muscled arms over his massive chest as he observed the crowd happily splashing around in the pond. Rolf rose when Julie made the introductions.

Shaking his guest's hand, Michael said, "As soon as y'all get defrosted, come on up to the house and we'll have a beer before supper."

The meal was served outdoors and, after the formalities of a prayer, was as casual and laid-back as the one at the Corderos' earlier that day. The fare was lighter but no less generous. While the kids babbled, teased, jostled and did what kids usually do, the adults talked about the drought, the state of the economy and the challenges of raising teenagers. Inevitably the discussion turned to Julie's job and the school administration.

"What can you tell me about the new school superintendent, Dr. Picard?" Rolf asked Michael.

"Not a whole lot. I know he came here from a district in southeast Texas, on the Louisiana border about a year ago, and he's brought order and discipline that was previously lacking. Truancy's down."

"TAAS test scores in English and math are up," Clare added.

Michael nodded. "The district has also received several awards and grants since he's been here, so he must be doing something right."

"I've met him," Clare told Rolf. "He's very personable. Seems to really listen. If anyone has anything bad to say about him, I certainly haven't heard it."

"Because there's a gag order in place," Julie remarked, and told them about the oath she'd had to sign.

WHEN ROLF WENT to help his children resaddle the horses, Michael pulled his sister aside and invited her to sit on the porch glider while he stretched out on the top step, his back against a pillar.

"I hope you're not getting serious about this guy," he told her.

Julie instantly felt the hairs on the back of her neck rise. The eldest, Michael took most after their father, and like Adam First, he had very strong opinions on a variety of subjects. Not all of them solicited. Not all of them welcome. And not all of them right.

She kicked the glider into motion. "I don't remember asking for your blessing."

Like her sister, Kerry, she tended to get her back up when challenged. For some inexplicable reason, her brilliant brothers never seemed to figure that out. They never knew when to back off...like now.

"You can do better, Julie," Michael informed her. "I know Jerome disappointed you. The guy was a jerk. I'm just sorry it took you so long to come to your senses."

Now he was calling her stupid—or a fool. She pumped her legs harder.

"On the other hand," he persisted, "when the time came, you did tell him to get lost. I guess that's all that matters."

Was she supposed to take that as a compliment? Sheesh, men were dense. "This is none of your business, Michael."

He pulled one leg up and laced his fingers below the knee. "You're my sister, Julie. You are my business."

Her feet firmly hit the ground, bringing the swing to a swerving halt. "I beg your pardon." She glared at him. "I'm not a piece of Number One property to be appraised and traded."

Michael closed his eyes and took a patience-gathering breath. "I'm worried about you, little sister. Rolf seems like a nice enough guy, but—"

"Excuse me, in case you haven't noticed, I'm an adult now. I pick my own friends," she said tight-lipped.

"Friends?" Michael raised his eyebrows and snorted. "I suspect it's more than friends. Do you think I can't see the way the two of you keep looking at each other?"

Her romantic interests were none of his concern. "Let me repeat, mind your own business."

"He's not right for you, Julie," Michael went on, undaunted. "He's got four kids and a living wife—"

Julie's feet were rocking on the boards again. "Ex-wife," she corrected him. "They're divorced and she's remarried."

Michael lowered his knee and stretched his legs out on the top step. "She's still the mother of his children. She could show up anytime and decide she wants her kids again.''

From the way Nancy described Sheryl, that didn't appear likely. But...

Her brother crossed his arms over his chest. ''What then, Julie? Either he dumps you and goes back to her for the sake of the children, or he takes a chance of losing the kids. How long do you think he'll love you if that happens?''

She should just get up and walk away. But that would be running, and she refused to be intimidated, especially by her know-it-all brother. ''Stuff it, Michael. This has nothing to do with you.''

''Think about it,'' he went on, oblivious to her pique. ''If Rolf asked you to marry him—''

''Hold it right there,'' she ordered as she brought the seat to another uneven halt. ''You're getting the cart before the horse. He hasn't asked me to marry him, and I haven't got a clue what I'd say if he did.''

Michael's smug grin told her she'd just made herself vulnerable.

She expelled a huge sigh and resumed the back-and-forth motion of the glider.

''Okay, I admit it. I find Rolf attractive, a lot more than Jerry ever was. Call it pheromones, animal magnetism, whatever. It doesn't make any difference. It's there. I can't define it, and I have no idea where this relationship is going. I don't even know if Rolf feels the same as I do. Either way, I'm certainly not going to justify myself to you. So why don't you just back the hell off, big brother.'' Then she added sweetly, ''Dear.''

''He could be after your money, of course,'' he muttered, as if he weren't actually addressing her.

She shook her head. Talking to him was like talking to a brick wall. "Rolf's a successful businessman. He doesn't need my money."

Michael smirked. "You sure?"

Julie closed her eyes and opened them again to see Rolf approaching from the corral where the horses stood patiently waiting. She climbed out of the glider, stepped over her brother's legs and descended the stairs. "Goodbye, Michael."

IT WAS WELL PAST DARK the following evening when Rolf drove up the long hill leading out of the box canyon in which the Coyote River had its origins. The Murdocks had had a busy second day. They'd gone horseback riding in the morning, then Adam gave them all an aerial tour of the Number One Ranch in his helicopter. By early afternoon other members of the First family were arriving. Michael, Clare and their kids. Gideon, Lupe and their three children. Only Kerry and Craig were missing, because they were overseas on one of Craig's many business trips. While the adults visited and pitched in on preparing Sunday dinner, the boisterous kids ran around to their hearts' content.

Now exhaustion was setting in. They voiced a few comments about the wonderful weekend, how sorry they were that it was over. But the chatter quickly dwindled, silence took over and four very tired children were soon swallowed up in the arms of Morpheus.

"You might have a little trouble getting them up for school tomorrow," Julie observed.

"It's been an exciting weekend," Rolf agreed.

She thought about the kiss they'd shared under the

pecan trees. She'd waited all day for him to kiss her again, but he hadn't. It was true they hadn't had many opportunities to be alone, but he could have invented some, she thought, a little disappointed.

"I'm glad you enjoyed it. My folks sure did."

"What about you, Julie? Did you have a good time?"

He was talking about the kiss; she knew it. Oh, yes, she'd taken pleasure in it. He must realize that.

"I did." Why should she deny it? "Very much. Maybe we ought to do it again."

She didn't miss the quirk of his lips in the faint reflection of the dashboard lights. "I reckon we should. Soon."

Tonight? She wanted to ask. Will you kiss me good-night?

They'd reached the paved public road. "I've been mulling over the question of the oath." His tone was serious now, the earlier playfulness gone.

"What have you decided?" she asked. "Still think I'm paranoid? Crazy?"

"I never thought you were crazy," he objected.

"Just paranoid." She slanted him a reptilian grin.

"Poor choice of words." He searched for others. "I thought you were probably being too sensitive. Overreacting."

"A flighty woman."

He glanced over, seriousness taking on a sterner demeanor. "Please don't put words in my mouth, Julie. I wasn't trying to insult you."

She chuckled, but she also believed him. "And now, Rolf? What do you think now?"

He breathed in and out. "Your brother and his wife gave a very favorable report on Picard. But you're right. The oath itself is disturbing—enough for me to have second thoughts about it.''

''Thank you, sir.'' She hadn't meant to be flip, but her words came out that way.

Her sarcasm annoyed him. ''What I'm saying is that I'm willing to check into this a little deeper. I can't promise anything.''

''I'm not asking for promises.'' She wondered if they were still talking about the oath.

CHAPTER FOUR

ROLF DEBATED with himself during the week that followed. His initial reaction to Julie's opposition to the oath had been that she was overreacting, exaggerating. Yet, there'd also been a lingering doubt that maybe she was right. He'd read Charles Picard's resumé in the local newspaper and met him at the school board meeting. He'd listened to the well-reputed educator articulate positions Rolf himself advocated; and he'd been impressed by the man's grasp of detail. In his early fifties, Picard carried himself with a dignity that Rolf admired but was not drawn to. Which hadn't bothered him in the least. There were many people he respected but had no interest in knowing on a personal level.

Rolf had been elected to the board when Frank Dalton was unable to finish his term because of failing health. Frank had served the school district for more than ten years and was highly respected. He'd enthusiastically endorsed his friend to succeed him. Unfortunately, Frank had passed a few days after Rolf took his place, so a valuable mentor was gone.

The person he felt most comfortable with was Herb Mellow, a retired military NCO who owned a well-drilling company. Herb had been on the board six years. Rolf decided to stop by the trailer he called his office. In his midforties, Herb had thinning brown hair which, he combed unaffectedly straight back.

"Things have improved considerably since Picard took over," he told Rolf as he leaned back in a rickety wooden chair. "There's a much stronger sense of order and discipline in the schools these days, and that's the first rule of education. Delinquency is down drastically. TAAS scores have gone up—"

Rolf had heard it all before. "They've been improving statewide," he pointed out.

"True, but ours have risen a bit faster than the average." He did a three-finger tattoo on the edge of the desk. Herb had recently given up smoking cigars and still didn't seem to know what to do with his hands. "Not a whole lot, I grant you, but the trend is definitely positive. A few more years and we stand a good chance of having the best district in the state."

Rolf settled back in the torn vinyl guest's chair, elbows on the frayed armrests. "How has he managed it?"

"Standards," Herb said unequivocally. "We went through a long period of accommodation and waiving academic requirements under the old administration. Picard's changed all that. No more social promotion. Teachers know what they have to teach, and they're held accountable for the results."

Rolf was all for that. Feeling good didn't accomplish anything, but accomplishing something made you feel good. It was a matter of keeping the horse before the cart. "What do the teachers think of him?"

"A mixed bag, as you might expect. Some love him. A few hate his guts." Herb opened his desk drawer, took out a paper-wrapped mint and offered it to his visitor. When Rolf declined, he extracted it from the cellophane and popped it into his own mouth. "Most simply accept him as the boss and go about doing their jobs."

The typical breakdown for any large organization, Rolf noted. "What about this loyalty oath you approved last year?"

Herb smiled. "I heard your friend Julie First raised a stink about it. Is that what this is all about?"

Rolf was stunned. Her version was that she'd asked a couple of questions, then signed on the line. She also reported that Bill Marcus had known about her hesitation, so it probably shouldn't be a surprise that other board members might have heard, too. Why was making what seemed like a reasonable inquiry garnering so much attention? Herb's referring to Julie as his friend shouldn't be a shock, either. Coyote Springs was at heart still a small town. No doubt his kids' bragging about their weekend at the First ranch had fanned gossip, as well. Still, it was unnerving to realize he lived in a fishbowl.

He chuckled. "She's really excited about her new job and mentioned this sworn statement was one of the mountain of papers she had to sign when she was hired. I'd never heard about the oath, though, so naturally it made me curious. You wouldn't happen to have a copy available, would you?"

Herb's brows rose. "As a matter of fact..." He went to a scratched-up gray metal file cabinet that might have come from army surplus. "I keep all my records... Here it is." He handed over a wrinkled paper.

Rolf read it carefully. The coercive tone was unmistakable. "Has this aroused any opposition?"

Herb shrugged. "About what you'd expect. A few

people have voiced misgivings. Others think it's a great idea. Most people simply accepted it.''

Again, the predictable breakdown. One-third for; one-third against; one-third apathetic.

''Whose idea was this, anyway?''

''Bill Marcus was the one who introduced it.''

''Not Picard?''

Herb shook his head. ''Picard wasn't even at the meeting when the matter was presented and voted on. As I recall, he was at a conference in Washington.''

''It all happened at one meeting, without being held over for further discussion?'' Seemed a bit precipitous for such an important issue. Hardly illegal, though.

''Bill put it on the agenda at the last minute.''

So there wasn't time to study the measure, to consider its possible ramifications. Still, none of this was either unprecedented or necessarily sinister. ''I understand the oath was accepted unanimously. Is that right?''

''Yep.'' Herb smacked his lips as he sucked on his candy. ''It was the right thing to do, Rolf,'' he added earnestly. ''I'm sure you remember what things were like a couple of years ago. Everybody was concerned about our poor showing on state exams, our low college admittance ratio and the rash of vandalism. No shootings or anything that dramatic, but there'd been a few fistfights on school grounds, and a teacher had her tires slashed in a parking lot one night when she was working late. A lot of name-calling within the ranks, too. Parents blaming teachers, teachers blaming administrators, administrators blaming board policies. Everyone was looking for a scapegoat. We decided the best first step in steering things back on track was to cool the rhetoric. It's worked. Things have been improving steadily ever since.''

It made sense. Stop the shouting and insults and people had a chance to hear one another.

"But why an oath?" Rolf asked. "It seems drastic.''

"Which is precisely why we went that route. Bill talked to the district's legal counsel, who pointed out that a policy statement would have no compelling force unless employees swore to obey it. As I say, it's worked. Can't argue with success.''

After a few more minutes, Rolf thanked Herb for his time and left. The decision had been unanimous, which meant his predecessor had voted for it, as well. Frank could be a maverick if he disagreed with something, so he must have believed this was the right thing to do.

Rolf hoped when he explained all this to Julie, she'd back off on the issue. If she didn't, he'd have to start questioning her motives. Was she trying to stir things up, make a reputation for herself? What better way than to take on the school superintendent or even the entire establishment? She was ambitious. He admired that. She also had a name and enough money to get away with things other people couldn't. That was also off-putting.

Her response to his kiss sure hadn't been off-putting, though. He'd like to sample those lips again. The past weekend with her had been like a trip to another world. Out on the ranch, it was hard to worry about mundane things like bureaucratic policies and the lumber business. There was a majesty about the place, a sense of being on top of the world. Riding a horse across open prairie, hearing the music of nature unmolested by machines and motors, gazing up at the stars at night made a man forget the millions of other people on the planet. Being with a beautiful woman in that eternal setting made a man feel complete and powerful.

Julie had him longing for the things missing from his life. He didn't think about Sheryl much these days, not in positive terms, anyway. But Julie brought back nostalgia for a time when his whole life seemed to revolve around loving a woman, a time when sharing experiences with her was his greatest joy and pleasure.

That Julie didn't look anything like his ex-wife made it easier. Sheryl had been tall, big boned and dark-haired, with deep-set brown eyes. Julie was small and delicate, with the grace and refinement of motion of a natural athlete. She'd demonstrated feminine elegance in the way she placed her foot in the stirrup and swept her leg over the rump of the horse. But it was watching her hips sway rhythmically in the saddle as she urged her mount on that was a study in pure erotic art.

Her kiss had taken him to a new level of awareness, to a dimension he wasn't comfortable in—but longed to be. She'd kissed him back, so apparently the pleasure of the experience hadn't been completely one-sided. But why would she be interested in a divorced man more than ten years her senior who had four kids?

JULIE KNEW SEVERAL of the teachers at Alamo Junior High, where she'd been a substitute teacher several years earlier. She ran into Myrna Watson from time to time in the supermarket or the library. They chatted, but it was the usual polite exchange of casual acquaintances.

On Wednesday morning, Julie made it a point to drop by Fabers', an old-fashioned drugstore and soda fountain on North Travis Street, where she knew Myrna went for lunch every Wednesday. Sure enough, the eighth-grade teacher showed up a few minutes later, and to Julie's relief, she was alone.

Myrna was an imposing woman, tall enough to gaze down on most of the adolescents she taught and bulky enough to intimidate them physically—if her piercing gray eyes didn't stop them in their tracks.

Her greeting for Julie was delighted and sincere. "Heard you took a job in the Ivory Tower," she said with a throaty laugh.

They ordered their sandwiches, exchanged small talk while waiting for them to be prepared, then moved into a tiny alcove and sat on uncomfortable wire chairs at a round table.

Myrna held up her egg salad on whole wheat. "I was hoping you'd stay in the classroom. You were good with the kids."

Julie had never told anyone but Jerry that she wasn't comfortable as a teacher. To learn it hadn't showed amazed her. "I may do that later."

Myrna shook her head. "It's a one-way street. I can't recall anyone ever returning to the classroom from admin. Cut in pay, for one thing."

"The money isn't important to me."

"I realize that." She sipped her cherry Coke through a straw. "Maybe you'll be different."

"You don't like admin, do you?" Julie ventured.

Myrna snorted. "Most teachers don't. We do the hard work—or as my husband would put it, where the rubber meets the road—and are usually looked down on as hirelings by the people in the Ivory Tower."

"I don't," Julie objected.

"You will." Myrna bit into the second half of her sandwich. "It comes with the territory."

"I won't," Julie insisted. Educating young minds was a team effort, and she didn't like being regarded as an adversary.

Myrna smiled. "Good. I'll hold you to that." She took another sip of her Coke. "I have a pretty good idea what brings you to see me, but why don't you spell it out."

For a moment, Julie was tempted to glance over her shoulder. It seemed like everyone was monitoring her. Rolf had accused her of being paranoid, and she was beginning to believe he was right.

"I had to sign a loyalty statement," she remarked in a low voice, though no one was close enough to overhear her.

Myrna's mouth sagged and for a moment her eyes darkened. "We all did. They hit us with it last spring when we were negotiating our contracts for this year. The message was simple. Sign it or no contract. None of us liked it, but there wasn't much we could do about it. I'm two years shy of retirement eligibility, Julie. I can't afford to throw all that away."

"That much pressure was put on you?"

Myrna shoved her empty plate away. "You remember Doris Berquist? She refused to sign their damned form, claiming it was an infringement of her civil rights. Her principal called her in and suggested she apply for early retirement while she still had the chance, because they weren't going to renew her contract."

"I—I don't believe it," Julie stammered.

"It cost her ten percent of what she would have received had she been able to hold on two more years."

Julie's jaw dropped and her hands went still as she stared at the woman across from her. "But she was a wonderful teacher."

Doris was one of those rare history teachers who got students excited about the subject because she always managed to fold in the human element and tie events of the past to what was happening in the students' own lives. Kids came away feeling they were part of history, not outsiders observing immutable and irrelevant incidents, that they could make a difference.

"The administration decided she wasn't a good role model to be in the classroom because she questioned authority." Bitterness sharpened Myrna's words, though she kept her voice low.

"You're serious?" This was unconscionable. Doris Berquist wasn't a radical. She was as patriotic as they came, and she loved her students. Teaching was her whole life.

"As a heart attack," Myrna said without a hint of humor. "That's an awfully high price to pay for questioning authority."

Myrna slipped Julie's empty plate on top of her own and moved the stack to the edge of the table.

"Anita Francis signed the paper last year, then made the mistake of criticizing it at a parent-teacher meeting. Two days later, she received a letter of reprimand and was told privately by the principal that if she didn't keep her mouth shut, her contract wouldn't be renewed this year, either. She can see the handwriting on the wall, so she's applying for early retirement at the end of this school year, too."

"But why is the administration doing this? Those women are exceptional teachers, exactly the ones you want to keep."

"Economics, for one thing. Seniority means higher pay and early retirement costs less in the long run," Myrna explained. "Getting rid of the old guard also gives the superintendent a chance to move his own people in. The experienced teachers they're hiring now come from Picard's old district."

"In other words," Julie observed, "they're his cronies, his puppets. Where does the teachers' union stand on this?"

Myrna sneered. "Not on our side, that's for sure. A few of us wanted the local to challenge the oath. But the bigwigs reminded us we have a damn good health plan, so shut up. The oath is a legitimate condition of employment."

"That's ridiculous. The union fights conditions of employment all the time. That's one of their biggest causes."

"I'm just telling you what they told us," Myrna retorted angrily, then gave a snort in apology for the outburst.

This was more than a little disturbing. "Who's behind this oath?"

"No question in my mind or anyone else's. Picard. Don't let his suave manner fool you. The guy's a shark with very sharp teeth."

The answer didn't surprise Julie. "Why is he doing it?"

"What I can tell you is that he called a special meeting of all the teachers in the district right after the oath was approved. When he made a decision, he explained, he expected us to salute smartly and obey, without question or reservation. Anyone who didn't like those rules could find employment elsewhere.''

"Were any members of the school board present?"

Myrna shook her head. "He didn't want witnesses. A couple of press people showed up, but he forced them to leave, and he warned the rest of us that if we discussed this with the media, we would be summarily fired for insubordination. It was a closed-door session. Him and us. And he made it absolutely clear he was the one wielding the big stick.''

"I'm amazed he's been able to keep this under wraps.''

Myrna frowned and lowered her head. "Believe it or not, there are teachers who support him, who think this is a good thing. Those of us who have a hard time with it also have the most to lose by speaking out. Picard's no fool. He knows how far he can push and how tight he can turn the screws.''

Julie could understand a person in a leadership position not wanting to be constantly questioned and criticized in public, but these measures were over the top and raised more questions than they avoided. Why would such draconian measures be put in place, except to intimidate? Why would intimidation be necessary if everything was on the up-and-up?

She resolved to ask Rolf those very questions.

JULIE STOPPED BY the lumberyard after work that afternoon to buy the materials she needed for her new shelves.

"If you'd like help installing these…" Rolf lifted precut, laminated white shelves off the rack one by one and carefully placed them in her cart. "They're not difficult to install, but they can be time-consuming if you've never done anything like this before."

She was busy counting out the brackets that would clip onto the vertical runners. He noticed her mouth was drawn and for a moment he thought she was about to tell him she was quite capable of screwing a few brackets into the wall. Then she glanced at him and he realized she'd simply been concentrating.

"Are you offering technical assistance?" she asked.

He was willing to give her any kind of assistance she might require—or desire. "And free labor."

"A strong man in my life. How exciting."

The sarcasm chastened him, and he cocked his head to one side. "Am I missing something? Did I say or do…"

Her movements halted and her shoulders sagged. "Sorry. I'm not in a very good mood right now." She lifted a bracket off the display rod, careful not to hit anything. The paint can display, she noticed, had been relocated.

"Anything I can help you with?"

She hesitated, then looked around to confirm no one was within earshot. "I've been checking on Picard."

Probably found out there was no sinister plot and was annoyed at having to admit it.

"So have I," he said. She regarded him with a crooked brow. "How about I come over to your place this evening, help you install these shelves and we can compare notes." The thoughtful purse of her lips was pure distraction.

"What about the kids?"

"Leah's over at a girlfriend's, working on a project. Derek has football practice until nine. And the twins are attending a birthday party. They won't be home until nine, either."

"So you're footloose and carefree."

He was on the verge of a smile. At this moment, he wished it were true. "Let's just say I'm unencumbered for a couple hours."

"I'll pick up a bucket of chicken," she announced, and gave him her address.

HE KNOCKED ON HER DOOR promptly at 6:30. "I hope you like chocolate mocha," he said when she answered.

She'd changed out of the pale-green floral dress into an old pair of cutoff jeans. Below their frayed edges, her bare legs begged to be stroked. The body heat they generated in him threatened to melt the ice cream in his hand.

"Good choice." She waited for his eyes to rise above her belly button. "It'll take the bite out of the Cajun-style chicken tenders I picked up."

He didn't need pepper at this point to break into a sweat. "How'd you know I like it spicy?"

She closed the door behind him and relieved him of the plastic bag containing the ice cream. He followed her into the efficiency kitchen and watched her put it in the bottom freezer.

"I noticed how you piled the jalapeños on your fajitas at the Corderos' last weekend," she commented over her shoulder.

"Observant lady." He was glad her back was turned so she couldn't observe the effect she was having on him.

She spun around. "Do you want to eat or work first?"

Now he had to contend with those incredible blue eyes. "Unless you're starving, I'd just as soon get the work part out of the way."

His attention was riveted on the sway of her hips as she led him to her bedroom. She pointed to the wall between the two windows facing the queen-size bed. "That's where I want them."

He had an urge to turn her in the opposite direction and lead her to where he wanted her. Sweat was beading on the back of his neck. He forced himself to survey the room. It wasn't fussy, but it was definitely feminine. A nineteenth-century china doll dressed in a frilly Victorian gown was perched on an old-fashioned wood-ribbed steamer trunk at the foot of a four-poster. Her bed. The place where she slept. He tried not to imagine her curled up under the fluffy down quilt.

She'd already laid things out on the carpeted floor. Drill and bits, level, tape measure, power screwdriver. Her efficiency gave him the distinct feeling she didn't need his assistance, but he was too distracted by the sight of her crouching over the well-stocked toolbox to figure out if he was pleased by that or not.

She explained how high she wanted the shelves. He did his best to concentrate on inches and fractions and not the rise of her breasts when she lifted her arms. He measured. He marked. He measured again. He drilled. All the time he kept sneaking glances at those incredible legs. He was definitely a leg man, and Julie's made him feel like a teenager again. It was a good thing he didn't have to use a hammer, he decided, or he'd probably have lost a thumbnail.

She readjusted the spacing of the shelves three times before she was satisfied they were exactly where she wanted them. He helped her stack the books and bookends. Novels. Mostly romances, a few thrillers and bestsellers.

"You've earned your keep." She dropped the tools into the box and closed the lid, then straightened and brushed off her hands. Their eyes met and he caught himself smiling at the jitters he saw lingering there. He felt even better when she fumbled with "Thanks" before declaring, "Let's eat."

In the kitchen, she set up a bamboo tray for each of them and placed the chicken she'd kept warm in a low oven on a third tray, along with the coleslaw and biscuits. She offered him his choice of soft drink from the refrigerator, and they carried dinner into the living room.

"I've been checking—" Rolf opened a paper napkin and smoothed it on his knee "—on the oath."

"Really? So have I. What did you find out?"

"Ladies first."

"Pretend I'm a feminist. Humor me."

"Are you?"

She slanted him a withering glare. "What have you learned?"

"That your concerns are unfounded. I've read the oath, and while I agree the wording is intimidating, I fail to see a diabolical plot behind it." He smiled. "It's merely an attempt to cool emotions so people can focus on doing their jobs."

Her eyes narrowed over the drumstick she was about to bite into. "Let me guess where you checked." There was a fine edge in her voice that came close to disdain.

He'd anticipated her not being happy with his conclusion, but he hadn't expected this level of hostility.

"You talked to someone on the board who voted
for the measure last year," she stated, "and he told
you it was all openly discussed and well intended."

He was taken aback. Of course that was how he
checked on it. What would she expect? Who else
could he talk to about it? The short-tempered anger
he'd experienced earlier was back. He felt like a fool.
"Bill Marcus introduced the measure right after Picard took over as superintendent, but Picard wasn't
even at that particular meeting. He was at a conference in Washington."

"How convenient."

"Instead of sniping at me—" he matched her flat
tone "—why don't you tell me what you found out.
I'd like to know what has you so riled."

She tossed her napkin onto her tray and rose from
the end of the couch. "All right. I talked to a teacher
I worked with several years ago when I was an intern.
She almost lost her job last spring when she questioned this loyalty oath. Another teacher was forced
into early retirement when she refused to sign it, and
a third teacher will also be taking early retirement at
the end of this school year."

"Are you sure you're not exaggerating?" She had
practical knowledge; his was theoretical. And it irri-
tated the hell out of him. "Opting for early retirement
isn't the same as actually being fired. Maybe it was
her perception that she was in danger of being let
go."

"'Let go.'" She repeated the words quietly, as if
she were examining them. "Is that what you call it?"
He could see she was simmering, ready to boil over.

"A person works for nearly thirty years to be a positive and productive influence on children and she's simply let go?"

As far as he could tell, no one had actually suffered any harm as a result of this policy. "This teacher who retired... How can you be sure it wasn't her choice?"

"Because I know her," Julie nearly shouted. "She's good at what she does, Rolf. She takes a subject that could be dull and dry and makes it relevant to her students."

"Maybe she's burned-out."

Julie threw up her hands in complete exasperation. "That explanation may salve your conscience, but it's bull. If you were acquainted with these women, you'd realize that. They're dedicated professionals who take their calling very seriously. Good teachers improve with time, Rolf. It's the lazy and incompetent ones who deteriorate, and I can assure you these women are the best."

She was standing in front of the cold, gas-log fireplace. He climbed to his feet and moved toward her. Opening his arms to her seemed completely natural. But she dodged his embrace.

"You claim the school board loves Picard," she reiterated. "I tell you the majority of teachers fear and despise him, but they're afraid to speak out."

"I can see you believe that," he conceded.

"Don't you dare patronize me, Rolf Murdock."

He hung his head in frustration. "Isn't there a chance you might be mistaken?"

"No," she shot back without a moment's hesitation. "I looked into Myrna's eyes when she was telling me about these incidents. Picard called a teachers' meeting right after the oath was approved and read

them the riot act. Cross him, he told them, and he'd
fire them for insubordination.''

"Has anyone actually been fired?" He flinched at
the daggers her blue eyes shot him. "It's a reasonable
question, Julie. All I have, third-hand, is that this
guy's a bully. But I haven't seen any evidence of it.''

Her chest pounded. She thought they'd been making progress, forming a bond that went beyond mutual
physical attraction, a bond that encompassed respect
and trust. At least, that was what she thought she'd
found in his kiss, his soft words, the erotic desire
simmering in his eyes. Obviously she'd been wrong.
He'd asked for evidence of bad faith, and she'd given
it to him. Now he was calling her a liar, a fraud, a
troublemaker.

"You haven't delved very deeply for proof that I
might be right, have you?" She lowered her voice,
but not its intensity. "Accepting the word of a school
board member who approved this thing is hardly making an unbiased evaluation.''

"Let me pose another question." His tone was
equally unbending. "If Picard is behind this, what's
his goal? What's he after? Why alienate the very
teachers and staff he's responsible for supervising, the
very people who can undermine his credibility?"

Rolf watched her mind work. He had the feeling
she wasn't searching for an answer so much as trying
to decide how to frame it.

"You're suggesting that they could simply not pro-
duce in order to discredit Picard."

"Something like that.''

Her shoulders sagged and she shook her head, defeated. "You still don't get it. Teachers don't go into
the classroom to make points with their superiors. The

good ones have only one mission—to teach children what they need to know. Their reward isn't in a paycheck or benefits or awards. It's seeing the light of understanding go on in a pupil's eyes, recognizing they've connected, imparted knowledge—and occasionally maybe even a kernel of wisdom. Teachers ache when students fail to succeed. The administration doesn't. Hell, administrators win pay raises because people think money will solve everything. Isn't that the current trend? If you pay incompetents more money, they'll magically become geniuses. Well, good teachers care about their students. They won't betray what they consider a sacred trust to make a point." She paused, forcing herself to calm down. "How many school board members did you talk to?"

"One," he conceded. "But I don't think he would intentionally lie to me." She snorted. He ignored her. "He admitted there were a few questions, even misgivings about the oath, but they saw it as doing more good than harm, and thus far, it's working. The atmosphere is less contentious."

"Because nobody's allowed to criticize."

"There's also less school violence, improved test scores. More scholarships awarded."

"So the end justifies the means."

"Tell me again what's wrong with asking people to be loyal to their organization?"

Disheartened, she huffed out a breath. "It depends on the organization, Rolf."

"What's wrong with the current school establishment that you want to be free to attack it?"

"We're going around in circles. I don't know because no one is permitted to talk about it."

He paced, as discouraged as she was.

"If Picard is behind this, as you seem to think, what does he have to gain?"

Julie shook her head. "I have no idea, except that he's on a power trip. That may be enough."

For some people power was an end in itself. "I'll look into this more closely, Julie, but frankly I doubt I'll find anything. Maybe there is a bit of a Napoleon complex at work here, but I can't see that it's doing any real harm." He raised his hand to stop her when she made an effort to speak. "What I'm saying is that I'll try to keep an open mind, but I'm not ready to condemn Picard yet, not until I see credible evidence he's doing something wrong."

CHAPTER FIVE

ROLF WAS STICKING BAR CODES on a new shipment of masking tape the next morning when one of the maintenance men from the district administrative building came in. Rolf had met him before. They'd passed the time, talking mostly about the drought and its effect on the price of pecans, since the guy had a dozen bearing trees on his property.

"Hello, Darren, what can I do for you today?"

"Howdy, Rolf. Need to match some paint. Brought a sample of the old stuff."

"Oil or latex?"

"Latex. I thought I still had the formula from when we painted that bathroom last time, but I guess it got thrown out."

"You purchased the paint here?"

"Yep. The district buys all its paint from you now."

"Shouldn't be a problem then. We'll have it on file." Rolf examined the small scrap of woodwork Darren handed him. "Hmm, lavender. Must be the ladies' john."

Darren snickered. "Miz Shaddick's *personal* john. We fixed it up for her a few months ago, and now she wants a private shower." He shrugged eloquently. "I guess it's one of the perks of being a bigwig. We had to take two stalls out of the regular ladies' room around the corner to accommodate her. Danged if I know why she needs it. How many people shower at work? But it ain't my place to question stuff like that. I just do what I'm told.''

They wandered over to the mixing bench, where Rolf consulted a computer terminal. ''Here it is. Spring lilac. Two gallons last January.'' He scribbled the formula on a notepad. ''Won't take but a few minutes to mix this up. One gallon this time?'' At Darren's nod, he asked, ''Need anything else?''

''Plumbing fixtures. I'll go check them out while you do that.''

Darren wandered away, and Rolf retrieved a gallon of tint base and set about adding the various dyes to it, tapped the lid back on with a mallet, clamped the can securely in the shaker, flipped the switch and went to join the maintenance man. He'd selected a high-priced, high-quality set of shower hardware.

''That comes with a lifetime warrantee, so be sure to save the paperwork.''

''I send it over to accounting. What they do with it is their business. I can't ever recall following up on a warrantee for something like this, anyway.''

Rolf wasn't surprised. Bureaucracies collected all sorts of papers, then couldn't find them when they needed them, or didn't know they had them to begin with. But then, most individuals didn't follow up on warrantees, either.

''How are things with the new superintendent?'' he asked casually as he realigned boxes on a shelf.

''The guy's all right,'' Darren said. ''Greets me by name when he sees me, asks how things are going in maintenance. It's nice to be recognized and not taken for granted. I don't recall the stuffed shirt he replaced even asking my name.''

"Good PR,'' Rolf noted.

"I get the feeling he listens, too.''

Even better PR, Rolf mused, and wondered why he was being cynical. "He seems to be keeping you busy.''

"We've put more hours in on the Ivory Tower since he came here than we did in the past five years.''

"Sounds like it needed attention.''

"Not all that much.'' He examined the kind of commercial-grade flush valve used in public rest rooms. "A couple of schools need it more. But I didn't say that,'' he quickly added.

"Like what?''

"Nothing. I shouldn't even have mentioned it.''

Noting the man's sudden nervousness, Rolf asked, "Heard everyone had to sign a loyalty oath last year. You, too?''

Darren's eyes went wide before he quickly averted his gaze. "Like you said, everybody did.''

Rolf tried to pass it off lightly. "Well, you don't have to sweat anything you say to me. I'm on the board, so it's not like telling tales out of school.'' He chuckled. His companion didn't. Rolf was about to pursue the matter, when a customer wandered down the aisle and Darren became very businesslike.

"I'll take this one. I can return it if it isn't what she wants, can't I?''

An unnecessary question. "Of course. That paint should be ready about now.''

After Darren left, Rolf became curious. Coyote

Lumber wasn't the sole building supply that sold to the school district. On his computer in his office, he checked figures. In the past six months, sales had doubled those of the previous administration, and the items were curious. Paint in colors that didn't seem appropriate for classrooms. Stylish wallpaper. Light fixtures that were more decorative than utilitarian. Ceramic tile that was definitely not institutional. Paneling that suited offices, not public spaces or classrooms. Clearly, a great deal of money was being spent on administrative space. That didn't mean equal and larger amounts weren't being spent on classrooms. The district could be procuring classroom materials from other retailers, but Darren said they were buying all their paint from him. Wouldn't even routine maintenance and repair of school buildings require paint?

Maybe Darren was only referring to the administration building. But Rolf didn't think so. On the other hand, maintenance often went in cycles. Routine work was performed on one building or series of buildings, then the repair crew moved to the next area, which would have different supply requirements. Perhaps the schedule had simply evolved to administrative space—or stalled there.

The way Darren had suddenly clammed up was more disturbing, as if he realized he was revealing too much, making himself vulnerable. Maybe Julie was right. Rolf had been talking to the wrong people. The only part of the Ivory Tower he'd seen was the entryway and the short corridor leading to the conference room. It was time he saw more. Visiting a few schools might be a good idea, as well.

THE CALL on Saturday afternoon was a pleasant surprise.

"Dad's taking the boat out tomorrow," Leah announced, "and we want you to join us."

"Have you asked your father?"

"It's okay with him. Will you come, please?"

She'd promised herself she would keep her distance, not because of her brother's comments, but because she obviously didn't have much credibility with Rolf. "What time?"

"Noon." The girl sounded hopeful.

She should decline the invitation. "I'll see you at your house about twelve o'clock then."

"Great. Dad said to bring your bikini so you can water-ski with us."

Not bathing suit. Bikini. A shimmer of excitement raced through her and her mind conjured up the memory of Rolf's bare torso, water drops suspended in the fine mesh of hair on his chest...

"Water-ski?" She hadn't done that in several years. "I hope it's like riding a bicycle—you never forget."

Leah giggled. "I bet you're better than all of us put together."

Julie laughed back. "Don't count on it."

She called out to the ranch and told Sheila she'd decided to stay in town this weekend but that she'd see them the next. When her stepmother didn't ask any questions, Julie figured the older woman was wise to what was going on. Not too much got past her.

The following day, at noon precisely, Julie halted in front of the Murdock house on Coyote Avenue and walked around to the back. Rolf's Express was backed up to the right bay of the garage, a good-size boat hitched to it.

The twins, who were stuffing blankets behind the back seat of the vehicle, greeted her, and Julie instantly realized she was in for a challenging day. Both boys were wearing exactly the same outfits. How would she tell them apart? She tried very hard to isolate a unique feature in their clothing. A different pair of shoelaces. A smudge or tear in their T-shirts or shorts. Nothing. She couldn't even find a skinned knee that would help her distinguish them. And knowing they were mirror images of each other, they awarded her identical smiles.

"Guess," taunted the one on the right.

That was all she could do—guess. Jeff tended to be the more aggressive, so she decided he was the one who had asked the question.

"Wrong," they agreed simultaneously, and grinned like cats.

She studied them more closely, again trying to find something that might give her a clue, but so far the secret eluded her.

"By the end of the day," she declared, "I'll be able to tell you two apart."

Simultaneously they raised their eyebrows, their expressions reflecting the fun they were having. But she had the satisfaction of detecting the tiniest smidgen of fear that she might succeed.

Feeling pleased with herself, she laughed and turned to the back door of the house.

Rolf was bent over, his nose stuck in the refrigerator, his shorts revealing long, heavily muscled legs that were dusted with curly dark hair. She stood there for a moment appreciating the view. "Quite a pose."

He pulled back with a jerk and peered over the top of the half door, a leer melting his features into a broad grin. His gaze wandered appreciatively over her bare legs, as well.

"Glad you could make it." His eyes twinkled playfully. "I hope you brought sunscreen. Today promises to be a scorcher. If you didn't, we have plenty."

His twisted broad smile suggested he'd be glad to apply it on her. The effect of that scenario was like instant sunburn. Her face grew hot.

"Thanks for inviting me." The high voltage between them was practically crackling. Willing her pulse to cease its stammering, she asked, "What can I do to help?"

"All that's left is to load this stuff." He nodded to the picnic basket and the cooler on the kitchen table.

Their hands met when they both reached for the basket.

"Oops, sorry." But he seemed in no rush to pull his hand away. "Can you handle this okay?"

Was he referring to the bulky hamper? She was sure she could manage that fine. She toted sixty-pound bales of hay when she had to. But if he was asking whether she could deal with his touching her, even casually, without her pulse skipping a beat and her tongue getting tangled, well, she wasn't quite as confident.

"I'll grab this," she told him. "Why don't you take the cooler."

"All right." He withdrew his hand.

They returned to the lakeside park where they'd gone fishing. He pulled up to the boat ramp and maneuvered into position on the first try. Ten minutes later, they were out on the lake.

In spite of a gentle breeze, the lake was smooth and relatively unpopulated. Derek was first up on the skis, handling himself with aggressive confidence and clumsy strength. Leah was less flamboyant but more graceful. Foster and Jeff were the clowns. Uncoordinated and totally entertaining. They took their dunkings with humor and verve.

Maybe it was the heat of Indian summer or the way Rolf's eyes seemed to caress her skin when her back was turned that made her hot. Whatever the reason, she felt invigorated when it was her turn to plunge into the cool lake. Rolf let the rope feed out, goosed the throttle and pulled slowly away, allowing her to gain her balance before gunning the engine to full speed.

She shot out of the water, rode his wake, thrilled by the speed, the wind, the sun and the look in the eyes of the man watching her from the wheel of the boat. He circled around in ever tightening arcs, carving figure eights on the placid lake. She skipped across the waves and zigzagged back to the hoots and cheers of the children. She never completely lost sight of their father, or his playful smirk just before he made another sharp swerve.

Somehow, she stayed vertical.

"Your turn," she called up to him almost breathlessly when Derek towed her to the side of the boat.

She watched the flexing play of Rolf's muscles as he bent and adjusted the foot straps on the skis. In a game of Truth or Dare, she'd have to admit she'd been sneaking glimpses of his sun-drenched body all afternoon. She wondered how he'd respond to a dare to touch that warm, exposed flesh.

"Hang on," she called out.

His brows went up, his mouth forming an O when she rammed the lever forth and shot ahead. Not quick enough to catch him completely off balance, though. His biceps bulged as he clutched the handle at the end of the rope. His flat belly rippled as he straightened his spine and leaned back against the force of the water gliding under his legs. And he laughed.

The happy sound sent darts of delight through her. She was torn between having to keep her eyes ahead or looking back at the sleek wet lines of his well-toned body.

With the kids egging her on, she cut a few sharp maneuvers designed to tumble him, but he was too quick, too dexterous, too able to anticipate her moves. She laughed with him when Derek finally gave him a hand on board.

"Got to be faster than that," he quipped. "I'm an old pro at this."

"I'll keep that in mind," she answered, a giggle disguising itself in a wide grin.

Rolf took over the wheel, brought them alongside the dock and shut off the engine. Leah and her brothers scampered out of the boat with unflagging energy and found a picnic table not too far away. Everyone settled down to lunch.

"I'm having second thoughts about the oath," Rolf confessed after the youngsters had gone off with friends to check out the fishing. Rolf stretched out on the quilt they'd spread on a small patch of grass.

"Why?" She bit into an apple and chewed.

"One of the district maintenance men came in the other day. We talked a little, but as soon as I started asking questions about school affairs, he clammed up."

"Negative evidence," she noted flippantly. "Doesn't prove a thing. Maybe he doesn't like to talk about work.'' She held up the half-eaten piece of fruit. ''Or he's done something wrong and doesn't want you picking up on it.''

Rolf's smile indicated he appreciated what she was doing—throwing his argument right back in his face. ''Could be,'' he admitted. ''But I did some checking. The district's spent an awful lot of money on the Ivory Tower over the past year.''

''The place is pretty plush,'' she declared, as if she were proud of the fact. ''You ought to come visit it.''

''I propose to, but I'll do it when you're not there.''

She got the message. He was trying to protect her. A grackle cawed harshly in a nearby mesquite tree. Julie ran her tongue over her front teeth, not sure if she was pleased that he wanted to protect her or offended that he thought he had to.

''A fancy admin building doesn't mean much,'' she pointed out.

''True enough, unless priorities are misplaced.'' He folded his hands behind his head and closed his eyes. ''Darren commented that a couple of the school buildings need attention. Do you know anything about that?''

She tossed the apple core into the plastic bag they'd brought for trash and wiped her lips with a paper napkin. ''I taught for a while at Grover Elementary and later at Alamo Junior High. We had a lot of trouble with rest rooms in both places.'' She settled onto her side, facing him, bending her elbow to support her head. Rolf had a strong profile. A straight nose, square jaw, firm chin. A very pleasant combination to gaze at.

''Aside from the plumbing, there were broken wall tiles, the sinks were stained beyond reclamation and several of the light fixtures were permanently out of order,'' she went on. ''Neither place had been painted in years, and there were a bunch of broken windows that had been taped up. Other than that, they were fine structures.''

His profile would be a nice thing to wake up to in the morning.

''Except when it rained, of course'' she went on. ''Fortunately, most of the leaks were in the hallways rather than the classrooms.''

''You're kidding, right?'' He opened his eyes and studied her. ''The schools aren't really that bad. Are they?''

She pondered the creases bracketing his mouth. Not laugh lines, she decided. Character lines. ''If you don't believe me, go see for yourself.''

He shifted his head back, again closed his eyes and remained silent for several minutes. ''When I first joined on board, Alyson Shaddick gave me a school tour. We went to—''

''Jefferson Elementary, Pioneer Junior and Memorial High.''

He stared at her. ''How did you know?''

''They're the showcases. They take all visitors there because those schools are in the better parts of town. They're the newest campuses and the best maintained.''

He levered himself up and rested on his elbows. ''You're telling me I was hoodwinked.''

''You said it. I didn't.'' She'd promised herself she wouldn't permit this subject to upset her. But it already had, and she didn't like herself for it. Antsy and annoyed, she climbed to her feet and strolled toward the lake.

She didn't have to glance back to know he was following. It wasn't simply the subject of the school board or the oath that was boosting her blood pressure.

Halfway to the dock, where the children were busy trying to untangle snarled lines, she spun around and faced him. Their eyes met, transfixed. She stopped breathing, dropped her gaze, then lifted it.

"I need to ask you... The answer's important." Several heartbeats later she peered up at him again. "I'm convinced something's not right in the school district. I don't know precisely what it is, but something's very wrong. My question is, do you agree with me, or do you think I'm just blowing smoke?"

He smiled, a soft, gentle, caring grin that twisted her heart. "I agree with you. The question now is what are we fixin' to do about it?"

She exhaled loudly, her chest rising and falling in great swells. Without thinking, she raised her arms and hung her hands on his shoulders, then leaned against him. The feel of his hard chest, the warmth of his body, the rhythm of his heart thudding in her ear awakened a desire so intense her breath caught. When he wrapped his arms around her, she instinctively snuggled against him. The sounds around them blended into a murmur as he tilted her chin up to his.

Awareness hit her like a gut punch and she suddenly pulled away. "People are watching," she mumbled.

His innocent smile came close to being angelic. He looked around. "So they are." Playfulness bubbled in his voice. "Would you like to go for a walk?"

She drew her lips between her teeth. "I think it would be wise if we checked on the kids first."

His eyes were laughing. "Good idea."

So they sauntered out on the dock and asked the fishermen what they were catching, commiserated on their rotten luck and wished them well, then casually wandered off as if their stroll was the most ordinary thing in the world.

He reached for her hand and guided her along a trail that skirted the parking lot before weaving its way through a thick growth of mesquite and live oak toward the next campground. At the midpoint, the path climbed a steep grade to the top of a hillock that gave a sweeping view of the lake.

Sailboats, speedboats, jet skis and a few rowboats dotted the corrugated surface of the water. The clear blue sky sparkled off the surface, giving it a crisp metallic gleam.

They'd fallen silent in their trek, a comfortable quietness. When he turned, his hand still holding hers, and brought his mouth closer, it was perfectly natural to let his lips bond with hers. When his tongue probed, it was instinctive for her to open them to him. And when their tongues met, it was irresistibly necessary to whimper with delight. Nature was definitely having its way there on this little promontory. Like his arms encircling her and hers hugging his waist, and the heat their bodies were generating between them.

Nature was producing other reactions, as well. Reactions that pleasured and tormented and left them both breathless. Reactions that made them smile and frown at the same time.

"I wish we could turn out the lights," he whispered, his lips close enough to hers that she could feel the physical warmth of his words.

She wanted to tell him they had to keep their eyes open, make sure they knew what they were doing. But she wasn't sure herself. He was eleven years her senior, a divorced father with four children. She had to remind herself of that, remind herself that life was more complicated than a kiss.

CHAPTER SIX

SCHOOL BOARD MEETINGS were held the fourth
Thursday of every month in the school administration
building conference room. They were public, but few
people attended when budgets were discussed unless
specific certain items were under consideration, such
as new football uniforms. Policies on appropriate student attire, lunch menus and school bus schedules
tended to draw larger crowds than buying new equipment for the chemistry lab.

Bill Marcus managed the office supply company
his family had established three-quarters of a century
ago. He'd been on the school board eight years, the
last three as chairman. Two of the other five members,
also ran their own companies. Matt Hargrove owned
a body-repair shop, and Chase Milsap held the franchise of a nationwide hardware store. Herb Bellows,
the military retiree, operated the well-drilling service.
Virginia Akers was a homemaker who was also active
in a wide range of social and charitable organizations.

Marcus tapped his gavel and called the meeting to
order precisely at six o'clock. He referred to the
printed agenda that had been distributed to the half-
empty room and made the usual request to waive
reading the minutes of the last meeting. The motion
was seconded, voted on and he proceeded to old business.

Most of the issues were routine and elicited little or no discussion. Finally, new business was introduced.

Rolf raised his hand to be recognized. "I'd like to discuss the matter of the oath that district employees have been forced to sign."

There was a pregnant pause. "It's not on the agenda," Marcus pointed out.

"I can bring it up during open discussions if you prefer," Rolf countered mildly.

"We'll take this up in executive session after the meeting," the chairman snapped.

"I'm wondering why such a sworn statement is necessary," Rolf persisted. He was disappointed when his query seemed to garner no reaction from the people in the audience.

When Marcus appeared unsure how to reply, Chase Milsap spoke up. "Mr. Chairman, if I may." He shifted in his seat to address Rolf, who was at the opposite end of the long table. "The oath was initiated last year after we went through a particularly difficult period. We felt it was necessary to calm the rhetoric and allow people to get on with their jobs."

This seemed to be the party line, which didn't make it wrong, of course.

"Criticism is annoying," Rolf acknowledged, "but it's part of the job."

"We haven't exempted ourselves from criticism, Mr. Murdock," the chairman informed him in a curt manner. "This is an open meeting. We're here to answer any questions the public might have about policy matters and to listen to their views."

"But not from members of your own establishment. Teachers and administrators are in an excellent position to give insight and advice. This oath effectively silences them."

The chairman's tone hardened. "Anyone attending this meeting is free to bring up whatever he or she chooses. No one's being silenced."

"May I also add," Dr. Picard chimed in from his seat next to the chairman, "that I for one greatly value contributions from teachers and other members of my administration. After all, they're in the best positions to explain the impact of any changes we may be considering."

When Rolf made an attempt to speak, Bill raised his hand. "Employees have ample opportunity to discuss policy matters with their supervisors and other members of the staff outside these meetings. That's their proper venue, not this public forum."

"Suppose an employee doesn't receive the response he or she feels is right?" Rolf challenged.

Sensing the chairman was becoming agitated, Herb Bellows noted, "Employees have a chain of command exactly like other organizations. If someone's immediate supervisor doesn't solve a problem, he or she can take it to that person's superior."

The logic was sound but conveniently missed the point. Rolf decided to drop the matter for the time being.

Dr. Picard proposed the district submit its application to a statewide recognition program. The motion passed without objection—a good note on which to end the meeting.

"What the hell's your problem, Murdock?" the chairman blared as soon as the press and public had cleared the room.

Rolf briefly considered playing innocent, but it

wasn't his style. "It's a legitimate question, Bill. Why does this bother you so much?"

"A legitimate question." Marcus's tone was scathing. "You might take a lesson from Herb. If you have a concern, you ought to consult the people who have the answers before voicing seditious comments in public."

"Seditious?" Rolf raised an eyebrow. It wasn't a term he would have expected.

"You'd better decide if you're going to be a team player, Murdock. A lot of us are beginning to wonder."

"I seem to have hit a hot button. Aren't you overreacting?" The very term Rolf had used to initially challenge Julie.

"I don't like being blindsided. The subject of this oath was not on the agenda. You had every opportunity to put it there, but you chose not to."

"Instead, you embarrassed all of us by bringing up a subject that was settled a long time ago," Chase Milsap contributed. "I have to question why."

"You could have probed any of us about this any time. Why bring it up here and now?" Virginia Akers asked quietly.

"Seems like you want to stir things up and cause trouble," Marcus insisted, his temper as cutting as before.

"As a matter of fact, I did talk to Herb about it last week," Rolf pointed out.

Bellows's face darkened. "I thought I answered your questions. If I didn't, you should have said so at the time."

"Rather than sabotaging this meeting," Marcus interjected.

Rolf's temper was beginning to rise. "Inflammatory words like *sedition* and *sabotage* are hardly conducive to calming emotions," he countered. "I didn't sabotage this meeting, and I don't understand why you're all so upset." He barely refrained from commenting that their reactions smacked of a collective guilty conscience. "I didn't come here with the intention of even raising the subject. Now I'm beginning to wonder if we ought to put it on the agenda for the next meeting and invite a full public debate over the issue."

He saw shock on the faces of the people around him.

"Mr. Murdock." Dr. Picard spoke up in a quiet adult tone. "I'm afraid this subject has gotten blown completely out of proportion, and like you, I'm not sure I understand why." He turned to the others. "Why don't we sit down for a minute, discuss this calmly and see if we can resolve it."

Bill was still clearly steaming, but he accepted the superintendent's lead. Shunning the raised dais where they'd been seated, Picard pulled around one of the chairs from the public area and motioned for the others to do the same. They sat in an informal semicircle below the platform.

"I wasn't here last year when the board adopted the oath you referred to," Picard stated in a dispassionate, very sincere manner. "Yes, I was aware of it, and I approved of it after the fact, but I had nothing to do with its drafting."

Bill's hands ceased their rubbing motion, and he glared at the superintendent. The old man leaned back in the folding chair, making it creak, and listened.

Picard went on. "Having said that, let me try to

explain why it was implemented. Over the past thirty years, I've worked in several school districts—as classroom teacher, school principal, administrator, assistant superintendent and now superintendent. I've seen the wonderful education we can give students when teachers and administrators are united in their efforts to maintain high professional standards. I've also seen how poorly we meet our public responsibilities to the youth of this country when we allow political infighting and petty bickering to distract us.''

Several heads nodded agreement.

''My predecessor was a good man, a devoted educator and a fine teacher. But I don't think I'm misstating the situation when I say he was not a very successful superintendent.'' Again heads nodded. ''During his tenure here, school budgets decreased. Test scores plummeted. Disciplinary problems grew. Teacher, parent and student discontent rose to unprecedented levels.''

Heads were lowered now, hands twisting and jaws working. These were the people who'd been in office during that period, and they apparently recognized the implied rebuke for their mishandling of the situation.

''I gather,'' Picard went on, ''that you feel the oath school district employees have been asked to sign is somewhat extreme.'' He smiled. ''To be honest, you're probably right. Had I been involved in its drafting, I would have recommended more conciliatory language. The fact remains, however, that it's accomplished what it set out to do—stifle dissension.''

Rolf was stunned. That was precisely his point and here the superintendent was conceding it. His expression must have been transparent, because Picard chuckled softly. "That surprises you."

Rolf admitted it did with a nod.

Again turning serious. Picard went on, his hands folded calmly in his lap. "It was absolutely essential that people stop yelling at one another so we could get things on an even keel. I think you'll find we've succeeded."

"No one's been fired for not taking this oath," Chase Milsap pointed out. "No one's been fired for violating it, either."

"Because everyone's afraid to speak up," Rolf ventured.

Picard smiled. "That's a specious argument, Mr. Murdock. Presumably people take oaths with the intent of honoring them."

Chalk up another point.

"Are you willing to modify the oath then?" Rolf asked.

The chairman was still red faced.

"At some point in the future I am," Picard agreed. "However, I don't think this is the right time. It's effective in its present form, and we have a considerable way to go before this district is where we want it. Things have improved, but a great deal still needs to be done. This policy hasn't been in force very long. Let's give it a little more time, and when emotions have cooled, we'll revisit it. Will you agree to that?"

Picard had very dexterously tossed the ball back in Rolf's court. If he said no, he would be perceived as a rabble-rouser. Which would be all right, if he could bring about change. But he was outnumbered on the present board. Any counterproposals he might make could be easily voted down. He'd already come across as a maverick and a troublemaker. Finding allies now seemed virtually impossible. But if he said yes, he all but became a co-conspirator. He had to ask himself, "A co-conspirator in what?" What were they conspiring to do? He had no answer.

"I'll table it," he conceded diplomatically, "with the understanding that I intend to bring it forward for formal discussion at a future date."

"Fair enough," Picard said, and made as if to rise.

"With one other condition," Rolf added.

Picard fell back into his seat. "What might that be?" He was the soul of patience.

Rolf had to give the man credit. Picard didn't seem upset by Rolf's challenge. "That no disciplinary action be taken against an employee for violating this oath before the matter can be reviewed by this board."

Brows rose at his audacity. Except Picard's. "Anybody have any objections to that?" he inquired equitably.

Slow, tentative headshakes indicated they didn't, and Rolf sensed a kind of relief that a crisis had been averted.

JULIE HAD CONSIDERED attending the meeting, but decided keeping a low profile might be better. Besides, Rolf would fill her in when he returned home. She'd been invited to dinner and had volunteered to stay with the kids that evening, rather than ask Bryn Haggerty or call Mrs. Tremain. After getting the kids to pitch in on cleaning up the kitchen, Julie helped them with their homework, then played a rousing game of Mexican Train until Rolf reappeared a few minutes after nine o'clock.

He didn't look particularly happy, but she resolved to wait until the others were in their rooms before questioning him.

"Can you come over and stay with us next time Daddy has to go out at night?" Jeff asked. The others hung on her answer.

"I can't promise I'll be able to all the time," she answered truthfully, without finishing the thought. The implied answer was "Yes," and they all accepted it without it being spoken.

"They give you any trouble?" Rolf asked a few minutes later in the kitchen. He offered her a long-neck beer from the refrigerator.

She nodded acceptance and watched him twist off the cap. When she reached for the bottle, their hands brushed, a casual contact that should have meant nothing, yet it was like touching a low-voltage wire, not enough to shock, just enough to tingle.

"Thanks. They were fine."

"Probably on their good behavior." He grinned. "They've taken to you."

"You can be very proud of them and of the job you've done raising them."

He waved her into the living room. She settled on one end of the couch, he on the other.

"They rarely mention their mother, Rolf."

Her brother's comment that Sheryl might show up at any time and want to be with her children had been quietly tormenting her. She had to know, yet she'd been afraid to ask. Afraid the question would imply she was interested in a relationship she wasn't willing to admit yet, even to herself. Afraid of what the answer might be.

"They must miss her terribly. Do they ever hear from her?"

Rolf went very still for a moment, wariness keeping him from making eye contact with her. "She's been gone over two years now. Not that she was here much before that. She sends birthday cards and Christmas presents."

"Where is she?"

He dangled the beer bottle off the arm of the couch, swinging it in a lazy circle. "Last time I heard, in the jungles of Brazil, studying native tribes with her new husband, the archaeologist."

The bitterness in his voice was unmistakable, and Julie regretted bringing up an obviously painful subject. But if the connection between them was going to mature beyond friendship, they'd have to discuss his ex-wife. Now seemed as good a time as any.

"Tell me about her," she persisted, despite his frown. He could refuse. What would that tell her?

He took a deep swallow of his beer, clutched the half-empty bottle and stared up at the ceiling. "She was tall and athletic. Worked out at a health spa a couple of days a week. Brunette, but in the sun it had reddish highlights. Brown eyes."

He spoke of her in the past tense, which was appropriate as far as his life was concerned, but it made her sound dead. Julie had already noticed there were plenty of pictures of the kids around the house, but none of their mother. Whose decision was that? she wondered. "Sounds attractive."

"She did a little modeling in college."

"Is that where you met her?"

"Rice University in Houston. It's a wonder we even bumped into each other." His face softened slightly at the memory, but not enough to form a smile. "It's a big school, and anthropology and business administration are worlds apart."

"How long were you married?"

"Fourteen years. Tied the knot right after we graduated."

He hadn't considered it "tying the knot" at the time, more like forming a union, exchanging vows. He thought she had, too.

"A long time to be together," Julie noted. "How much of it was happy?"

Rolf drank more beer, but he didn't really taste it. "The first few years were." Looking back at them now, they seemed somehow a fraud, as if they'd been playing at love and marriage without really participating in it.

"She had a teaching job at TUCS," he went on. "I should have seen that was her first love—anthropology. Studying other people's cultures. Then Derek came along."

He'd been thrilled when she became pregnant. Only in retrospect did he understand that for Sheryl it had been a disappointment. At the time, he'd thought she was worried about her pregnancy, concerned about not being the perfect mother. It had taken almost fourteen years for him to realize she'd never wanted to be a parent in the first place. He still wondered how he'd been so blind. She claimed she'd tried to tell him, but he wouldn't listen. Maybe she was right. Maybe he'd been so awed at being a daddy that he couldn't imagine her not wanting to be a mommy.

He took a sip of beer. "I was a freelance management consultant in those days, didn't own the lumberyard yet. My hours were fairly flexible. She cut back her teaching schedule, and between us, we made sure one of us was always with the baby. Then Leah came along. We'd intended to have just two children.''

That wasn't precisely correct. Sheryl had convinced him two was enough, that it would be irresponsible to contribute to overpopulation, that financially they couldn't support more than two without lowering their standard of living. Intellectually, he agreed with her, though deep inside, he yearned for a big family. As an only child, he'd always envied kids who had brothers and sisters.

''Mother Nature had other plans,'' he added. ''Sheryl developed a problem and the doctor recommended she stop taking the pill. The twins were the result.''

An accident for which she blamed him. As if he were the one who was oversexed. He hadn't been the one who'd had an affair.

He tipped his bottle again and realized it was empty. He held it up. ''Another?''

Julie's was barely half-finished. She declined. ''But you go on.''

He considered for a moment, then shook his head and deposited the bottle on the end table.

''I reckon that's when she began to change,'' he continued, though the restlessness had been developing for some time—if only he had opened his eyes to them. ''She wasn't happy about being pregnant again.''

She horrified him when she'd suggested getting an abortion. For several months he'd worried she'd do it behind his back. He was relieved and grateful when she didn't, but his attitude toward her wasn't the same after that. He'd vowed to be a dutiful husband and he intended to keep that promise, but trust and respect were gone, and so was love.

"Sheryl had planned to teach full-time again and do anthropological research on location when Leah started school. The twins meant she had to retrench. A few years later, I bought the lumberyard, my spare time disappeared and Sheryl was left with raising the kids."

"That's what caused the breakup?"

He worked his jaw. Clearly this was the most painful part. "As soon as the twins started school, Sheryl resumed a full academic load, and that first summer she went to explore a dig with Walter Hemming, an archaeologist at the university. I suppose I should have seen it coming, but I didn't."

"They fell in love," Julie concluded quietly.

He nodded.

"I'm sorry."

"The irony is that by then the lumberyard was beginning to make money, and I had more time to spend with her and the kids. We could have afforded to go on trips... But it was too late."

Julie thought she could understand Sheryl's leaving Rolf, even if she didn't agree with it. But how could a mother abandon her children, she asked herself anew? It was unthinkable.

Rolf had picked up his beer and was slowly scraping the label off the bottle, though she doubted he realized he was doing it. What thoughts, what emotions were going through his mind? Guilt that he'd been a poor husband, a poor father? Shame that his wife had left him for another man? Guilt again that because of him, his children were growing up without a mother?

Julie polished off her beer. "I think I'm ready for plain water now."

He jumped to his feet. "Coming right up."

"So what happened at the meeting tonight?" she inquired as she trailed him to the kitchen.

His facial muscles relaxed at the change of subject. "I have to tell you, Picard is good. I raised the subject of the oath, and Bill Marcus went ballistic. It was Picard who calmed everyone down. We had an informal meeting after everyone else left, which turned out to be the most interesting part of the evening."

Rolf took two bottles from the refrigerator, handed her one and they returned to the living room. "Picard claims to have had no part in writing the oath or the decision to implement it."

"Do you believe him?"

"At the time, I wanted to." He resumed his former seat, extended his arm across the back of the couch and took a slug of spring water. "Judging from the scowl on Bill's face during the discussion, though, I suspected Picard may have talked him into ramrodding it through when he wasn't present so he could give himself deniability. Picard also admitted the purpose of the oath was to—and I use his words—*stifle dissension.*"

"That's a pretty damning admission."

"I thought so, too, until I had a chance to think about it on the way home." He cocked an eyebrow at her. "What else could be the purpose of it other than to keep people quiet? It sounds like a confession, but of what? There can't be any other reason for asking, or telling, people to keep their mouths shut."

"How did he justify it?"

"With the same reasoning Herb Bellows gave me. Too much unproductive, loudmouth name-calling going on that accomplished nothing, except to further inflame matters."

Julie tipped her bottle and took a small sip. "I have to admit he's probably right. We had two terrible football seasons in a row, lost the basketball championship by ten points, TAAS scores were down and the roof at one of the elementary schools had been torn off in a storm—"

"And we were being faced with higher school tax assessments," Rolf added.

"None of that justifies a gag order, though. What about First Amendment rights to free speech?"

Rolf grinned. "Picard admits the language of the oath is over the top. He just doesn't think this is the time to soften it. It's accomplishing its goal—"

"By suspending people's civil rights. Last time I checked, that was a tried-and-true method used by dictators—and with the same rationalized justification—to establish order."

"Chase Milsap pointed out that no one has been fired for not taking the oath, and no one has been fired for violating it."

"Quibbling," she scoffed. "Forced retirement amounts to firing. People haven't violated the oath because they're scared to death of losing their jobs."

He held up a finger. "I got the group to agree that no one would be disciplined or fired for violating it until the board had a chance to review the situation."

Julie brightened. "It's a start, I suppose, but you're not likely to get anyone to open up on your say-so alone." She rolled her water bottle between her hands. "I'll see what I can research at the office. I'd like to compile a list of employees who have left the district's employ since the oath went into effect, as well as any who might have moved into lower paying positions."

"We can probably interview the ones who left," Rolf said. "I don't know about people who've been downgraded. The oath hasn't been rescinded, so they're still vulnerable."

She studied the man sitting a few feet away. The tension he'd demonstrated while talking about his ex-wife was gone. But he wasn't completely at ease. The lines on either side of the bridge of his nose still reflected discomfort.

"What's made you change your mind, Rolf?"

He pushed back against the sofa cushion, expanded his chest and smiled. "You, first of all."

He had a wonderful smile, and when he shared it exclusively with her, as he did now, it intimated a relationship that definitely went beyond the boundaries of platonic friendship.

"You thought I was blowing this out of proportion, a flighty female—"

"I never said that." He was still smiling.

"Yeah, you did." Her narrowed eyes dared him to contradict her.

"There are other factors, too," he went on, avoiding her challenge. "The chairman's defensiveness put me on guard."

"My brother and his wife had very positive comments about Picard."

Rolf considered that. "In her own way, maybe not even consciously, Clare qualified her approval when she noted Dr. Picard is a very personable man. The guy's a charmer, Julie. Hell, he almost had me convinced he was on the side of the angels when we were talking this evening. He's not stupid by any means.''

She finished off her drink. ''It's late. I better get going. Busy day tomorrow.''

He rose and drew her into his arms. Before she realized what was happening, he ravaged her mouth with his. The intensity of his hunger startled her. Then she melted into the taste of him.

''Be careful,'' he murmured against her lips.

THE MORE ROLF THOUGHT about the two meetings he'd attended, the more angry he became. Being new to the system and unfamiliar with how it functioned, he'd naturally adopted a wait-and-see attitude, willing to take the lead from the more senior members. He'd asked questions and expected straightforward answers. A different pattern was beginning to emerge.

At the first board meeting, they'd approved reallocation of maintenance funds from schools to admin, purportedly to meet emergency repairs. They also authorized the purchase of new desks and carpeting to complete renovations that had been previously approved, but that, it turned out, hadn't included the missing items. Poor planning, but okay, it happens. The original prices quoted in the planning stage turned out to be higher at the point of purchase. That, too, could be explained—by fuel costs, for example. The problem was that this seemed to happen all the time, and no one was seriously questioning it.

He drove to the admin building on Monday at noontime, knowing Julie would be out for lunch. He checked the directory inside the main entrance. The conference room was on the ground floor, the records section in the basement. He took the stairs to the second floor. He'd never been up here. Impressive, he decided. The walls were papered, not painted, the floors thickly carpeted, not asphalt tiled. He poked his head into a few unoccupied offices. Furnishings were premium quality. No wonder the building was referred to as the Ivory Tower.

He returned downstairs. A young woman approached him. "May I help you, sir?"

"I'm looking for the records section."

"Downstairs. In the basement." She pointed to a plaque on the wall with an arrow to the lower level.

He grinned sheepishly. "Pretty sneaky, putting directions right there in front of me."

She smiled and let him pass.

He descended the concrete steps. An older woman was there, eating lunch at her desk.

She rolled the remains of her deli sandwich in its paper wrapper and threw it into the wastebasket. "Hello, Mr. Murdock. What brings you to my dungeon?"

It took a moment, but then he recognized her. She and her husband had come to the lumberyard several weeks ago to purchase treated lumber. He searched his memory for a name.

"Ever build your deck, Mrs. Nolan?"

She chuckled. "Almost. John still has to replace the ladder with steps."

"We have ready-made ones that'll probably fit the bill."

"You do?" Her face brightened. "I should have checked with you sooner. I suspect John's been procrastinating because he's not sure how to build them."

"Tell him to stop by when he gets a chance. Assembly is required, so he'll be able to brag he made them."

She laughed, enjoying their little conspiracy. "I'll do it. Now, how can I help you?"

"I'd like copies of the last three audit reports."

She eyed him curiously. "Audits?"

"They are a matter of public record, aren't they?"

"Sure," she responded quickly. "It's just that no one ever bothers to read them."

"You know how it is. I'm the new kid on the block, so I figure I better do my homework."

She rose, wiped her hands on a paper napkin and walked over to a row of file cabinets. She pulled out three separate reports, each of which was professionally plastic-bound in chocolate-brown covers and embossed with gold lettering. "I'll have to inform the superintendent you took these." She handed them over.

"Why is that? Do you tell him every time someone wants a public record?"

"No, of course not. He just likes to know about audits, copies of the minutes, things like that."

Rolf snapped his fingers. "I knew there was something else I wanted to ask for. I need the minutes of the board meetings for the past two years."

Her eyes went wide. "Two years? You realize you're talking about more than thirty meetings?"

"That many, huh?" He acted surprised, though he'd figured it would be at least that number. He also knew there wouldn't be any records of executive sessions, which was where a good deal of the infighting took place. "Well," he said with a smile, and a shrug, "I guess I have plenty of reading to do."

"It'll take me a few minutes to assemble them all."
She sounded apologetic. "If you want to come back
later—"

"That's all right. I can wait."

She shrugged. "You might as well sit at my desk.
I'll be a while."

"Thanks."

He read the executive summaries of all three reports and immediately noted a big discrepancy. The
oldest two reports confirmed that commonly accepted
accounting principles had been used in a consistent
and accurate manner, and that all monies had been
carefully and accurately accounted for. In other
words, a clean bill of procedural health.

The most recent one noted that changes in accounting procedures were made in the third quarter of the
accounting year, and that some difficulty had been
encountered in maintaining a clear audit trail.

"The changes in accounting procedures," it read,
"do not conform to generally accepted standards of
accrual accounting employed by both private commercial and government agencies. All monies appear
to be accounted for, and we found no evidence of
fraud or other violation of the public trust. We are
concerned, however, that continued use of this irreg-
ular system could result in fraud or other misappro-
priation of funds. We strongly recommend a return to
well-established accounting practices."

Rolf remembered the article in the local newspaper
reporting the audit. "All monies are accounted for
and we found no violation of the public trust."

Something was definitely going on. Julie had been
right in her "paranoia."

CHAPTER SEVEN

"ARE YOU SETTLED IN?" Alyson Shaddick asked. It had been several weeks since Julie was hired.

Julie smiled up from her desk. "There's a lot to grasp."

Her long blond hair was piled loosely on top of her head, a provocative style, since it gave the illusion that it was about to tumble down at any moment.

"Students think they're the only ones in the learning mode," she remarked. "They don't understand the tests they take in school are easy compared with the ones life will throw at them. Some lessons you have to learn on your own."

Julie wondered if there was a subliminal message in the woman's philosophical ramblings. "My father tried to tell me that once, and I didn't believe him."

"Speaking of tests, that's the project I need you to work on." She sat in the chair beside Julie's desk and crossed her legs, not bothering to pull down the tight skirt that rode halfway up her thighs. "As you know we'll be administering the TAAS at the end of the year. At times I suspect we put too much emphasis on scores, but they're what we're judged by, so we'd best meet the challenge. I'd like you to review the past three years' tests and develop a bank of practice questions that will prepare students for this year's exam."

"Be glad to," Julie agreed. She enjoyed constructing tests. It wasn't nearly as easy as people thought. Wading through a stockpile of old exams was a good place to start.

"Last year we reached the 'Recognized' standard for the first time," Alyson said. "But of course our goal is to be 'Exemplary.'"

Advancing from eighty percent of students passing the tests in reading, writing, mathematics, social studies and science to ninety percent wouldn't be an easy task and not likely accomplished in one year.

"Our students deserve no less," Alyson pointed out.

Julie agreed and set immediately to work. First, she had to assemble the tests themselves.

To her surprise, they hadn't been loaded onto the computer. She trekked to the file room in the basement and spoke to Mrs. Nolan.

"They were supposed to be computerized," the older woman agreed. "I guess Betsy never got around to it."

Betsy Wilford was Julie's predecessor. She'd retired last year after almost forty years with the school district, and moved with her husband back to their native Arkansas.

"Well, let me have them and I'll do it," Julie offered. "It'll be a good way for me to become familiar with them."

She carried the instructors' copies of the past-three-years' tests, the ones with the correct answers marked on them, and returned to her office. Typing them into files on the computer would take hours. Her research had already identified the scores for each of the tests. Indeed they'd gone up two points overall, from seventy-nine to eighty-one. Not a huge improvement objectively speaking, but significant since it crossed the crucial eighty-percent line. She established a silent goal for herself. This year the overall average would go up three points.

She stopped in at the lumberyard that afternoon, supposedly to find out if they carried dimmer switches for the overhead light in her bedroom, but really to see Rolf, to be around him. When he asked how her day had been, as she knew he would, she told him about her first real assignment. Exchanging the news of the day with him felt so right.

"I'm doing an analysis to determine which questions were easiest and which ones were the toughest. No use wasting time on the slam-dunks. But I also need to know which wrong answers are usually chosen. That's extremely valuable to teachers, showing them how they can restructure their lesson plans to be more effective."

He shifted the base of a kitchen cabinet to align with another on display. "You like your work, don't you?"

"I'm doing what I'm good at, something that's worthwhile and, I hope, will make a difference." She couldn't help but appreciate the flexing sinew in his forearms as he tugged another modular component into position. "Test analysis is tedious. A lot of teachers ignore it, which often leads to erroneous conclusions."

He pulled a red bandana from his hip pocket and wiped his brow. "In what way?"

She leaned against a sink across the narrow aisle while she tried to think of a good example. "Suppose a question on a test is, At the end of which century did Columbus discover America? If most students answer the fourteenth, is it because they don't know the great explorer made his historical journey in 1492, or because they don't comprehend that the 1400s constitute the fifteenth century?''

He was glad she wore skirts and dresses to work. It meant he got to see more of her wonderfully distracting legs. "Hmm. I see your point."

"A few practice questions on Columbus and century counting will pinpoint the problem."

"You say the individual tests aren't on the computer," he observed, more fascinated by her presence than the subject under discussion.

She groaned at the thought of having to wade through thousands of individual exam booklets to perform her analysis. "Since I have to start somewhere, I'll check the last test, the one where students achieved the best scores, and build on that."

"How about coming over to the house and having dinner with me and the kids tonight?"

"Wish I could," she told him, and meant it. She was beginning to feel as comfortable at his place as her own. Better, because he was there. "But I have a sorority meeting this evening."

The next morning, she returned to the file room.

"Julie," Mrs. Nolan said, "do you know how many individual tests you're talking about? Fifteen thousand. We don't even keep them here. No room. I'd have to requisition them from the archives."

"Oh." Julie should have realized. Her project wasn't for one school but for the entire district. Maybe she could do a sampling. "How about getting me the tests for an individual class in an individual school?"

The older woman compressed her lips in thought. "That's more doable. It still might take me a couple of days, though."

"In the meantime, I can work with what I have." She filled out a requisition slip for the tests books of two classes, one at a school that normally made a poor showing and the other from an honors class in the best school in the district.

To her surprise, they arrived the next afternoon— two large boxes of them. Isolating the ones she wanted took her until quitting time. She ended up with two stacks: one containing thirty-five tests, the other twenty-two.

It was while she was segregating the booklets that she discovered the scores opposite the names on the screen didn't match the handwritten numbers on the actual tests. Strange. She double-checked. All the grades on the screen were two points higher than those on the paper copies.

Baffled, Julie checked a few other scores. Again, the numbers on the screen had been inflated by two points.

Confusion slipped into apprehension. If what she thought she'd found was correct, the district had falsified TAAS results.

Julie compared the numbers on other tests. All of them had been raised. She ran a quick tally. The sample confirmed that there had, in fact, been no improvement in student achievement in the past year.

Who had done this? The person responsible could face criminal charges. This had to be reported. But to whom? How would she be confident she could trust the person she notified? And what should she do with the evidence sitting in her office?

Mrs. Nolan knew she had the files. Was she aware of what was going on? Probably not. She handled paperwork; she didn't read it.

Betsy Wilford, her predecessor, would have reported test results. Julie had a hard time imagining the elderly woman being part of a criminal conspiracy. She'd slowed down in her last years and should probably have retired earlier than she did, but her waning energy didn't make her dishonest.

"The final results wouldn't have gone from Betsy directly to the Texas Education Agency," Julie told Rolf that evening. This time she'd accepted his invitation to join him and the family for dinner. He'd stopped off at a Chinese restaurant and picked up take-out, one of the kids' favorites, though Jeff insisted on picking out the water chestnuts and bamboo shoots. Julie waited until they'd left the table before bringing up the problem.

"The head of administration would have reviewed them, then forwarded them on to the superintendent."

"You think Alyson's the culprit?" he asked.

Julie used her chopsticks to pluck up another piece of Orange Chicken. "Picard could easily have upped the scores before he sent them to Austin. There was a uniform two-point addition to each raw score, so it couldn't be the result of marking on a curve. I considered the possibility that additional credit was granted for a question that was eliminated, but I found no documentation to support it."

Rolf was paying attention. "How are test results reported?"

"Once Betty entered the information into the database, she would have composed a consolidated report and sent it to Alyson and the superintendent."

"So Betsy could have done it."

"Could have, but why?"

He didn't have an answer. "Would she have noticed if they were changed by someone above her?"

Julie tilted her head. "Not likely. She wouldn't have much reason to go back into the file. Besides, there are thousands of scores. Unless she happened to focus on a particular one and noticed a discrepancy, she'd never have any reason to suspect a thing."

"Okay. Eliminate Betsy Wilford."

"Which leaves Alyson Shaddick and Dr. Picard."

Rolf picked up a shrimp egg roll. "What about Alyson?"

"She wouldn't have anything to gain, either."

They remained silent for a minute or two.

"The obvious culprit," Julie ventured, "is Picard. He came here with the express promise to improve the district's standing. Now it has, and his reputation has soared."

Rolf nodded.

"There's one way to narrow it down between Alyson and Picard," Julie decided. "I'll compare the tests from the previous two years with the scores reported to the TEA. If results were falsified before Picard arrived—" she shrugged "—I don't know who to blame. But if it started after he took over, it's a safe bet he's the one who's been cooking the numbers."

That was the logical and the right thing to do, but it still left a sour taste in Rolf's mouth.

THE OFFICE OF THE MAYOR of Coyote Springs was in a three-story art deco building several blocks from the century-old Victorian courthouse. The massive furniture fit the room but dwarfed petite Georgina Hampton. Fifty-seven years old, with short, shiny, dyed mahogany hair and a generous armor of gold jewelry on her wrists and ears, she looked very efficient and feminine in her gray pinstripe suit and lavender silk ruffled blouse.

Circling the front of the desk, she extended her hand. "Hello, Rolf. Don't think I've seen you here before. How are things at home?"

"Fine, thanks."

"I understand both Jeff and Foster are competing in the state spelling bee next month. Any guess on which one will win?"

Sharp lady, he thought, and smiled in amazement at the skill of politicians for disarming their constituents. Not many people who didn't have a personal stake in something like a spelling bee would even bother to read an article about it in the local paper, much less remember the names of the contestants.

"I'm not taking any bets," he said proudly. "They never fail to surprise me."

She returned behind her desk and sat in the high-backed leather chair. "What brings you to see me?"

"School board business."

Her finely trimmed eyebrows went up at the same time she pursed her lips. "That's an independent body over which I have no power." In fact, the office of mayor was largely ceremonial, exercising very little statutory control of anything.

"I realize that, but you do have influence."

"Probably less than you do as a board member. But what precisely is it you think I should be influencing?"

"I'm concerned about the school budget. According to my analysis, we're way over this year."

"Again—" she was clearly trying to fathom where he was headed with this "—you're in a position to have an impact. The board approves expenditures. I have no say one way or another in the matter."

"But you do help shape tax policy."

"City taxes, not school taxes," she pointed out with a wary expression. "That's why it's called an independent school district."

"Do you think people really draw a distinction?"

Georgie's brows again drew together. "What precisely are you getting at, Rolf?"

"Unless school spending is curbed, school taxes will have to be raised. When that happens, people will start examining all taxes and how they're spent."

He saw her eyes flicker. A discussion of taxes always generated a politician's interest. It was the Monopoly money they had to play with.

"That sounds a little like a threat." The hardness in her eyes contradicted the smile on her lips. "I hope you don't mean it that way."

"What I'm suggesting, Mayor, is that you may have a potential problem looming."

She studied him for several seconds. "Would you care to elaborate?"

Time to level. "I'm concerned about Dr. Picard. Are you aware of a loyalty oath school district employees have to sign, in which they give up their right to publicly criticize any decision school officials make?"

She steepled her long-nailed fingers. "I believe it was implemented last year at the behest of the board chairman. What does it have to do with Dr. Picard?"

"It essentially gives him a free hand to run the district in any way he wants without any checks or balances."

Her gray eyes didn't waver from his. "Excuse me, Rolf, but isn't that precisely what the school board is charged with—overseeing school policies?"

At the meeting, Picard had managed to twist his arguments around on him, and now the mayor was doing the same thing. Rolf was getting tired of politicians.

"If you have a problem with oversight policies," she pressed, "why don't you take them up with your colleagues. Isn't that why you were elected to the post?"

He was beginning to wonder. "I've talked to Bill about it," he explained. "He's not very open-minded."

"He introduced the policy—" she snorted "—so I don't suppose he is." Georgina studied him again. "I have to admit to being a bit confused. You tell me you're worried about a directive implemented by the governing body you're a member of and in a vague way about the school superintendent. I confess I don't understand your worry, or why you're coming to me with these concerns, since my office has nothing to do with school matters."

"You're in a unique position," he elaborated, "to ask questions about public policy. I thought you might raise this issue of the loyalty oath."

"I don't see why I should." Her voice was becoming more starchy. "I have no indication there's anything wrong. What am I supposed to express concern about?" Before he could explain further, she went on. "Let me put things in perspective for you, Rolf.

Like many cities and towns across the country, we're concerned about our public education system. Coyote Springs's past record isn't particularly good—or bad. We experienced low TAAS scores and increasing disciplinary problems. When Ferron Mansfield was persuaded to retire last year, we conducted a very careful search for a replacement, a person with a proven record for turning schools around. A select committee made up of the school board and several other concerned citizens—I was honored to be one of them—narrowed the list down to six people. We interviewed all of them. Dr. Picard came out on top, and we have considered ourselves very fortunate to have hired him.''

She rested back in her chair and placed the tips of her fingers on the edge of the massive desk.

''The evidence to date indicates we made a good choice. Since Dr. Picard has taken over, our scholastic record has improved. Public confidence in the local school system has risen, and we've garnered a growing number of state, federal and private foundation grants. We have a good chance of receiving several prestigious awards, and more of our graduates this year are likely to go on to college than ever before.''

He was bucking her pride, which meant that without hard facts to contradict her litany of accomplishments, she wasn't inclined to listen to him.

''The school budget is a shambles,'' he noted.

''You approve expenditures, Rolf, not I. If it's a problem, do something about it. But I advise you to be very careful about what you sow, because you may not like what you reap.'' Her eyes were level with his, and he realized she had a raised seat.

''I'm glad you've brought up budget concerns,

though," she continued. "There's a matter I've been meaning to discuss with you. Your lumberyard does a good deal of business with the school district as well as the city. Neither is under any obligation to buy from you, of course. In fact, your selling to us might be considered a conflict of interest now that you're on the school board. Frankly, I've been concerned lately that the state auditor-general might decide to probe the way we do handle procurement and criticize us for purchasing goods and services that in the aggregate exceed the dollar amount requiring competitive contracts."

Rolf recognized a threat when he heard one. Play the game or suffer the financial consequences. If he had only himself to worry about, he might call her on this blatant attempt at intimidation and take his chances. He could always find another job in another place. But he wasn't alone. He had four children to raise. And Madam Mayor knew it.

"Please understand, there's no pressure at this time to alter the city's purchasing agreements with local vendors," Georgina Hampton went on in the most benign fashion, "but other cities have run into this kind of scrutiny. I don't agree with it. I believe we do very well by buying from local sources, and I'm convinced all of our merchants here in town have treated us fairly and honestly. I just thought you ought to know."

"I appreciate that." In other words, I get the message.

She rose from her chair and came around the side of the desk, the hand of friendship once again extended.

"Tell those twins of yours to work hard. I suspect

they'll be up against tough competition. I have to be neutral, of course, but that doesn't prevent me from offering them my best wishes."

He smiled and shook her hand. "Thanks. I'll pass on your wise counsel."

She gave him a mirthful chuckle, and this time it sounded genuine. "If they take it, they're different from my kids. Mine never thought I knew diddly about squat."

He laughed back. "Yeah, kids are like that. It's at least as hard for them to believe we were their ages once as it is for us to remember what it was like to be that young."

To think that he could solve this problem through the political route had probably been naive. Georgina Hampton had close ties with the business community, and with the cost of campaigns these days, she couldn't afford to alienate its most powerful members.

JULIE WAS READY to leave the office, when the telephone rang.

"Hi, beautiful. This is Rolf." As if she wouldn't recognize his voice. But he sounded rushed, nervous.

"Hi back. I was about to walk out the door."

"I'm glad I caught you then. Look, I was wondering if you could do me a favor. Zack Oman, one of my workmen, fell off a ladder. He might have a broken arm."

She could hear confusion in the background. "Oh, Rolf, I'm so sorry."

"Would it be possible for you to come over and take care of the kids for me this evening? I realize this is short notice, and you might have other plans...

I can ask Bryn, if you can't do it, but they would much rather spend time with you than her. It would mean fixing them dinner—''

"I'm not a gourmet cook, but I bet I can rustle up something without poisoning them."

"Then you'll do it?" He sounded so hopeful and relieved.

"Of course I will. I'll stop at my place to change, then rescue Bryn from the kids." The way she dressed for work wasn't suitable for preparing meals and lounging around in afterward. June Cleaver, she wasn't.

"You're a lifesaver. And a doll. Thanks."

"What time do you expect to be home?"

"Can't say for sure. A few hours. I've never known anyone to go to an emergency room and get out quickly, especially when there's a broken bone to set and cast. Zack doesn't have any family around here, so I don't feel right leaving him."

"I'm glad to help. And don't worry about the kids. I'll see to it they brush their teeth and wash behind their ears."

"Thanks, sweetheart. I'll see you as soon as I can break away."

"Whenever." She felt lighthearted. He needed her and that made her feel good. Was that why he called her beautiful, a doll, sweetheart?

In spite of the emergency, Rolf seemed reluctant to break the connection. "Rough day?"

"Let's call it interesting."

"Maybe you can tell me about it when I get home," he said.

She liked the idea of sitting in his house, waiting for him. Even more, she liked the notion of their spending more time together. She wanted to share her new information and concerns with him, a man whose wide shoulder she could rest her head on and take comfort from. "Yeah, I'd like to."

Forty-five minutes later, Julie parked in Rolf's driveway and walked next door to his neighbor's house.

Bryn met her at the door. "Hi, Julie. Rolf called to say you'd be over. He really didn't need to bother you. I could have taken care of them for a few more hours."

Julie felt Bryn sizing her up. *I'm the competition,* she realized, and sensed the other woman's hostility. Correction—Julie nearly smiled—*she's the competition.*

"I think he feels guilty about imposing on you so much," Julie replied diplomatically. She knew the kids weren't enthusiastic about spending time with Daniella and her mother.

"You're here!" Leah called from the living room. Judging from the tight expression on Bryn's face, she didn't miss the note of relief in the girl's voice.

"Appears that way," she quipped.

"Did you bring Mexican Train?"

Julie's face lit up. "As a matter of fact, it's out in the truck. If y'all finish your homework in time—"

"What's a Mexican train?" Daniella had silently moved up behind her mother.

"A dominoes game," Jeff replied from behind her.

"Dominoes are dumb," the fourteen-year-old snarled.

"Yeah, right." Derek retorted derisively as he squeezed by her and made his way toward Julie and the back door. "How would you know? You've never even played it."

Julie had noticed Bryn's daughter was a sulky girl who rarely seemed to approve of or be pleased with anything. Rolf's children were all younger, which may have partially explained her attitude. Derek showed no interest in her, even though she was already breasty and quite proud of it. Give him another year, she decided, and he'd notice.

"Come on, kids. Let's move it on out. We'll eat and then you have homework to do before we play any games. Don't forget to thank Mrs. Haggerty."

Two minutes later they were crowding in the back door of the Murdock house. "Boy, I'm glad Dad called you." Leah sighed as she dropped her books in the middle of the kitchen table. "I don't know what's wrong with Daniella lately. She's a real pain."

"Girls are always a pain," Derek informed her.

"Boys are such jerks," Leah countered.

"Okay, you two. This is a good time to hit the books. Dinner in half an hour."

"What're we having?" Foster wanted to know.

"You have a choice. Braised kidneys or fried liver."

"Oh, yuck. Gross." Leah made an ugly face.

"I like chicken livers," Foster told her. "Can we have onions with them?"

"Gag," his twin brother intoned. "I hate onions."

But not liver? Julie chuckled. From what Rolf had told her, they'd consumed more than their share of hot dogs and hamburgers at Bryn's house. She'd stopped off on the way over and picked up two roast chickens and a quart of buttermilk.

"No agreement on either of those two selections, huh? Well, how about roast chicken and biscuits?"

"All right." Derek shot his fist into the air.

"No hot dogs?" Jeff asked, surprising her by sounding disappointed.

"No hot dogs," Julie informed him.

"Good," he said flatly, and walked out of the room.

"Yeah, I'm tired of hot dogs, too," Foster agreed, and followed.

"Where did you buy the biscuits?" Leah asked.

"I didn't. I'll make them from scratch."

"You know how to make biscuits?" The girl's eyes were wide. "Can I watch?"

Julie wouldn't have thought making baking powder biscuits would be such an adventure. Elva, the woman who took over as cook and housekeeper after Julie's mother died nearly twenty years ago, made them routinely. "No, you can help... But how about your homework?"

"I did most of it in school. It won't take me long to finish the rest."

Leah and her brothers chattered throughout the simple meal. Julie had found two large cans of corn in the pantry and put them on to go with the salad she'd bought. But the biscuits were the big treat. She was a little worried they'd get sick eating so many, until she remembered they were growing children who burned up the carbohydrates in pure enthusiasm.

After she checked everyone's homework to make sure it was done, they settled down into another round of Mexican Train. It was fun watching their spirits rise and fall as the dominoes were played; interesting to see how they strategized. The game was one in which a player could help an opponent or shut him or her out, and these siblings did both. When one of them was way down, another player would come to his or her rescue. Inevitably, they crowed about winning and razzed the big loser, but they did so without being too overbearing.

At nine-thirty, Julie gave orders for bedtime. They grumbled, suggested one more round but gave up gracefully when she turned them down. She checked the TV listings. There wasn't anything she was interested in, so she picked up the book she'd brought with her, tucked her legs under her on the big wingback in front of the cold fireplace and began to read.

Which was how Rolf found her, sound asleep, when he arrived home at eleven.

CHAPTER EIGHT

SHE WAS SO BEAUTIFUL, curled up on his chair, her head tilted against the side of the wingback, legs tucked under her, book fallen to the floor. Sweet and content. He couldn't resist. He moved to the chair, leaned over, placed his hands on its arms and brushed his lips against hers. She stirred slightly before her eyes shot open and she gaped at him in momentary confusion.

"Hi, sleepyhead." His face was mere inches away from hers. "Have a good nap?"

"Rolf." His name was a faint whisper, a bedroom sigh and incredibly sexy. "Rolf," she repeated. "I didn't hear you come in."

She started to unravel herself, and in the process, her head came closer to his. He wasn't about to let the opportunity pass, not without another taste. He took her face between his hands, held it, smiled and brought his mouth down to hers. Not a skimming this time. A full, searching kiss. A kiss she answered with teeth and tongue—and hands creeping around his neck. She held him as their mouths passed messages words could not convey.

Her eyes were still closed when he broke off. Then she opened them and grinned at him. Desire became a fire in his belly, searing and intense. She stretched her arms over her head. Her breasts rose. It took every ounce of control to rein in the savage rush that whipped though him. With his breath caught in his throat, he backed away.

"What time is it?" Her voice was still husky, licked with sleep.

"Almost eleven."

"How's Zack?"

"Fine. Or as fine as a guy can be with a broken arm. They wanted to keep him overnight since he lives alone, but a friend offered to put him up for a few days until he's able to more or less take care of himself."

She stood and Rolf watched her tuck her shirt into her jeans. His blood, already hot, now pounded, as he fantasized his hand fanned out on the flat of her stomach and insinuating itself under the waistband. He was torn between the erotic impulse to touch her and the need to turn away. But averting his eyes was impossible. Not when he was faced with the points of her nipples tenting her T-shirt. He managed to shut his mouth a microsecond before her eyes met his. Or did he? An amused grin tugged at the corners of her mouth. She ran her tongue across her teeth.

"How did it happen?"

He moved toward the kitchen, trying to distract himself from the swelling heat of embarrassment. "He was using a wooden ladder to replace one of the overhead fluorescent lights and one of the rungs snapped," he said over his shoulder. "Thank heavens no one was near enough to be cut by the exploding tube. Instinct had him closing his eyes—otherwise he could have been blinded."

Julie shivered. A split second could change a life forever.

"Anyway, he's all right and no one else was injured." Rolf held the swinging door to the kitchen for her. "I know it's late, but do you have time to stay and talk for a while? I ran across a few things today that I'd like to share with you."

He liked the sound of the words. Sharing things with her, thoughts, ideas…kisses, touches. He had a bed upstairs… But not while his children were in the house.

"Me, too."

He wished they didn't have to worry about getting up for work in the morning. An all-night gab session felt about right at the moment. Not just talk, but he wouldn't think about the other possibilities.

"I'm thirsty," she said. "Did you eat anything? Are you hungry?"

Starved, but not for food. "I grabbed a bite in the cafeteria. I must admit hospital fare's a lot better than it used to be. But I could go for something to drink."

He popped the tops on a couple of noncaffeinated soft drinks and they carried them back to the living room.

While she told him about her latest discovery of test-score tampering, he studied her hands as they curled around the soda can. Soft hands. Competent hands. He remembered the feel of them on the back of his neck when he bent to kiss her. Warm, gentle, erotic. He tried to ignore the desire to have them touch him again, touch other parts of his body. But certain wanton images were too powerful to suppress.

He recounted his meeting with Georgina Hampton and her not-so-subtly veiled threat if he didn't back off.

Julie resumed her seat in the wingback. "What will you do?"

"Dig deeper." He slouched into the corner of the sofa. "I have a feeling this goes beyond an ill-advised oath and a few adjusted test scores. For all her political savvy, the mayor overplayed her hand. I don't take well to intimidation."

"She's threatening your livelihood, Rolf," Julie reminded him.

"And that makes me mad," he acknowledged. "I went to her with the best of intentions—to give her a heads-up about a potential problem, a possible scandal in her town, and she as much as admitted she was part of it. She could have pretended to take me seriously, could have promised to investigate the matter and sent me away, pleased with myself. It would probably have taken months before I realized she wasn't doing anything. Instead, she went for the big push. Wrong move, lady." He threw back his head for a deep chug of his soda.

Restless, he climbed to his feet and walked over to the mantel, then turned to face Julie. "It's time for me to take the offensive."

"Be careful." Julie had once been ready to go in shooting. "Let's make sure we have facts to back us up when we begin exchanging salvos."

He had to smile. She was in effect advising him to do the same thing he'd told her.

"Since you have access to the ISD computer system, do you think you can dig up information for me without arousing suspicion?"

"Depends on what it is." She brushed back an unruly lock of hair.

"What I want is probably a matter of public record,

but I don't want to tip my hand by visiting the courthouse and asking for it.''

''What specifically?''

''A copy of Picard's resumé. Not the PR release that was published in the paper, but the one he used when he applied for the superintendent's job.''

''Shouldn't be a problem.'' Her eyes narrowed in thought. ''We might even be able to get it from your computer here.''

He hadn't considered that. He knew there was an incredible amount of information on the Web, but he rarely tapped into it. He'd put a parent guard on the computer, restricting Web site access in case his kids decided they wanted to explore on their own.

''Come on.'' He led her into his den, a small room in the back of the house behind the kitchen. ''You're more adept at computers than I am.'' He switched on the terminal and held out the chair for her while the machine booted. ''Let's see what we can find.''

She located in a matter of minutes what it would have taken him hours to uncover. Picard's credentials were impressive. He'd received his bachelor's degree in American history in his home state of Louisiana and earned his masters and Ph.D. in education at the University of Texas in Houston. He'd taught at several junior high schools in southeast Texas, then returned to Louisiana, where he was an assistant principal, then principal in a very large high school. He'd held several such positions until eight years ago, when he became superintendent in two different districts, one in south Texas, the other in the Panhandle. During those years, he was recognized as Outstanding Educator of the Year at the local and state levels and received half a dozen national awards for his work with minority and disadvantaged children.

"Based on this, I can understand why he was hired," Julie admitted.

"Who does he give as references?"

She checked that section and saw half a dozen names. Three were fairly well-known—a congressman, a famous trial lawyer and an actor renowned for her populist views. Neither Rolf nor Julie recognized the other three people.

"He keeps company with powerful and very influential people," she pointed out.

"Is there any way of finding out if anyone checked those references?"

"I don't think...wait a sec." She poked a series of keys and the screen changed. "There's no report here on the specific references."

"They probably would have been discussed in executive session," Rolf noted, "and there won't be any minutes of those meetings."

Julie moved the cursor to a block at the bottom of the screen. "According to this, the person in charge of checking them was your predecessor, Frank Dalton."

Rolf put his hands on the small of his back and straightened. "He never mentioned a word about it. Of course, he was pretty sick by the time he nominated me. Well, it doesn't matter. I can call them myself and find out what information they passed on. Maybe they'll be willing to send me copies of their replies."

Julie tickled more keys.

"What are you looking for?"

"These various awards. I'm wondering if the nomination write-ups are on file. Here we go."

They both read the narrative on the screen.

"The usual overblown rhetoric," Rolf commented.

Julie moved on to the next Web site. Essentially the same things, but that wasn't unusual. Nothing said you couldn't be given multiple awards for the same achievements.

"Can you print these out for me?"

"Sure." Julie's fingers danced across the keyboard, and in a matter of minutes the printer was spitting out paper.

He picked the sheets up and glanced through them. "I'll check on these statistics, too."

"I'll verify test results for past years, as well." She turned off the computer, and they returned to the living room.

"I'm not sure that's a good idea, Julie. I've been thinking. When I asked for the audit reports, Mrs. Nolan said she had to let her boss know I'd taken them. I imagine she'll do the same thing with your request for tests."

Julie brushed his concern off with a shrug. "So what? Alyson gave me a job to do. Neither she nor Picard can fault me for being thorough."

"Are you sure that's how they'll see it?"

She smiled. "What other explanation could there be?"

He wasn't convinced. "I don't want you putting yourself in danger."

"Rolf, relax. As long as I don't give any indication I'm comparing individual grades against official records, I doubt Alyson will pay any attention."

"I hope you're right."

"Besides—" she wrapped her arms around his waist "—what's the worst they can do? Fire me?"

JULIE WAS CONVINCED intentional fraud was involved in the TAAS testing program. It would have been nice if she could have confided in her supervisor to determine if—remote as the possibility seemed—there might be a reasonable explanation for the discrepancies. She would much rather have called Alyson an ally than a potential enemy, but Julie didn't trust the older woman. Her boss was very pleasant and friendly, even solicitous about how things were progressing. Nevertheless, for vague reasons Julie couldn't explain, Alyson made her uncomfortable.

So when the tall blonde stuck her head in Julie's office the next day and casually asked how the practice question project was coming along, Julie was instantly on the alert.

Had Mrs. Nolan told her about requisitioning tests from the archives? Or would Julie be giving herself away by even mentioning it? Deciding the truth was easier to handle than a lie, she told her about the requisition.

"Unfortunately, Betsy Wilford either didn't perform a test item analysis or didn't post it, because I haven't been able to find it in the system. I can't do a very good job of targeting areas for improvement until I know where the weak spots are, but I also don't have time for a complete analysis," she went on to explain. "The best I can do under the circumstances is a rough sampling. I figure my probability of error isn't more than plus or minus five points."

"That's fine, Julie." Alyson leaned against the

door. "Just don't get bogged down in too much detail."

Julie laughed. "No way. With fifteen thousand answer sheets to choose from, I can't possibly do more than a random sample."

"I'll need your first list of questions by the end of next week."

So she was turning on the pressure, establishing a deadline that would make it impossible for her to more than skim through mountains of paper. "You'll have them."

Julie tried to gauge her boss's mood. Was she making a routine progress check on the project, or did she harbor suspicions about her new curriculum developer?

Since it would be a day or two before the other class tests she'd requisitioned showed up, Julie spent her time composing questions from the information she had available. She seriously doubted the additional forms would change her approach. Her real objective was verifying the raw scores against the ones forwarded to the state authorities.

Her office was tiny, but it did have a window. She rarely looked out because the view it afforded was limited to the parking lot. Late that afternoon, as she was clearing her desk and preparing to shut down for the day, she happened to notice Alyson getting into her car. Again, there was an uncomfortable feeling of something wrong. Precisely what, Julie couldn't identify, except that Alyson seemed uncharacteristically nervous, furtive. Julie hurried down to her own car and pulled out of the parking lot in the same direction she'd seen her boss take, though it was the opposite way to her apartment. Julie didn't know what she expected to find, but her curiosity was definitely piqued.

A ripple of excitement tingled down her spine. She felt like a spy out of a James Bond movie as she trailed half a block behind Alyson's candy-red Volvo. The car was distinctive, so following it from a distance wasn't difficult. Her own little white truck was common enough that even if Alyson checked her rearview mirror, she wasn't likely to see a vehicle that stood out.

Alyson finally turned into a supermarket parking lot. Julie felt let down. Her boss was grocery shopping. Except… She didn't pull up near the other vehicles clustered in front of the store but drove around the side of the building. Julie recognized the black Mercedes waiting there.

Julie whipped into a spot in the middle of a pack, facing in the right direction so she could observe what was going on. The car parked directly in front of her prevented Alyson and her confederate from seeing the school sticker on the truck's bumper. Hoping the lowering sun was glaring off her windshield, Julie sat very still and watched Dr. Picard leave his car and go around to the passenger side of Alyson's. He crawled in, kissed her quickly on the lips and slid down below the bottom of the window. He wasn't visible when Alyson drove blithely past Julie on her way out the parking lot.

Holding her breath in stunned shock at what she was witnessing, Julie bit her lips to stifle the guffaw threatening to burst out of her. Picard was divorced. Alyson had never married. If they wanted to have an affair, it wasn't anybody else's business. But this silly subterfuge, this cloak-and-dagger rendezvous made her laugh.

"ROLF, YOU NEED to see this." Jake Tarns stood in the doorway to the office, holding a piece of wood.

"What's that?"

"The rung of the ladder that broke the other day."

Rolf had called Zack that morning at his friend's house. The nineteen-year-old was still asleep, but his buddy, who was a student at the university, said Zack was doing all right, though he was a real klutz at trying to do things with one hand. He'd probably be staying with his friend several more days. According to the doctor, the break was a simple fracture that, given the kid's youth and general good health, should heal quickly with no permanent damage.

"What about it?" Rolf now asked his assistant.

"Take a gander at this." Jake placed the split wooden step on top of the desk. "The metal reinforcing rod is missing, and it appears someone cross-cut the underside of the rung."

Rolf stared. There was no mistaking the clean straight line of a saw. His mind tried to come up with a reason for it, but there seemed only one possible explanation. "You say the stabilizing rod is missing?" With it in place, even the weakened rung might have held a lightweight like Zack, who probably didn't top a hundred and thirty-five pounds.

"I thought at first it became dislodged when Zack fell, but I haven't been able to find it."

Was the ladder sabotaged? Had somebody intentionally engineered an "accident" and put a life in danger? A cold shiver of dread turned to a hot shaft of rage. "Who knows about this?"

"No one. I brought it directly to you." Jake stood there patiently for several minutes as Rolf considered all the angles. It sounded melodramatic, but someone was out to get him. That someone was willing to hurt other people in the process.

Admission brought panic and his concerns immediately shifted to Julie. Except for expressing her initial reservations about the oath, she'd kept a low profile. Rolf alone had been the one asking questions at public and private meetings. They were after him. Were they after her, as well? Might she be in danger?

He picked up the phone and dialed a number he had memorized but had never used.

"Are you going to call the police?" Jake asked.

"No choice." He held up a finger as the phone on the other end rang. No answer after five rings. Rolf checked the clock over his door. After four-thirty. She was gone for the day. Would she come here? Or would she go home first? It was Friday. Might she have gone to the ranch? She hadn't mentioned anything about it.

He hung up and dialed another number. "I'd like to report a crime."

Julie showed up just before the police arrived. She looked so fresh and inviting, standing in the doorway, the sun behind her, transforming her blond hair into a golden halo. He had the urge to run to her, drag her into his arms and hold her tight. The black-and-white pulling into the nearly deserted parking lot persuaded him that would have to wait.

She came forward, then stood aside as the policemen approached Rolf.

"Give me one minute," he told them, and walked directly to her. Only then was he able to see her eyes clearly. Incredible eyes. "Are you all right?" he asked, reaching out his hands to hold hers. He had to touch her, to make sure she was real, that she was safe.

Confusion furled her brow. "I'm fine, Rolf. What's going on?"

"I'll tell you about it later." He could see she didn't like being put off. He didn't like doing it, either, but he had no alternative. "Julie, please go over to Bryn's house, take the kids home and keep them inside until I get there." He could see from her expression that he wasn't helping matters.

"What's wrong? What's happened?" He could hear the note of panic in her voice.

"It's about Zack's accident. I need to make a report. I'll be home in an hour or so, or I'll call you if I'm not. I'll explain everything then."

She wanted to argue with him. The policeman standing behind him dissuaded her. "Okay, but call me if you'll be more than an hour late. I'll fix supper for the kids."

He leaned forward and kissed her on the cheek. He would have preferred a more intimate show of affection, but he could feel the impatience of the cops behind him. He watched her leave, eased by the assurance that nothing had happened to her. But how could he be sure nothing would?

An hour later, he said goodbye to the two policemen. They'd been thorough and professional. The ladder was defective, but there was no real evidence it had been tampered with. For one thing, it had been moved several times since the accident, so the metal rod could have gone missing at any time, thrown out with other junk. And the saw marks were dirty enough that there was no way of proving they had been recent. The ladder could have been defective for some time and simply not been noticed. Rolf and Jake both had to admit they hadn't inspected it in months, and even then hadn't specifically checked the underside of the individual steps.

"Mr. Murdock," the senior policeman concluded, "I don't see any evidence here of a crime. Accidents happen. I reckon that's what this was. If you find anything that supports your allegation or that clearly indicates someone is intentionally damaging your property, give me a call." He handed Rolf one of his cards. "But right now, I don't see that we have anything to go on."

Rolf drove home angry and confused. The cops almost had him convinced he was imagining things. They'd agreed to file a report, but there was nothing they would do with it except stick it in a drawer with a bunch of other unsubstantiated complaints.

A committee of inquiry met him. Julie said very little while the children quizzed him about the police coming to the lumberyard. He told them more or less the truth—that he and Jake had thought someone might have purposely messed with the ladder Zack fell off the other day. But it appeared after further examination that it was simply a product defect. Only Julie gazed at him with doubt in her eyes.

After they finished eating and the kids were attending to their homework, Rolf invited Julie out to his workshop behind the garage. She didn't question the strange request.

He waited until they were inside and the door closed. Then he swept her into his arms and kissed her hard on the mouth. She welcomed the taste of him, hot, frantic, nearly out of control. When they broke off, he planted his head in the crook of her neck. "I was so worried about you," he murmured in her ear.

She eased him away enough to gaze into his eyes. "You don't believe it was a simple accident, do you?"

"For a few minutes they almost had me convinced," he admitted. "I don't want to think I've put you in danger."

She stepped out of his embrace and turned away from him, her back arched before she faced him again. "I can take care of myself, Rolf."

He wanted to lock her in a tower, one to which he alone had the key, but he also recognized he'd be disappointed if she agreed to let him.

"I know," he agreed, perhaps too easily. "But I worry about my kids, too. There's no telling who might have used that ladder."

"Oh, Rolf, it could have been you."

He clutched Julie's waist. She didn't protest, though she did make a muffled sound when he pressed his lips to hers.

"It might have been you." He recalled all too vividly her climbing that ladder the first day they'd met, the sight of her legs as she mounted the rungs. "I'd never forgive myself if anything happened to you, Julie," he murmured. "I want to keep you in my life. I want you more than I can tell you."

CHAPTER NINE

ON SATURDAY AFTERNOON, while the kids were at the movies with their friends, Rolf invited Julie to join him on a visit with Bertha Dalton, the widow of the man he'd replaced on the school board.

"You don't have to worry about Bertha," Rolf assured her. "She's utterly trustworthy."

Bertha was a tall, angular woman in her late sixties with yellowish-gray hair, which she wore in a pigtail down her back. Her gingerbread house in one of the older parts of town attested to her expertise in handicrafts. The windows were festooned with stained-glass doodads. Luxurious macramé flowerpots were suspended on the front porch, and inside, Rolf knew they'd find everything from beaded bookmarks to needlepoint samplers. The house was cluttered, yet it felt homey rather than cramped.

She greeted him with a wide smile and soft hug. "It's about time you stopped by. I haven't seen you in months."

He was about to apologize, but she forestalled him with a throaty laugh.

"Don't bother giving me excuses. You're busy. With four kids to bring up and a lumberyard to run, I'm sure your time is full. If you can only make it every six months, I guess I'll just have to accept that."

He introduced Julie.

"Julie First. My, my." She smiled fondly. "You won't remember me, but when you were still in diapers, I worked with your dear mother on the literacy council. I didn't realize it had been so many years."

Bertha had already closed the door behind them and was walking toward the kitchen.

"Hot coffee or iced tea?" she asked over her shoulder.

They chose tea.

The three of them sat on the enclosed back porch. It felt cool, not only from the air-conditioning, but from the tall pecan trees that shrouded it in a woodland grove. Hanging pots of trailing blossoms and vines blurred the transition from outdoors to in.

Rolf and Bertha exchanged news of what was happening in their lives.

"They say it gets easier with time," she told her guests, "but I still miss Frank. I keep turning to tell him something, only to realize he isn't there." She sipped her tea and brightened. "Don't misunderstand. I'm not ready to join him yet. I have plans of my own. Things I want to do. Grandkids I'm dedicated to spoiling." She smiled happily. "Now, what can I help you with?"

Rolf hadn't had any illusions that she would take his dropping by as purely social, though he felt guilty that it wasn't. She and Frank used to come over to his house every once in a while for dinner or just to visit. He could have told her she knew where he lived, too. But as she'd indicated, she had her own life.

"Frank was supposed to check the references on Charles Picard before he was hired. Do you know if he ever did?"

Bertha frowned. "He never said anything about it, and he usually told me everything involving the school board." She sipped her tea, never quite taking her eyes off Rolf. "He was worried that the board was moving in the wrong direction. Which was why he nominated you. Figured you'd keep them honest."

"Moving in the wrong direction? How?"

She pulled her pigtail over her shoulder. "He couldn't put his finger on it, but he felt the members were too comfortable in their jobs. Too well established."

"In what way?" Julie asked.

"They weren't paying enough attention to money matters, for one thing. Everything was getting spruced up except the classrooms."

Julie tossed Rolf a glance. She'd told him the same thing—that buildings were not being properly maintained.

"What did he think about Dr. Picard?" Rolf asked.

Bertha wobbled her head, as if unsure how to respond. "Frank was pretty sick by the time they selected the new superintendent. He'd met Picard when he came for his interview. Oh, Frank was impressed with him, all right. Called him a smooth operator, which wasn't a compliment in Frank's book."

"But he voted to hire him," Rolf pointed out.

"He missed the executive session when they selected him. I remember he was furious when he found out the way they'd handled it. Executive sessions were normally held before public meetings, especially if there was anything controversial on the agenda. But for some inexplicable reason, Bill decided to call a special session following the regular meeting—right after Frank left because he wasn't feeling well. He usually hung around to socialize, you know. That's when they made the decision to hire Picard. Frank was in the hospital by the time of the next meeting and Bill announced that the board had unanimously agreed to hire Picard. It wouldn't have been unanimous if Frank had been there.''

"He would have voted against him?" Julie asked.

Bertha leaned back in her rocker and shook her head. "He thought Picard was too slick.''

"Right after Picard took over as superintendent," Julie said, "the board unanimously approved a loyalty oath for all school district employees.''

Bertha's forehead furled. "Loyalty oath?"

Julie explained its provisions. "Your husband voted for it," she concluded. "Did he ever talk to you about it, or tell you why he approved of it?"

Bertha shook her head emphatically. "Frank would never have voted for something like that. It goes completely against all his principles. He was a firm believer in the First Amendment right to free speech.'' She thought a moment and then stared at Julie, then Rolf, her mind in her eyes, working.

"After this guy Picard took over, Frank attended only one more meeting. I know for a fact a loyalty oath wasn't discussed, because I went with him.''

Rolf and Julie exchanged eye contact.

"According to the minutes of the meeting—" Julie started.

"That session was a travesty," Bertha declared. "It was almost an hour late getting under way because Bill insisted on reading the minutes of the last meeting, which in the past had always been waived, and then nitpicked them to death. Suddenly, nearly forty-five minutes into old business, he called for an executive session. They'd never done that before, not in the middle of a public meeting. Frank had had chemo that day and he was too drained to stay for it. So we left. I heard later it was another two hours before the public meeting resumed. Practically everyone had left by that time. If the minutes reflect a board vote on the oath, I'm willing to bet that's when they did it—when no one was around to ask questions.''

Rolf climbed to his feet. *Sneaky* was a temperate word for the games Marcus and Picard were playing. ''Frank was there at the beginning of the meeting, so the record would show him as present. It would have been appropriate for them later to note he had left, but my guess is they were counting on no one challenging the minutes at the next meeting.''

''Especially,'' Bertha pointed out, ''since reading them was sure to be waived. No one wanted a repeat of the ordeal Bill had caused at the previous meeting.''

''My guess,'' Julia added, ''is that if anyone had actually questioned the omission, the chairman would have brushed it aside as an administrative oversight—''

''And one of no significance,'' Rolf interjected, ''since Frank's vote wouldn't have changed the outcome. Cute.''

Bertha rolled her eyes. ''That's exactly the kind of shenanigans Frank was becoming concerned about.''

Rolf wished Frank had told him about this. ''Why did he nominate me as his replacement?''

The glow of Bertha's smile took years off her face. ''He knew you were honest and that you wouldn't put up with any crap. He was sorry he didn't get to break you in properly, but by then he was declining fast and had other priorities.''

Rolf missed his old friend and wished he'd spent more time with him. He and Julie left a few minutes later, after he elicited the older woman's promise to come by the house on Coyote Avenue for a visit.

''I think we've turned a corner,'' Rolf commented once they were in his car. ''We're on our way to finding out what this conspiracy is all about.''

It would be nice to go off somewhere for a few hours, he thought as he drove along with Julie beside him. Maybe go to her apartment to check out her shelves. The four-poster. But there wasn't time before the kids would be home, and in a town this size, there was no way to maintain anonymity. No way to slip off for an afternoon delight.

JULIE HAD BEEN on the job several weeks before she was given her welcoming audience with the superintendent. She didn't know why it had taken so long. Newcomers normally received an interview in the first few days of being hired, but Julie didn't dwell on it. Picard was the boss. Scheduling was at his option, not hers. When Alyson announced that Dr. Picard wanted to see her, she stopped what she was doing, made a quick visit to the ladies' room to apply fresh lip gloss and check the hint of eye shadow she wore, then went to his office.

The secretary, a tall, very pretty, slender blonde, not much older than Julie, announced her. The superintendent's corner office was expectedly large, with two windows in each of the outside walls. His paneled desk in the corner between them had a glass top, and, except for a green shaded banker's lamp and

a wooden basket for incoming and outgoing corre-
spondence, it was completely bare. The walls were
covered with plaques, framed awards and pictures of
people, a few of them instantly recognizable personalities.

He was standing with his back to the doorway, gazing out a window, hands clasped behind him, when
Julie entered. Turning almost with a jerk, as if he'd
been roused from deep thought, he smiled and came
around the side of the desk. Julie had met him on
several occasions, most recently at her graduation
when she received her master's degree, but this was
the first time she had occasion to speak with him.

His thick dark-brown hair was sprinkled with gray
at the temples, giving him a distinguished appearance.
He wasn't tall, but he was slim and lithe, and though
he wouldn't be described as handsome, he had a char-
ismatic air many women found charming. His per-
sonality and manners were less impressive to men,
but even they tended to call him a "nice guy" or
"sharp" in the good sense. Julie quickly realized his
brown eyes were capable of drilling into a person.

"Ms. First." He moved toward her with out-
stretched hand. "How nice to finally meet you."

The secretary closed the door behind her. As it
clicked, he squeezed Julie's hands. His touch was
warm and dry, friendly and sincere.

"I'm sorry to have taken so long to personally welcome you to our organization. I hope you're beginning to feel at home here."

"Yes, thank you." She wondered when he was going to release her hands.

As if reading her mind, he let go and waved her
toward the conversation pit in the corner of the room

opposite his desk. A low square table was the center-piece for two couches against the inside walls and two armchairs facing them. Following his direction, Julie took the inside corner of one of the couches, expecting him to sit in the opposing chair. Instead, he lounged beside her. With Rolf, she would have welcomed the proximity. This man raised the hairs on the back of her neck.

"Tell me a little about yourself," he prompted as he positioned himself sideways on the cushion to observe her. "I've reviewed your employee record," he admitted, "but those are cold facts. What about you the person?"

The legendary Picard charisma wasn't working, not on her, at least. Maybe it was because she'd seen him sneak out of a grocery store parking lot, crawl into a car and kiss a woman who was not his wife.

Julie found herself uncomfortable with the man, though he hadn't actually done anything overtly wrong or inappropriate. But his sitting so close bothered her, and the way he studied her made her feel, if not naked, at least as if she'd left a couple of buttons on her blouse undone.

"I graduated from TUCS last spring—" she tried not to let her nervousness show "—with a master's in elementary and secondary education."

"Yes, I know that." He was smiling at her. "I remember you at the ceremony. But I'm more interested in you as an individual. What are your goals, your ambitions? Are you married?"

Perhaps it was a reasonable and logical question, but it upped her anxiety nevertheless.

"No," she replied.

"Seeing anyone?"

Fight or flight. Those were basic instincts in a dangerous situation. She could simply say no...or yes—she was seeing a member of the school board. But either response would be fleeing, and Julie's daddy hadn't taught his children to run from a problem but to meet it head-on.

"Excuse me, Dr. Picard, but I don't know what that has to do with my working here."

He wasn't put off by her offensive. Rather, he seemed humored by it, even pleased by her spunk. "Of course it doesn't. I'm a man of curiosity. An attractive young woman like you must have many friends. I was just wondering if there was anyone special in your life."

Her nerves popped into overdrive. She was about to snap at him that it was none of his business, when he preempted her with a disarming question. "Tell me, Julie, what are your professional ambitions? I know you've taught school, and now you're in administration—a lot earlier than most educators, I might add—so tell me where you hope to go from here."

These were the questions she'd expected. Yet his timing, or perhaps the gleam in his eye—a sparkle that said she amused him—was making her skin crawl.

"For now," she answered quietly, "I want to do the best job I can at refining our curriculum. Our educational system has received so much bad publicity in the past few years that I want to do my part to correct the situation."

"We all do," he agreed. "And you're extremely well qualified to help achieve that laudable goal. But a sharp, intelligent young woman like you doesn't want to stay in curriculum forever. I'm sure you have further ambitions. What are they?''

He was right, of course. She didn't want to stand still. ''From here, perhaps I can become an assistant principal, maybe even the principal of a school.''

''And after that—superintendent?'' He smiled conspiratorially, as if they were sharing a secret. ''I plan on being around here for a while yet, but when I leave...well, maybe you'll be ready for the job.''

''You must expect to be here a very long time.'' She forced a chuckle, hoping to break the tension.

He smirked rather than laughed. ''Maybe I will. I'm not all that old, you know. I can still keep up a pretty good pace.''

As though to punctuate the statement, he moved closer and took her hand in his. ''There's a lot of politics involved in administration, Julie. Do you think you're up to it?''

She had to forcefully extricate her fingers from his grip. ''What are you suggesting, Dr. Picard?''

Apparently undaunted by her pulling back, he commented, ''You have to be able to get along with a lot of people when you lead an organization. That means stroking them, appeasing them, making them feel good. Can you handle that?''

Her heart was pounding, her palms clammy. Without wanting to, she looked into the deep dark eyes of Dr. Picard. The calculation and amusement she saw there intensified her anxiety.

She stood up abruptly. ''Do you know what sexual harassment is, Dr. Picard?''

He leaned back against the side of the couch and beamed up at her, not in the least disturbed by her outburst. ''Be careful, Julie.'' His words were low and level and filled with a kind of banked threat that made her shiver. "I would be extremely cautious if I were you about throwing around unfounded accusations."

He rose to his feet. "We're alone, Julie. There aren't any witnesses to this conversation. You'll find, if you make unsubstantiated accusations, your reputation will suffer far more than mine. I'd hate to have to tell people that you came on to me, a man of authority old enough to be your father."

"You're not serious," she sputtered, before she realized she'd vocalized the thought scrambling through her head.

His smile now was icy cold. "As serious as a pink slip, Julie. Except that getting fired will be the least of your worries." He calmly folded his arms. "Let me remind you that you signed a pledge—more than a pledge. People don't take kindly to someone breaking an oath, so I recommend you be very judicious about any statements you make outside this room."

He was the man in charge, the man in control. He walked past her and crossed the room to the door. With his hand on the knob, he let his eyes twinkle at her. "Keep that in mind."

He pulled the door open with a sweeping flourish. "Thank you so much for coming, Ms. First." His tone was bright and chipper, completely at odds with the menacing manner of seconds earlier. "I'm sure you'll be a tremendous asset to our team, and I wish you every success in your career."

His ingratiating smile turned her stomach. She also knew he'd already put her on the horns of a dilemma. Should she walk out playing the friendly new employee role, he'd be able to use it to show there hadn't been a problem between them if she chose to bring up the meeting at a later date. On the other hand, should she leave in a huff, she had no doubt he'd follow through on his threat to make her the villain of the piece and fire her. For the moment, her best course of action was to exit on a neutral note that wouldn't do her any credit but that he couldn't use to his advantage, either.

"Thank you for seeing me, Dr. Picard." Her voice was too loud. She stepped through the doorway but didn't look at the secretary or acknowledge Alyson, who was over by a file cabinet, apparently checking a folder.

Julie's heart was still pounding as she walked down the long corridor. She was convinced her knees were about to buckle out from under her. Her hands hadn't stopped trembling by the time she reached her office. She crumpled into the chair behind her desk, expecting Alyson to appear any minute. To bubble over and pretend everything was fine? Or to close the door and tell her she'd better watch her step—or pack up.

Julie hated the feeling of powerlessness Picard had given her. She'd received catcalls on occasion and even been propositioned a few times, but she'd never considered herself the victim of sexual harassment. The whistles and calls were intended as compliments, which was how she'd regarded them. Even the propositions, while insulting on one level, had never been menacing.

Which was what made Picard's *suggestions* so unnerving. Intellectually, she'd known what sexual harassment was, but now she understood emotionally how it felt. Out of control. Belittled. Demeaned. Picard was using his position of authority to threaten her.

He was absolutely right. Without a witness, it was her word against his. He had enough stature to portray her as a woman spurned. She might be able to cause him embarrassment if she went public with her account of the interview, but he had the ear of the media, the support of public officials and the admiration of a large segment of the public. Chances were her reputation would be the one ruined. She could find herself the target of a civil action for slander. Even if she won, nothing would be gained. Picard's reputation would continue to grow.

As Julie's pulse slowly settled, her thoughts became more orderly. Yes, she was at a disadvantage. But she wasn't totally powerless.

With steady fingers, she directed her mouse to the word processor on her computer and entitled a new document "sexual harassment." If anyone was monitoring her work station, there wouldn't be any doubt what they'd find in this file. Carefully, she composed a detailed narrative of the interview—including, to the best of her recollection, the exact words Picard had used—and precisely described his physical touching. It didn't take long. She reread it, made a few corrections and put two lines for signatures on the bottom. A minute later, the laser printer spewed out a single copy.

She read it one more time and walked down the hall to the file room. Her friend was there, today wearing a blue dress with a wide patent-leather belt.

"Would you do me a favor, Nancy? I'd like you to witness my signature." She put the paper on the counter.

"What is it?" The older woman began reading. Her jaw dropped and her eyes grew wide. For a fleeting moment, she appeared frightened.

"You're not swearing to the accuracy of the contents," Julie assured her. "Simply vouching for the authenticity of my signature."

Nancy sucked in her cheeks, her eyes gleaming now. "You've got guts, girl. Good for you. It's about time someone spoke up. Where do I sign?"

ROLF HAD ALREADY figured out that as long as Bill was in a position to personally profit from school district expenditures, he was little inclined to curtail their spending. Marcus's Office Supply was an old-fashioned store, nostalgic and cozy, with squeaky, hardwood floors and converted gaslight fixtures. In spite of the row of computers, printers and other hi-tech components Bill had added in the past few years, it wasn't a popular place. What reportedly kept him afloat was his middleman contracts involving truckloads of bond paper, pencils, erasers and staplers for the city, county and school district. Rolf didn't begrudge him any of it. But he did draw the line at corruption.

Two members on the board couldn't possibly have a profit motive for being there—Virginia Akers and Herb Bellows. The retired military man had already voiced his support for the chain of command and the status quo. Rolf didn't question Herb's sincerity or honesty, but he sensed no sympathy for Rolf's concerns, either. Perhaps Virginia Akers would feel differently.

Ginny's husband was a salesman in a local department store. He wasn't an owner, received no commissions on sales, therefore, neither she nor her husband would have any personal stake in the school district's actions.

"Sure I voted for the oath," she told Rolf after inviting him to the backyard, where she'd been tending a beautifully maintained rock garden.

Rolf sat in one of the lawn chairs on the edge of the patio. "You didn't have any misgivings about it?"

She continued to churn up the black soil. "Why should I? Bill explained the reason for it and how it would shut whiners up for a while so we could move forward, instead of constantly defending ourselves. Made sense to me."

"Don't you think teachers and administrators have a right to speak out if they see something wrong?"

"'Course I do." Ginny dug a little hole with her spade and placed a peat pot of dianthus in it, then sat on her haunches and brushed back a hank of slightly damp black hair from her forehead with her wrist. "They can bring their problems to their supervisors and let the people in charge do their jobs."

"Suppose the boss won't fix them."

"This isn't a perfect world," she observed with a coldness that surprised him. "Things don't always go the way we want them to. The boss always has good reasons for doing what he does, even though people working for him or her don't know what the reasons are. Seems to me we have to have faith the right thing gets done."

"And if it doesn't?" Rolf harbored no illusion he would convert her to his way of thinking, but it was interesting listening to her reasoning.

"Then you go above him—or her."

"If the next guy in the chain disagrees with you, you're in big trouble, though. How long have you been on the board?"

"Five years," she answered proudly while packing dirt around the next planting.

"What made you decide to run?"

"I still had a couple of kids in school back then. Felt it was my duty to go to meetings, PTA, school board, things like that. Never missed one, so when there was an opening, Bill suggested I throw my name in the hat. We'd already become pretty good friends, since we saw each other at all the meetings. I wasn't sure I was the right person for the job. I mean, it's not like I'm anybody important here in town, but Bill offered to sponsor me. You know, let everybody know I was his choice for the job." Virginia chuckled good-naturedly. "You want to know the truth—nobody else was interested in running."

And the chairman knew he had a sheep. Rolf was willing to bet she voted exactly the same way he did every time.

Rolf decided to venture off in another direction. "I'm a little concerned about the budget. We seem to be overspending."

"Nothing to worry about." She pulled a grass runner invading the bed. "It always looks that way at the beginning of the school year because we have to buy so many things up front, but it levels off later and everything works out fine."

If that was true, he thought, good planners would front-load the budget. He wondered how well she understood the process. It was a subject that made some people's eyes glaze over.

"Is that what happened last year?" he asked.

She leaned forward and plucked deadheads from a flowering coreopsis nana. "Last year was no problem. The books balanced. They always do."

Rolf blinked slowly. "By tapping into reserves."

"That's what reserves are for, aren't they?"

Her remark answered his question. Probably what Bill Marcus told her. Rolf was tempted to explain it was like drawing money out of savings every month to bolster the checking account. Eventually there wouldn't be any savings left and the bills would still have to be paid. But he wasn't sure the example would accomplish anything positive. As long as Bill said everything balanced, she was satisfied and didn't question how it got that way.

"At this rate," he pointed out, "the school district will be bankrupt in another year."

She laughed. "Bill won't let that happen. He's a businessman, after all. He understands these things."

"I'm a businessman, too," Rolf reminded her.

She smiled politely. "Bill's company's been around for nearly seventy-five years."

And it was on the verge of bankruptcy.

"I really wouldn't worry about the budget," she assured him. "Dr. Picard got us a fistful of grants last year, and the way things have been improving around here, I bet we'll receive even more of them this year."

Rolf left a few minutes later, wondering if Julie could have handled the interview better. Not that there was much to be gained. The two women were so completely different. Rolf couldn't imagine Julie blindly taking another person's word for a thing as important as a school budget or the right of free speech.

What was it Ginny had said? Picard obtained a bunch of grants. So where was the money? Rolf had studied the financial statements for the past three years. He hadn't seen any grant money reflected as income. Maybe that was another area to investigate.

CHAPTER TEN

ALL AFTERNOON, Julie smoldered, seethed and conjured up ways to settle accounts with Picard. Rolf would no doubt have his own ideas about how to deal with the lecher. If he was anything like her brothers, his first impulse would be to confront the superintendent, probably with clenched hands in the parking lot behind the administration building. Which would make Picard the victim. Maybe it would be better to keep this to herself.

She immediately rejected the notion. Informing Rolf was the right thing to do. Hadn't she bragged to Jerry Benton that when she met a man she could truly love, they would share everything fifty-fifty? That meant the bad as well as the good.

How comforting it would be to share not just this problem, but her most inner thoughts with Rolf. To tell him her joys and fears, the things that made her feel good and those that troubled her. To lean against his broad chest while she explored her ideas and dreams, her hopes and aspirations. To put her head on his shoulder when she was worried or sad. Most of all, to know he would be there when she needed him. A man who would sympathize and encourage unconditionally.

Some married couples found that level of trust. Her dad had it with Sheila, Clare with Michael.

Julie's heart told her she'd discovered in Rolf that soul-deep bond that would allow them to endure life's trials and grow stronger because they had each other.

She waited until after the kids had traipsed off to their rooms for the night to bring up the subject. The twins had abandoned a game of chess, and now she and Rolf were sitting across from each other, mulling over the chaos they'd left.

"I had my newcomer's interview with Dr. Picard today." She moved her king into a protected square.

He put her queen in jeopardy. "How'd it go?"

She shifted a pawn for protection. "He made my skin crawl."

"How's that?" Worry creased Rolf's forehead. "He's usually pretty smooth, everybody's friend."

"Especially with women." She studied the pattern of pieces. "Even more so if they're blondes."

Startled, his head shot up, his glance quizzical, almost accusatory. "Julie, are you telling me he made a pass at you?"

She took herself back to the superintendent's office, to the leading questions, the feigned interest in her ambitions and aspirations. For a moment the sick feeling returned, but she shoved it aside. She was safe here. She was with Rolf, a man who cared about her, not one who wanted to exploit her. Reassured, she struggled to keep her tone light. "Yep."

"He what?" Rolf's voice was raised and hard. "Did he touch you? Tell me he didn't touch you."

His anger confused her. Was it directed at Picard or at her for being in the situation? She'd never considered that he might hold this against her. But men sometimes did blame women for being "available," as if they were an attractive nuisance, guilty of seducing a man simply by being female.

"He touched my hands," she replied evenly, though her heart was beginning to pound.

"Your hands?" He sounded incredulous. "Only your hands?"

"Nothing more, Rolf." For a fleeting moment, the sense of helplessness she'd earlier experienced returned, and her stomach felt hollow. The vulnerability was a mere spark; the fire it ignited was hot temper. "Because I wouldn't let him."

He gaped at her, clearly shaken by her rebuke, then rose from his chair and sat on the couch beside her. She hadn't been aware of her hands shaking until he covered them with his own, until he drew them up and kissed them tenderly, then folded her in his arms. The shelter of his embrace brought unexpected tears to her eyes.

"I'm sorry, sweetheart. I didn't mean it to sound as though I was angry at you. I'm mad as hell at him and at myself for not being there to protect you."

She wasn't sure why she was weeping. She hadn't shed a tear all day over the incident. But now, her eyes wet, her throat burning, she leaned into him, grateful for the solid warmth of his shoulder, the comfort of his body close to hers. They held each other for several minutes, until she pulled away and swiped at her damp cheeks.

"I'm sorry," she mumbled.

He kissed her lightly on the lips. "You have nothing to be sorry for."

"I don't know why I did that," she confessed.

"Because he hurt you." He paused. "Because you weren't sure of me." He tipped her chin up and gazed into her brimming blue eyes. "I'm sorry, Julie. I care too much about you to ever want to cause you pain."

She threw her arms around him. They held each other and she listened to their hearts beat.

"Can you tell me what happened?" he asked after a while.

She fudged a smile, pulled back and climbed to her feet. "Of course I can."

Pacing, she began her narrative, repeating Picard's words, describing his gestures. Physical movement and verbal expression emboldened her. The old defiant spirit returned.

"That son of a bitch," Rolf swore when she finished. He jumped up, held her again, as much for his own comfort as hers. "I'll fix him for this. I'll—"

"No." It felt good to grin at him. "It's already taken care of."

He pulled his chin back. "What do you mean?"

"This is something I had to do on my own, Rolf. I hope you understand…and accept it."

She sat back down on the couch and stretched out luxuriously while she described the statement she'd written and had Nancy witness. "Then I took it to my lawyer this afternoon."

"You'll sue his ass?" He smiled. "Good."

"Not yet," she corrected him. "We discussed options. I can file formal charges, but without witnesses or any corroboration, it would be little more than a nuisance suit. A case of he said–she said. With all the character witnesses Picard would undoubtedly put on the stand, I couldn't possibly win."

"What about this affidavit you wrote and had witnessed?" But before she could answer, he broke into a broad grin. "You're pretty smart, you know that? In fact, brilliant."

His glowing smile sparked a warmth inside her she hadn't expected. Her lawyer had been pleased with her, too, but Rolf was proud of her.

"Let's see," he said. "You documented his harassment, left a copy of it on your computer for anyone to find and had Nancy sign and date the paper copy. She'll blab to other people about it. If Picard pulls a stunt like this on another employee, she'll know what to do, and you'll have your corroboration. Yep—" he swept her into his arms "—positively brilliant."

"I thought so," she admitted smugly. "Of course, nothing may come of it."

He shook his head in disagreement. "His kind of behavior is compulsive. Picard came on to you. I'm sure you weren't the first, and you won't be the last." He stretched out his hand and drew her up against him. Caging her hips against his, he smiled at her with the promise of pleasure in his eyes. "You're a woman after my own heart, Julie First. I like having you in my life."

As she drove home that evening, she kept touching her lips, recollecting the feel of his mouth on hers. Kisses that had left them both panting.

ROLF'S MAJOR CONCERN after his divorce was to provide his children with a stable home life. He knew nothing could compensate for a missing mother, even one more devoted to her books and research than being a nurturer and homemaker. But a dependable routine, one they could count on would go a long way in giving them a sense of belonging. Bryn next door had helped.

Then Julie had come along. The kids had taken to her easily and naturally. Especially Leah, who looked up to her as a combination fairy godmother and big sister, and Julie had reciprocated so automatically he couldn't ignore the dynamics building between them. But it wasn't his children's responses that kept him awake at night. He'd come to realize that a day without Julie in it was incomplete and a solitary bed very difficult to sleep in.

"I won't be able to watch your children for the next couple of weeks," Bryn announced when he went to her house Friday afternoon. She said it casually, as if it were no big deal.

"Oh?"

She scooped back the hair that had fallen across her face. "Dannie and I have signed up for an exercise class every day after school, and right after that, we're going to learn to throw pots. Isn't that exciting?"

Exercise classes. Throwing pots. Exciting. "When did you decide this?"

"We've been talking about it for a while," she said with an offhandedness he didn't believe for a minute. "I've been worried about her putting on so much weight. And, well, I guess I could probably afford to take off a few pounds myself."

No, he hadn't been aware of her concern. Their diet of hot dogs and pizza certainly didn't suggest it. Daniella was naturally on the chubby side, and probably always would be. That was her build, her genes. On the other hand, her sitting around eating junk food and never engaging in sports didn't help. She had a pretty face and a beautiful complexion. Rolf could hardly criticize Bryn's decision. As for the woman herself, a little toning up probably wouldn't hurt.

But Rolf had the feeling this move wasn't purely about getting in shape or losing weight. Bryn could have told him beforehand she was considering this to give him time to plan, instead of dropping it on him at the last minute. Mrs. Tremain would probably be available on a temporary basis, but he didn't think she'd want to be tied down with this schedule permanently. It might be different if she lived close by or on an established school bus route, but her retirement community was on the other side of town.

"When do your classes start?" he asked.

"Monday. For two weeks," she reminded him. "After that we'll decide if we want to continue with them."

In other words, Bryn was giving him a couple of weeks to miss her and her services. He wanted to laugh. Subtlety wasn't her forte.

"Thanks for the heads-up. I'll work out something."

His casual lack of concern seemed to panic her. "I suppose they could come to exercise classes with us—"

"That won't be necessary. Thanks anyway."

She looked a little crestfallen when he and the kids left a few minutes later.

"Is it true," Jeff asked, "that we don't have to go to her house after school anymore?"

"For the next couple of weeks, at least."

"Good."

"I bet Julie'll stay with us," Foster contributed.

"She has to work." Rolf wished she could take

over from Bryn. Julie was only a dozen years older than Derek, yet she handled herself with a maturity and authority all the children looked up to. The kids were always in a good mood when they were with her. Ironically, it wasn't because she let them get away with things as Bryn often did. They liked the order and structure Julie brought and her willingness to treat them like adults.

The woman foremost in his thoughts showed up as he was lighting the gas grill in the backyard.

"We can't go over to Bryn's anymore," Leah told her gleefully.

She glanced at Rolf. "Why not?"

"She's taking her fat daughter to exercise class and—"

"Leah," Rolf interjected sternly, "I don't want to hear you talking like that."

"Well, she is."

"It doesn't make any difference." He used a wire brush to clean the heated grate. "It's impolite."

"It also says a lot more about the kind of a person you are than she is," Julie emphasized. "Is that how you want people to think of you? As someone who calls other people names."

Leah screwed up her mouth distastefully. "I guess not," she capitulated in a small voice, then brightened. "But we can't stay over there after school, because she won't be home."

At Julie's quizzical expression, Rolf explained about the exercise and pottery classes.

"What will you do?"

"I'll call Mrs. Tremain a little later and see if she can come over in the afternoons."

"Ah, Dad. All she ever wants me to do is chores.

Put the dishes away. Fold the laundry. Clean my room.''

Running his tongue across his teeth, he commented, ''Well, maybe if your room wasn't always such a mess—''

''It's always my fault, isn't it?'' Leah stormed up the back steps and slammed the screen door behind her.

''Oops.'' He pursed his lips.

''Sounds like you touched a raw nerve,'' Julie observed.

''She seems to have a lot of them lately.''

Julie followed him into the kitchen.

He moved to the refrigerator, took out the chicken pieces he'd been marinating and placed the dish on the counter. ''Would you mind opening a can of baked beans and putting them in that cast iron pot? I'll heat them on the grill while the chicken's broiling.''

Automatically Julie went to the pantry and retrieved the item.

''Do you think Mrs. Tremain will be available?'' she asked as she followed Rolf back outside.

He shrugged his big shoulders. ''She's very good with the kids, though they're not very fond of her, either. I guess I wouldn't describe her as a fun person.''

''Julie can come over,'' Jeff interrupted shooting hoops to contribute.

''I've already told you,'' Rolf countered, ''she has to work, too.''

''What time do you get home?'' Julie asked the boy.

''Me and Foster—''

"Foster and I," Rolf corrected him.

Jeff sighed resignedly. "Our bus drops us off at 3:30 most days. Leah's bus drops her off around 4:00, but Derek doesn't get here till 5:00, 'cause he has track."

"If we were talking about only a half hour," Rolf noted, "and Derek could be here the whole time, I might let him be in charge—"

"No way," Jeff objected. "He's always bossing us around."

"Relax." Rolf turned a piece of chicken. "I said if."

"Good," Derek chimed in as he bounced through the back door in shorts and tank top. "'Cause I don't want to be in charge of these squirts."

"My workday doesn't end until 4:30, guys, so I don't see how I can help. Wish I could."

Rolf brushed barbecue sauce on the chicken.

Julie moved up beside him and stirred the beans. "You don't close in the evening till six." She pursed her lips. "I have an idea."

His movements hitched. "Like what?"

"Is the school bus route anywhere near the lumberyard?"

"It goes right by. Why?"

"If the bus can drop them off there, they can do their homework in your office. I'll come by around a quarter to five and pick them up, bring them here and stay until you arrive."

"Yes!" Foster punched the air.

"Hmm." The corners of Rolf's mouth were turned down in thought, but his eyes sent a different message. "It might work," he mused slowly. "You wouldn't mind?"

"It'll only be for a couple of weeks, right?"

"Yeah, until Bryn's classes are over, or I can make other arrangements."

"I guess I can handle a couple of weeks of your kids. The question is, will they be able to put up with me?" She winked at him. "I see a few chores around here that need to be done."

"God bless you."

ROLF PLUNKED HIMSELF DOWN in an easy chair in the living room. "Are you sure you don't mind?" The kids had finally gone up to bed and the two of them were alone. In the room, but not in the house. "I'm sure you have other things you need to do after work."

She couldn't help but titter. "Yeah, like put the dishes away, fold the laundry, clean my room—"

He grinned at her. "Your room didn't look too bad to me." His voice was low, probably so it wouldn't carry upstairs, but it hinted at a different kind of intimacy.

She recalled him filling her bedroom, except in her imagination he wasn't in work clothes but the way she'd seen him at the swimming hole, bare-chested, tousle-haired, his skin shiny wet. She took a deep breath. That kind of picture left her damp and slick. And now she'd committed herself to spending every afternoon with his children and seeing him every evening. That wouldn't exactly be a hardship. But keeping their clothes on might be.

"So what did you learn at the *Gazette* today?" she asked.

He rose and retrieved his attaché case, apparently equally relieved to be off the subject of her bedroom.

She sat on the couch beside him. If the glance she'd caught meant anything, his thoughts hadn't been confined to installing shelves in her bedroom, either.

"Picard has indeed received several awards over the past year." He pulled out a thick folder of papers that had obviously been printed off a computer screen and placed it on the coffee table in front of them. "He's also received several grants from various organizations. A few went to him personally, so how he uses the money is his business, but other funds were given to the school district. The thing is, none of the money appears in the school budget, either as outside income or as reimbursement for expenses."

"Are you saying he's spent district money without accounting for it?"

"Without accounting for it and possibly without being authorized to use it."

Julie grimaced. "Fraud. Maybe even embezzlement."

"Maybe. It's too early to know for sure."

"Why? If the money went to the district and he's using it without authorization—"

"We don't know for sure the district ever received the money, since it doesn't appear on the books, or that he spent it."

"I see your point." She snorted. "This gets complicateder and complicateder."

"That's how fraud thrives," Rolf agreed. "In any large organizations, accountability becomes convoluted and the number of interlocking elements so confusing that things fall through the cracks."

"Okay, so what do we do now?"

"Now—" he slid across the few feet separating them "—my first move will be to kiss you."

A shimmer of warmth rippled from her chest up to her neck and down to her belly. "Will it?"

His eyes were focused exclusively on her, his lips curled in a lazy smile.

"Indeed it will." His thigh touched hers, contact raising desire to craving. He snaked his arm behind her back and placed his other hand on the side of her rib cage. The hand moved up, torturously slow, a gentle, tantalizing skimming along the outside of her breast. Briefly, he cupped her, making her nipples tingle and harden. He continued his teasing journey up to her shoulder, the side of her neck. Her heartbeat drummed a savage tattoo as he insinuated his fingers in her hair. Her breathing stopped altogether when he leaned forward and brought his face closer to hers.

She whispered his name. It was supposed to be a warning. But of what? To whom? She wasn't afraid—exactly. She was still in control.

His eyes sparkled. "Julie." The word was a murmured prayer.

A sensation, feverish and liquid, eddied through her veins. The first contact of his lips triggered a hunger, an ache that drew her into the kiss. She wasn't in control anymore, and she gloried in her captivity.

His soft lips pressed against hers. Parted. His tongue traced their surface and probed deeper. She met him, coyly at first. Then the minuet began. Sway and dip. Whirl and spin. Touch and taste and savor. Was she humming a love song or groaning with pleasure? It didn't matter.

When he withdrew, they were both breathing hard. Frustration tormented his smile. "I wish we were someplace else. Alone."

"Shh." She pressed a finger to his lips. The lips

that had just kissed hers. "I should be leaving." *Before I forget there are children in the house. Before I give in to lust and my need for you.*

"No." The harshness of the word made her smile.

"Now—" her voice was husky, uncertain "—about Picard."

He groaned and threw himself back against the couch, his arm still behind her shoulders. Not touching, but she could feel its intimate presence.

"Hmm, Picard, yes. Picard." He closed his eyes, as if taking inventory of himself. "Thirsty?"

"After that kiss? Yeah."

He raised his arm over her head and climbed to his feet. Half turning, he extended his hand to her. His fingers curled around hers as she rose. Warm fingers. Strong and possessive.

He held the swinging door to the kitchen to let her pass. From the refrigerator, he extracted a pair of soft drinks, and gave her one. They sat at opposite ends of the table. Their hands didn't meet, but their eyes did.

"What were we talking about?" he mumbled.

She fought to remember. "Picard."

"Damn him." He settled against the wooden chair. "I'll call the agencies that reportedly sent us money, identify myself as a new member of the board and explain that I'm trying to straighten out an accounting mess. Once I know when the funds were transferred and to whom, we may have the foundation for a case."

"It's about time," Julie said. "This whole situation is becoming extremely frustrating."

His mouth quirked and the gleam once again

danced in his eyes. "I know the feeling." He took a long draw on his drink. "Which is precisely how people get away with fraud and embezzlement. Not only is investigation often time-consuming and complicated, it's usually embarrassing to the victim. Nobody likes to admit being a sucker. Large corporations frequently bury cases of employee fraud and embezzlement and simply write off the losses because they don't want to acknowledge, especially to their stockholders, that their security systems failed or were compromised, that they were hoodwinked."

"You think that's what Picard is counting on?" she asked.

Rolf lifted his shoulders and let them fall. "We don't even know at this point if he's actually done anything wrong."

"What have you learned from Picard's references?" she asked.

"Nothing yet. I should be hearing something in the next few days."

ROLF'S PROBING into Dr. Picard's activities in the school district was no longer a secret. He'd expressed reservations about the oath, approached the mayor about the expenditure of school funds, visited the newspaper to check on the awards and grants garnered by the busy superintendent. Not that Rolf was really trying to hide his activities. In his opinion, the more people who were aware of possible misconduct on the superintendent's part, the more alert they'd be.

Rolf soon realized he'd miscalculated, however. He hadn't counted on the opposition. In his naiveté he'd assumed they'd run for cover when the heat was turned on. Instead, they closed ranks against him.

Rolf had bought the lumberyard six years earlier after having worked there for several years. The yard had been a lot like Marcus's Office Supply—out-of-date and failing. The previous owner, an elderly man who'd inherited it from his father, had been unwilling to explore new technology or markets. Rolf had seen its potential and had immediately inaugurated radical changes. He'd extended the merchandise line from lumber and associated hardware—nails, screws and a few basic tools—to plumbing and electrical supplies, ready-built cabinets, household appliances and decorating materials. The do-it-yourself retail store quickly became the most visible part of the business, but the largest profits were still from wholesale trade with builders and other commercial enterprises.

Rolf's rude awakening that this was about to change came on the following Monday morning. Tubby Vannon showed up at the store and demanded to see him. Vannon did renovation work and bought a fair amount of his materials and supplies from Rolf.

"Hi, Tubby. What can I do for you today?"

"Not a damn thing," the barrel-shaped man snarled. "I came to tell you I won't be a party to your Picard bashing. I don't know what you think you're doing by attacking a man who's done nothing but good for this community. He's given us pride in our school system, and all you seem to want to do is make him out to be some sort of criminal." The man's round face was bright red.

Rolf was stunned by the vitriol of the attack. "I haven't accused him of anything, Tubby." He wasn't foolish enough to make accusations in public that he couldn't defend.

"That's not the way I hear it."

"From who?" Rolf shot back. "I haven't said a thing to anyone against the superintendent, so I'd be much obliged if you'd tell me who's spreading these rumors. I'd like to straighten this out."

Tubby refused to reveal his source. Rolf suspected it was Bill Marcus, but until someone confirmed that, it was pure guesswork. Tubby left a few minutes later, still steaming that Rolf had it in for the superintendent.

Several of Rolf's regular commercial customers routinely sent him blanket purchase orders before the first of the month, so their workmen could sign for the things they needed. The company would then receive a single itemized invoice at the end of the month instead of a pile of smaller ones. The system made things easier for both parties. When the purchase orders hadn't come in by the fifth of the month, Rolf decided to give the companies a call to let them know and to assure them if any of their people came in for supplies, he'd honor their signatures.

"We're not cutting a P.O. for you this month," Enid Schroeder from Shield Construction told him over the phone.

Rolf was instantly on the alert. "Is there a problem?"

"The problem is the way you're persecuting Dr. Picard," she informed him stiffly.

"I don't understand." But he did. The picture was becoming all too clear. "What has Dr. Picard got to do—"

"We don't like the way you're treating him, and until that changes, we have no intention of doing business with you."

"Do you mind telling me who's told you I'm attacking Dr. Picard? Because it's not true. I haven't done or said anything against him.''

"You were elected to the board to help make our district better. Dr. Picard is doing that,'' she insisted without answering his question. "But all you seem to be interested in is stirring up trouble.''

"Don't you think I have a right to tell my side of the story?''

"Why, so you can lie?''

"Enid, we've dealt with each other for more than five years now. Have you ever known me to lie to you or to anyone else?''

"Just because you haven't been caught before doesn't mean you haven't.''

Outrage lurked inside him, but the prominent emotion he felt was a weary sadness. Bonds of trust were being destroyed, and though they might later be reestablished, they would never be quite the same. Scars would always mar them.

"I'm sorry you feel that way, Enid. Perhaps one day in the future we can get past this.''

She slammed the phone in his ear.

By the third such conversation, concern and anger were turning to panic. The combined sales from the four people who had closed their accounts averaged over twenty thousand dollars a month. He might be able to make up part of it in retail where profits were higher but volume lower, but it would be extremely difficult. The summer fix-it season was over. Home improvements tended to drop off toward the end of the year.

There was one account that hadn't been closed, and it was a biggie. Rolf's major regret now was that he hadn't himself closed it months ago when he'd joined

the school board. The city and school district had
joined forces for a combined purchasing of goods and
services. It simplified paperwork and allowed them to
take advantage of volume discounts. The consolidated
P.O. had arrived on schedule the previous Friday in
spite of the mayor's threat to drop it. Rolf knew precisely why. It could be used against him later if trouble developed. Honoring this purchase order could be
made to appear as if Rolf were profiting from corruption, as well.

Cutting himself off from this lucrative account,
however, could be financially disastrous—unless he
found other large accounts to take its place—which,
under the circumstances, didn't seem likely. Abro-
gating the agreement now could also be perceived as
an attempt to hide his past involvement, a slick ma-
neuver to cover his tracks.

What he preserved, however, was his integrity.

Taking a huge breath and holding it for a long minute, he picked up the phone, called city hall and can-
celed the open purchase order with the city and with
the school district. He had just crossed over the break-
even point. Unless he found a way to expand his business in ways he hadn't thought of yet, he was facing
financial ruin.

CHAPTER ELEVEN

MONDAY MORNING, Rolf was in the lay-down yard overseeing the offloading of pallets of two-by-fours from a flatbed truck, when his assistant, Jake Tarns, rushed out of the building.

"I just received a call from the police department," he shouted above the whine of the forklift. "That cover we installed over the handicapped entrance at Tillman Middle School collapsed."

A cold shiver raced down Rolf's back. "Dear God. Was anybody hurt?"

"They don't think so."

Rolf let out a rush of air. "What exactly happened?"

"Apparently water collected from the storm last night and the weight caused the thing to collapse."

That didn't make sense. The structure was nothing more than an awning for the back door of the building, where a ramp had been installed a few years ago for handicapped students and teachers. There were gutters for runoff that should have handled even the heaviest downpour.

The torrential storm, shortly after midnight, lasted only a short time. What had gone wrong? Was the collapse the fault of the installation or the materials themselves? One of Rolf's areas of expansion included the purchase of a franchise for minor construction, things like carports, awnings and outbuildings for storage. Most of the products were prefabricated and in kits. If the materials were defective, the manufacturer was responsible, but Rolf wouldn't escape liability. Insurance might cover all his expenses, but his reputation would be seriously tarnished.

Damn it, this was no time for him to be thinking of his reputation. Children's lives had been in jeopardy, and he could never forgive himself for that.

"I better go over there."

Tillman was one of the oldest schools in the district. The original building, dating back to the twenties, was a single-story oblong structure of yellow stone and white stucco, with a few chipped, decorative orange Spanish tiles along the roofline. A year and half ago a wing was added to the back to accommodate children with physical disabilities, but one bureaucratic muddle after another delayed its completion and use. A few months ago, while work was still under way on the inside, the board had approved the construction of a cover from the door to the edge of the parking lot. Rolf was one of three people to compete for the job. His bid came in considerably lower than both his rivals'.

The area was now a madhouse. Police cars were parked in front of the building. School buses, some already packed with children, were lined up, their engines belching black diesel fumes. Rolf pulled around to the rear of the building. A fire truck stood nearby, as well as a paramedic van. There was a sense of purpose in the air but not panic.

The awning was a tangled mess of leaning steel beams and twisted corrugated metal, its sharp edges glinting in the sun. Rolf got out of his truck, approached one of the policeman guarding the perimeter and identified himself. "Was anyone hurt?"

"Not that I know of." The young officer lifted the yellow police-line tape to let him pass.

Bill Marcus was talking to several men gathered around the back of the construction site. Rolf recognized Chet Marler, the city's building inspector, and the fire chief.

"What happened?"

"It appears the downspouts were blocked, so the rain collected," Chet explained. "The weight of the water, combined with the heavy winds we had early this morning, caused the bolts to snap. The lack of stabilizing wind rods didn't help, either."

Rolf put his hand out for the bolt the inspector was holding and frowned when he examined its smooth head.

"It's the right size," Marler noted, "but the wrong tensile strength."

"This is a grade two," Rolf agreed. "It should be an eight."

There were three grades of bolts: two, five and eight. Two was the softest, designed to sheer off under pressure. Eight was the hardest and what should have been used for this project. Raised marks on the head would have indicated its high tensile strength.

"I don't understand how this could have happened. I'll have to check the specifications that came with the kit." The fabricating company furnished most of the customized materials and identified what bolts and other standard components to use.

Bill Marcus, his wide frame and yellow hard hat making him resemble a caricature of a bulldog, fired Rolf a narrow-eyed glare. "I understand you're refusing to do any more business with the city and school district now," Bill grumbled ominously. "This wouldn't have anything to do with that decision, would it?"

The temptation to lash out and go on the defensive was almost overwhelming. "I'm not refusing to sell anything to anyone," Rolf replied with a crispness in his voice. The sick feeling was intensifying, but he refused to justify himself by adding that he simply wanted to avoid any appearance of a conflict of interest. "I'll honor individual purchase orders from any agency within the municipality."

Marcus's response was a dismissive sneer. His awareness of Coyote Lumber's change in policy, however, set Rolf's teeth on edge. Perhaps, as chairman of the board, Bill would be informed of this type of procedural shift, but Rolf doubted it. More likely, people who were suddenly uncomfortable with his decision were keeping Bill in the loop.

"Don't think your position on the school board will save you. You won't get away with this. Because of your pinching pennies, children's lives could have been at stake."

Rolf glowered and his voice was far from even now. "Are you suggesting I intentionally sold inferior materials to the school for a few bucks' profit?" He put his hand on the man's shoulder, turning him to face him. The shock of being touched, even on the padded shoulder of his suit jacket, had Bill Marcus's eyes bulging with apprehension.

"I would never, never do anything," Rolf enunciated, "that might endanger children. I very much resent your insinuating that I would. I have kids of my own."

"Not attending this school you don't," Marcus shot back nervously.

"Gentlemen—" the inspector raised his hands "—calm down. No one here is making any accusations against anyone else. Until my investigation is complete, we don't know what happened."

"I'd be very careful about making public statements, if I were you, Marcus," Rolf said between his teeth. "One word to suggest I'm responsible for this accident, and I'll sue you for slander and defamation of character. I don't take lightly to being accused of endangering the lives of children."

Placatingly, Chet Marler intervened. "He's right, Bill. I wouldn't go around making any unfounded accusations."

The chairman ignored him. "You do your investigating, Inspector, then we'll see." He stomped away.

Rolf again examined the bolt in his hand. "You have a problem here, too, Chet. This structure passed inspection just a few days ago," he commented. "Who passed it?"

He gnawed the corner of his mouth. "I'll have to check the records." Marler excused himself and left.

A few minutes later, Rolf drove back to the lumberyard, all the time trying to analyze the situation. He had a pretty good idea that whoever was responsible for the inspection had either signed off on the paperwork without even seeing the construction or had done nothing more than a quick drive-by. It wasn't unusual with builders they trusted. Had Sam Dossard, his foreman on the job, screwed up?

Or had the work been sabotaged, and if so, when and by whom? Above all, why? Rolf's business was already in trouble, and now he was in danger of losing the one thing he was counting on to save it: his good reputation.

Jake's expression was apprehensive when Rolf came through the doorway. "You don't look happy."

"Come with me." Rolf marched to his office at the rear of the building. "Tell me again about why Sam Dossard left last week."

"Sam?" Jake's forehead furled momentarily, then he seemed to recognize the significance of the question. "He came to see me Thursday afternoon. Right after you signed out for lunch. Said he was quitting. I asked him why. He told me he'd received word that morning that his mother was sick, and he didn't know if she was going to make it. I told him I was real sorry and asked if there was anything we could do. He said no, he had to hit the road and would let us know where to send his final check. I offered him my condolences. We shook hands. He climbed in his truck and took off."

Rolf slouched against the front of his desk. He had a host of questions he wished he'd thought to ask earlier, not that they would have made any difference.

"If he found out about his mother in the morning, why did he wait until the afternoon to cut out?"

"I asked him the same thing." Jake sank into the chair by the door, clearly uncomfortable. "He said he called home during his lunch break and found out his mom had taken a turn for the worse. The doctor recommended he get home right away."

"Did you believe him?"

Jake glanced down at this hands. "Didn't have any reason not to, Rolf, not at the time." He looked up. "All I could think of was that the poor guy's mom was dying.'' Which was natural enough, considering Jake's own mother's failing health.

"Did you offer to hold his job for him?"

Jake nodded. "But he said if she recovered, he'd want to stay there, close by, and if she didn't…he'd have a bunch of things to take care of.'' Jake closed his eyes and took a deep breath. "I'm sorry, Boss. I had no idea something like this—"

"No way you could have," Rolf consoled him. "He was a good worker. Where's home. I forget."

"I don't remember the name of the place. A little town outside Baton Rouge, I think."

Louisiana. Picard's home state and the last place Picard had served as superintendent. What were the chances of there being a connection?

"What did Dossard do that day?"

Jake scratched his head. "Spent the whole morning over at Tillman. I figured he was just being conscientious about finishing up at the school before having to take off.'' Jake studied his boss curiously. "What's this all about, Rolf?"

He moved around, sank into his swivel chair, inhaled deeply and raised his head. "It appears the reason for the collapse over at Tillman was clogged downspouts, the wrong bolts being used and no wind rods being installed."

Jake slumped in his seat. "I can't believe Sam would be so careless."

"I don't want to believe it, either," Rolf intoned, wringing his hands nervously in front of him. "But from what I saw, it's true."

"At least there weren't any kids around. From what I've heard, that wing won't be ready for use until the spring."

"Yeah." Rolf pushed away from the desk and went to a dusty black file cabinet in the corner of the cluttered office. He removed a buff-colored personnel folder.

"You think Sam screwed it up and hightailed it out of here because he knew what would happen?" Jake asked.

"I'd say it's a good guess." He flipped through the pages. "According to his job application, his mother died ten years ago."

Jake pounded the arm of his chair, emitted a coarse expletive and sprang to his feet. "That son of a bitch. Why in the name of...why would he do this?" He shook his head. "The guy had a good job. He seemed to be happy with his work. He certainly knew sheet metal. That was one of the reasons you hired him, in spite of his record."

Sam had spent two years in prison for grand theft auto—the result of youthful bad judgment and keeping the wrong company. Rolf had been willing to overlook the criminal record because the twenty-six-year-old had gone straight for the five years since his release and was savvy about metalwork.

Rolf shared Jake's outrage and feeling of betrayal. He'd liked Sam. He didn't excuse what he'd done in the past, but he didn't think the young man had been a bad kid so much as a foolish one. Apparently he'd misjudged.

"I need you to do something for me," Rolf said. "Check the specs and see what tensile strength bolts he was supposed to use. Then dig out the invoices and see what he ordered."

Jake moved to the door. "It might have been a

simple mix-up, and when he realized what he'd done, he panicked and ran.''

"Could be, but Sam worked for me long enough to know I wouldn't fire him if he came to me and owned up to a mistake. My first concern would be to correct it, then see what we need to do to make sure it didn't happen again.''

Jake nodded agreement. "It'll be interesting to see if he actually sends us an address for his final pay.''

"Any bets?''

Jake made a bitter attempt at a chuckle. "Not from me. I'm still having trouble believing he did this.''

The phone on the desk buzzed. An outside line. He hoped it was Julie. The sound of her voice would be the one bright spot in an otherwise miserable day. He could picture her sweet lips close to the phone, and almost laughed at the echoes of an old country-and-western song. "Coyote Lumber—''

"Murdock,'' Bill Marcus shouted loud enough that the telephone wire probably wasn't necessary. "Special executive session at my house this evening at eight. Be there.'' The line went dead.

NANCY CAME BARGING into the room. On reflex, Julie hit a key to change the screen on her computer. She was checking the Web for one of the foundations that had given Picard an award for outstanding service in the advancement of secondary education.

"Have you heard?'' Nancy blustered.

"Heard what?'' Julie let herself relax. Nancy didn't know what Julie was up to, but she wasn't confident the woman would keep her lips sealed if she found out.

"The roof at Tillman Elementary collapsed. No telling how many people, kids, are trapped."

"Dear God."

"Haven't you been listening to the radio?" Nancy rushed to the credenza behind Julie and turned up the volume. Julie hadn't even noticed that the light rock she used as background music had been interrupted.

"The collapse of the new cover for physically challenged students at Tillman Elementary, one of the oldest schools in Coyote Springs, came as a complete surprise, according to the city building inspector who was on the scene minutes after the disaster was reported. The new annex, scheduled to open in the spring, was unoccupied. Thankfully no one was injured. The cause of the failure of the new construction is not known at this time, but the head of the Coyote Springs school board, William Marcus, informed this reporter that it may have been due to the use of substandard materials. He said an investigation is underway. This station's sources inform us," the newscaster went on, "that the minor construction project was being performed by Coyote Lumber. Rolf Murdock, its owner, has not been available for comment."

Julie squeezed her eyes shut, took a deep breath and picked up the phone. Rolf wasn't there, of course. He hadn't yet returned from the construction site, and Jake didn't know when he would.

She glanced at the clock on her desk. Her workday ended in another hour. "Tell the kids I'll pick them up at the regular time."

ONE GLANCE AT ROLF coming in the kitchen door and Julie knew he was in a depressed mood.

"Where are the kids?" he muttered.

"Down the street with the Davises. Mitch won three large supremes from Rodrigo Pizza and has a new computer game, so most of the kids in the neighborhood are there. Under the circumstances—"

He pulled out a ladder-back chair and sank onto it, his hands in his lap, his head drooping. "Thanks for your help."

She snagged a bottle of beer from the refrigerator, used a dishtowel to unscrew the top, set it on the table and took the seat next to him.

"So what happened?" she asked, knowing there was no point in beating around the bush.

He took a long pull on the cold beverage, smiled gratefully and gave her the lowdown.

"You think this was engineered, don't you?"

"I can't believe anyone would put handicapped children at risk. But what else can it be?" He swallowed more beer, then began peeling the label with his thumbnail.

"Let's examine the facts." He held up fingers to enumerate them. "Sam Dossard knew his job. That's why I hired him in spite of his criminal record." At her shocked expression, he explained the circumstances. "We did some checking this afternoon. The specification for the awning called for grade eight bolts. Sam ordered eights in sufficient quantity to do the job, and the order arrived in time. We found them in his storeroom. But he installed grade twos. Why? There's only one reason." He breathed loudly through his nose. "He had an incentive."

"What kind of incentive?" Julie asked.

"Blackmail is a possibility. His criminal record, which wasn't widely known, also made him vulnerable."

"But why, Rolf?"

"That's what I don't know, not for sure, anyway." He rubbed the back of his neck. "Drive me out of business? I have competition, but none of us seems out to destroy the others. I was low bid on this project by quite a lot, but in the case of Brunner Builders, I think they purposely bid high because they really didn't want this small job. Anchor Walls has enough work to do that this contract wasn't really important. So why would they want Sam to sabotage it? It doesn't make much sense."

"What happens now?" she asked.

Rolf worked his jaw. "The city will investigate, determine the construction was shoddy and that I'm liable for the damages."

"It doesn't seem fair," she said.

"I'll be fined and have to pay damages. Fortunately, no one was hurt. Otherwise I could be faced with criminal charges as well as lawsuits by individuals and their families. The franchiser will probably decide he doesn't want to deal with me and terminate my contract." He shook his head. "I called my lawyer this afternoon and told him briefly what's happened. We're getting together first thing in the morning at his office to review my options."

"Would you like me to tag along—for moral support?"

He wrapped his arms around her. "Thanks. I appreciate it, but I can handle this part by myself. Besides, you have your own job to go to and things to do there."

She gave him a gentle kiss on the lips, pulling back before he could deepen it. "I can't offer you a pizza supreme," she murmured, "but I bet I can find something to feed you."

He brought his hand up to her cheek and held it there, enjoying the soft warmth, the hint of tension under his fingers. "You've done so much for me already."

"It's been my pleasure," she murmured.

The breathless tremor in her voice made him want more. As he gazed into her blue eyes, his pulse hammered a staccato beat. He ached for her, for much more than words and gentle touches.

He shifted his pelvis. There could be no doubt how she affected him, how the feel of her aroused him. Her lids drooped. Her jaw sagged. The pout of her lips was all the invitation he needed. The taste of her was sweet, intoxicating, more mind-altering than any wine. He fondled her breast. Her hard nipple was in the palm of his hand when they heard the clatter of feet and the enthusiasm of young voices.

Inhaling deeply, he released her and stepped back. The children barged in and greeted him.

"Did you hear what happened at Tillman?" Foster asked with the fascination of youth for disaster. "The roof caved in."

The twins seemed disappointed when he told them it was only the new awning and that no one was hurt. He might have laughed at their reactions had it been a computer game or TV action-adventure. Real life was different. A lesson they would learn. He hoped it wouldn't be too quickly or too painfully.

He glanced at his watch. Seven-thirty. "I have to be over at the chairman's house in a few minutes. Special executive session."

Julie removed his empty beer bottle and dropped it

in the trash. "I don't suppose you know when you'll be back," she said over her shoulder.

Awareness of her unwillingness to let him go was a balm to his ego. "This could take hours."

Jeff poured himself a glass of milk. "That pizza had fish on it. Yuck."

"Anchovies," Derek explained. "Actually, they were pretty good."

"You're weird," his brother informed him.

"Oh, damn." Rolf looked directly at Julie. "I haven't even asked you if you can stay."

She studied his somber face and wanted desperately to kiss it. "You don't think I'd abandon you in a situation like this, do you?"

His smile was rueful as he rested an arm on her shoulders, buddy-style. "You know something? I've decided I like having you around."

"Really." She grinned playfully.

"We do, too," Leah chimed in.

Reminded his children were still present, he released Julie and moved toward the kitchen door.

"We may have to discuss this a little more later." He turned the knob and winked at her over his shoulder.

CHAPTER TWELVE

THE MEETING at Bill Marcus's house was far from friendly. Nerves were on edge, tempers seething below the surface of not just Rolf and the chairman, but of all the other members, as well.

"The first order of business," Bill announced, "is to decide what we should do about Tillman Elementary."

"It'll cost a fortune if we have to relocate all the classes," said Chase Milsap, the hardware franchise owner.

"What's the physical danger to the students if they continue to attend classes there?" Herb Mellow asked. "That has to be our primary concern."

"Agreed." The chairman glared at Rolf. Under other circumstances, it would have taken willpower to keep from looking away. In this case, pure anger was sufficient to maintain eye contact. "I discussed the matter with the building inspector late this afternoon. He tells me there's no threat of further collapse—"

Matt Hargrove interrupted. "Kids are drawn to disaster. That rubble heap will be an attractive nuisance until it's removed."

"That won't be until after the building inspector finishes his investigation," Chase Milsap pointed out.

"We're talking about the safety of children," Herb

reminded them. "We have no choice but to relocate them temporarily."

Virginia Akers arched an eyebrow at Herb's vehemence. "But where? And how long will it take us to set up new classrooms? Every day of school missed has to be made up."

"We still have the temporary buildings behind Middlefarm Junior," Matt noted. "Our plan was to remove them now that their renovations have been completed. Why don't we hold on to them for a little longer, until we know it's safe to go back to Tillman."

Virginia Akers seconded the idea. "We can have the school buses drop the children off there instead of at Tillman."

"That'll add to the schedule," Marcus reminded everyone. "The two schools are at opposite ends of town. Either the kids lose classroom time or we implement earlier pickup and later return, which means extending hours for the school bus drivers. Another expense."

"Damn the expenses." Herb thumped the table. "This is no time to be counting pennies."

"I agree with you," Marcus said, "but we're not talking about pennies here. Our budget is already overdrawn."

Rolf had heard enough. "You're all overreaching. We don't have to relocate classes—just cancel them for a day or two while we install safety fencing."

"Cancel classes?" Virginia was shocked at the notion.

"Just like for snow days," Rolf elaborated. "We put extra days in the school calendar every year for contingencies. This is one of them."

"Fencing costs money," Milsap pointed out.

"The Evenstreet Foundation awarded the school district forty thousand dollars last quarter that hasn't been reflected in the budget. It's more than enough to cover this expense."

There was a moment in which brows were raised, as if the other members were unaware of the grant or had forgotten about it.

"State grant programs are also available for emergency situations such as this." Rolf surveyed the others around the dining room table. "Matt, would you be willing to join me as a committee of two to check into them?"

"Since you may be found responsible for this *accident*," Marcus objected, "I don't think you should be the one—"

"What Bill means to say," Rolf interjected, "is that my company had the contract to put up the awning. We don't know if the materials were defective, the installation was the problem or someone tampered with it later. It passed city inspection just last week. If officials find that my foreman screwed up, I'll make good for any damage done."

Marcus slammed his hand on the table. "The law will see to it that you do."

Rolf ignored him. "But the city's building inspector will have some questions to answer, as well." Everyone listened attentively. Bill Marcus continued to scowl.

"I draw three things to your attention," Rolf added. "We don't know for sure at this point why the structure failed. We don't know who is responsible for that failure." He held up his hand to emphasize the next point. "And third, it would be very unwise to make unsubstantiated public statements about this situation that could turn out to be libelous.''

"That sounds like a threat," Marcus snarled.

"I'm not into threats," Rolf countered, strangely calmed by the other man's bluster. "It's advice. Your attorneys will undoubtedly tell you the same thing." He made eye contact with each of them before proceeding. "Now, about looking into this matter of financial assistance—"

"If you don't have time, Matt," the chairman persisted, "Chase and I can work on this."

Rolf shook his head emphatically. "You'll be too busy with other things, like arranging for installation of the fencing as soon as possible." He peered at Marcus. "And walking a diplomatic tightrope in explaining this to the public." Rolf addressed Hargrove, the man sitting across from him. "What do you say?"

Hargrove nodded. "Glad to help."

"Unless there's something else, I suggest we adjourn," Rolf offered. "I don't know about y'all, but I've had a very long, trying day, and I need to get home to my family."

Since no one moved or proposed further discussion, he climbed to his feet. It was a signal that prompted the others to do the same.

"Thanks for your hospitality, Bill," Rolf said with friendly politeness, as if they hadn't been ready to throttle each other throughout the evening. "I realize this has been a rough day for you, too. I'm sure you'll keep us all informed of anything new you learn." He pushed his vacated chair neatly against the edge of the dining room table. "This situation is messy, but with patience and careful planning, I'm sure we can do this school district proud."

Rolf wished on the way home that he felt nearly as confident as he'd pretended. He knew there was no retreating. The gauntlet had been thrown. Enmity declared. Failing business or not, Bill Marcus was still a pillar of the community, a man who wielded a great deal of influence, if not direct power.

It was after ten o'clock when he pulled into the driveway of the house on Coyote Avenue. By now, the kids would be in bed. He regretted not having a chance to sit down at the supper table with them as a family and explain what was going on and what they could expect from it. They'd no doubt hear unpleasant things at school about the disaster at Tillman—if Bill's venom was any indication. He needed to prepare them and help them learn to cope with malicious tongues. He'd have to do it tomorrow morning, though he knew the first sleepy hour of the day wasn't their best time.

He found Julie at the computer in the den. Her blond hair was pulled back in a ponytail, a few stray wisps at the base of her neck.

"Hi," she greeted him. "How'd it go?"

He walked up behind her, placed his hands on her shoulders, bent and kissed her on the right temple. "Hmm, peachy keen." Which was how her hair smelled. Clean, fresh and alluring. The need for a sympathetic touch had him pressing his cheek against hers.

"Rolf, are you all right?" She swiveled in the seat and regarded him. He could see her eyes wanted to smile, but the anxiety in her expression held the joy in check.

He lifted her gently to her feet and wrapped his arms around her, empowered and consoled by the warmth of her body pressed against his. The soft thrust of her breasts against his chest slowed his breathing to a deep, greedy act of desperation. Her eyes were shining with startled delight. Strangely, he couldn't smile back, even as he soaked in the joy he saw there. Her jaw was slack, not in awe but anticipation. He brushed his lips across hers, savoring the smooth velvet friction between them. Teasing pleasure. She let out a delicate moan. He captured her mouth with his and slid into its silky warmth. She locked her arms around his waist, the captive holding the captor.

"Okay? I am now," he murmured. They set each other free. *Not free,* he told himself. *On parole.* He couldn't imagine ever being free of this woman.

"You hungry?" She turned off the computer.

He shook his head. "Not for food." He placed his hand over hers. Soft, warm and feminine. He shouldn't be thinking about how much he wanted her right now, how he needed her. But it was no use. After the events of the day, her touch was his one solace.

"What happened at the meeting?"

They moved into the living room and sat at opposite ends of the couch, as if getting too close would block communication. He gave a brief account of the session.

"Why is Bill so hostile?"

He raised his arms over his head and stretched. The old man's animosity was almost visceral, although he'd been friendly enough when Rolf had first joined the board. "He's scared. A year or so ago, his company wasn't doing too well. Then he started receiving big sales contracts from the district. My dropping my

contract has him worried somebody will question why
he hasn't. If there's enough pressure applied, he'll
have to, which will mean almost certain disaster, a
personal as well as family failure, since the company
appeared to be thriving when he inherited it."

Rolf couldn't bear the separation any longer. To
hell with the school board and business solvency. He
slid down beside her and draped an arm along the
back of the couch so his fingers could roam the slender column of her neck. "How was your day? Did
you play Mexican Train with the kids again this evening."

She smiled, and as always it lit up her face. "Just
a short session."

He toyed with the delicate skin below her ear. She
couldn't resist tilting her head into his touch. Her
pulse throbbed under his fingertips. "We need to get
away."

"That would be nice." Her vision lost its focus as
she half closed her eyes.

She didn't know what it was about Rolf's touch
that was so completely different from any other sensation she'd ever experienced. It wasn't just his
kisses—though the very anticipation of his tongue
tangling with hers sent heat surging in secret places.
This man stirred desires she'd never before felt so
helpless to resist. He was strong and gentle, firm yet
yielding, determined but patient. He made her laugh
with joy and brought her to tears of longing.

"Maybe we can all go out to the ranch this weekend," she muttered.

"The kids would definitely enjoy that." He smiled
seductively at her. "But I'm not sure I can get away
right now."

She splayed her hand on his chest. Her touch was like an electric shock, jolting his heart, making his blood race. "Even for a night?" she asked softly. "Clare called this evening. She wanted to know what the situation is at Tillman. Their youngest is in the fifth grade there. She also suggested we come out to the ranch this weekend. They're planning a trail ride for a bunch of their son Dave's friends from school and she thought your kids might like to join them."

He perked up.

"They're riding out on Saturday afternoon, camping overnight and returning sometime Sunday."

"I won't be able to break away until pretty late on Saturday." He frowned. "Too late for them to make it."

"I was thinking," she said casually, "I could take them to the ranch and leave them there, then come back into town. I have chores to catch up on. Exciting things like doing laundry." Her eyes promised more than her words.

"Would you like to use our washing machine? It's heavy-duty, you know."

She leaned over and planted a kiss on his lips. "Heavy-duty, huh? I admire strength and endurance."

He sucked in his cheeks. "I'll keep that in mind."

JULIE WASN'T SURPRISED that the kids were hyperactive bundles of energy the rest of the week. The prospect of spending a night on the Number One and camping under the stars on one of the biggest ranches in Texas made them remarkably willing to do anything she asked. Like yard work. Personal laundry. Cleaning up their rooms. Even washing windows. Derek volunteered to straighten up the garage for his dad, and he fixed the chain on Leah's bicycle, which had been broken for almost two weeks.

By Friday evening, they were so antsy Julie was tempted to drive them out to the ranch immediately following supper, except that hadn't been the deal. As much as she wanted to spend a night alone with Rolf, for now anticipation would have to be her sole pleasure.

Shortly before noon on Saturday, Julie chauffeured the four Murdock children to the Number One. In no time, they had disappeared into the barn with the other kids.

Michael and Clare were on the floor of the mudroom, picking beggar's lice off the last of Seneca's pups. They'd found good homes for five of the six young golden retrievers. Julie suspected this one was destined for the Home Place. Her father loved pets and hadn't had a housedog for several years, since his favorite black lab died of old age.

"Hi," Clare greeted her. "The kids all right?"

Julie sat down on the floor beside the older animal. Everybody went into raptures over the pups, forgetting their mama. Seneca raised her head with what could have been a smile when Julie began petting her.

"They headed for the barn and horses as soon as we parked," Julie answered. "Thanks for taking them this weekend."

"With this Tillman fiasco, getting away will probably do them good," Michael observed. "I've heard some ugly rumors that Rolf substituted cheaper materials in that construction project."

"It's not true," Julie answered, trying very hard not to sound bitter at the way Rolf and his children were being treated by people they thought were friends. "Dossard, the guy he hired to handle steel erection and sheet metal jobs, used the wrong bolts, then took a hike."

"Too bad," her brother observed, though Julie couldn't detect any real sympathy in the words. "Not that it makes a whole lot of difference. Murdock's responsible."

"He knows that," Julie all but snarled. Clare frowned at her husband in a silent warning to lighten up. "But he'd still like to find out who put Dossard up to not following specifications."

Michael combed through the fur of the patient pup's hind leg. "You mean he thinks it was sabotage, not an accident?"

"It's remotely possible it was an innocent screw-up," Julie conceded. "But Rolf doesn't think so."

"Is he being sued?" Clare asked.

Julie shook her head without enthusiasm. "Not yet, but it may be only a matter of time."

"Has he got the capital reserves if he is?" Michael asked.

She could feign ignorance, but what would be the point? She knew where her brother was going with his question. She didn't like it. Still, there was nothing she could do about it. "His insurance will probably cover any judgment. But he's lost several lucrative contracts over this mess. Legal fees alone could drive him into bankruptcy."

Michael sat back on his haunches and regarded her. "I hate to say I told you so—"

"But you will anyway," Julie snapped. Only Seneca's soft fur kept her from bunching her hand into a fist.

"You didn't want to think your wealth was important to him before, but maybe now it's become a bigger factor in your relationship. Has he asked you for money?"

Julie closed her eyes and took a deep breath. "No, and he won't."

"Are you sure? What will you say if he does?"

"Damn it, Michael," she snapped loud enough to make Seneca lift her head and peer at her. "What I do with my money is none of your concern. Now, for the last time, mind your own damn business."

He stroked the spot where he'd removed the pesky little burrs. "In other words, you don't know."

Furious, Julie began to rise, but Clare reached over and put her hand on her sister-in-law's arm. "I don't for a minute think Rolf Murdock would do anything that might endanger people's lives, especially children's. To save a few bucks? Absurd. His reputation is too important to him."

Gratefully, Julie let out a painful chestful of air. "He wouldn't. It's just that…proving it may be hard to do, especially with the forces lined up against him."

"Remind him he has friends, too," Clare told her.

It was a simple statement, delivered undramatically but sincerely. She glanced over at her brother. With a slow blink, he nodded. He would support her, but because she was family. "Let me know if I can help."

Julie had a late lunch with her father and stepmother. She gave them the current lowdown.

Sheila shook her head. "He seems like such a nice man, and a good father. This is all so unfair."

"You're getting pretty serious about him, aren't you?" Adam ventured.

Julie could have told him it had gone beyond getting serious. She was in love with him. "Michael thinks I'm making a big mistake." She munched on one of the whole-wheat crackers Sheila had served with the green salad and grilled chicken.

"Rolf strikes me as an intelligent, hardworking man," her father commented. "The kind I'd like as a friend."

Julie felt the first stirrings of hope. Her brother was negative, but her father appeared to be much more objective.

"If you're seeking my advice..." Adam smiled sympathetically. "I'm the last one you should come to. My record for choosing husbands for my daughters isn't very good, so take anything I say with a grain of salt."

She knew what he was referring to. He'd forced her sister, Kerry, into marrying the man who'd gotten her pregnant—with disastrous consequences. Father and daughter had made peace, but he'd never forgiven himself for his mistake.

"We men regard ourselves as very logical creatures. In matters of the heart, women are more insightful, though."

"I wish I had that on tape," Sheila quipped, shooting her husband an amused grin.

"Michael says Rolf's too old for me, that his children's ages—Derek is thirteen, more than half my age—could be a problem, and that Rolf is interested in my money."

"They're all valid considerations," her father concurred gently.

"Have you discussed these things with Rolf, dear?" Sheila asked.

Julie shook her head.

"I think you need to," her father remarked.

She remained silent, her fingers toying with her fork.

Adam reached over and covered her hand with his. His rough calluses were strangely reassuring. "If, after you've asked all the hard questions, you're convinced Rolf Murdock is the man for you, sweetheart, you'll have my unqualified support," he told her sincerely. "You know that. But you have to ask the questions and decide if he's giving you truthful answers."

JULIE DROVE back into town with the radio turned off and her mind active. Why did love have to be so complicated?

It was after six by the time she arrived at Rolf's house. He wasn't home yet, but she wasn't surprised. She'd stopped off at her apartment and picked up her dirty laundry, then gone to the market to buy something for dinner. Stir-fry. Quick and easy. She was still slicing zucchini, when she heard his van pull into the driveway and peeked through the kitchen window. He moved with his usual straight broad-shouldered carriage, but the shadows under his eyes belied his confident stance.

She greeted him with a kiss on the cheek and watched as he transformed from beleaguered merchant to friend and lover. He rested his hands on her hips and gazed deeply at her. "This certainly is a pleasant way to come home after a hard day in the salt mines."

Her eyes danced with his. "Salt, huh? Sounds thirsty. There's a bottle of Llano Johannisberg Riesling in the fridge, if you'd care to pull the cork. Unless you're too tired, of course.''

He snaked his hands behind her to draw her closer, his feet planted outside hers. ''I might be able to work up the energy.''

She patted the side of his face. ''I'm counting on it.''

Final preparations for the meal took little time. He poured the wine and they sat, exchanging glances across the kitchen table as they ate and sipped.

''I'm sort of sorry we couldn't join the kids on their ride tonight.'' He popped a piece of mushroom into his mouth. ''A night under the stars, surrounded by the sounds of nature—''

''The babble of the young people,'' she reminded him.

''Surely on five hundred thousand acres, it would be possible to escape—''

She laughed. ''I 'spect you're right.''

''On the other hand,'' he went on, ''having the house all to ourselves for the first time in history isn't exactly a hardship.''

''There are the dishes.''

''Spoilsport.'' He put his tongue to his upper lip and he fixed his eyes on hers over the rim of his wineglass. ''I was thinking of how much more comfortable a bed is than a sleeping bag.''

''There is that,'' she agreed.

They finished their simple meal in near silence. Words weren't necessary when their eyes were saying so much. They sipped white wine but didn't have a second glass.

It took only a minute to relegate their plates to the dishwasher. She was straightening up when his arms enfolded her from behind. She pushed back against his hard chest and rested her arms on his. His powerful hands, splayed on her belly, made her breathing abate, her vision dim to a haze. She rested her head under his chin and soaked in the rhythm of his slow breathing.

"I think we're done in here," he murmured.

Or maybe we're just beginning, she thought, as she rotated in the circle of his embrace.

Instantly his mouth found hers, and she gave herself over to the pleasure and the urgency of his kiss. Her head was light when he took her by the hand and led her out of the kitchen and down the hall to the foot of the stairs. He turned her to face him and was about to say something, but she pressed her finger to his parted lips to seal them. Still holding his hand, she slowly climbed the stairs, one step ahead of him.

She'd never been in his bedroom and didn't know what to expect, but once inside, she knew it was his. The room was large, simple but not plain, masculine but not unfriendly. She dismissed thoughts of the woman he'd shared it with, except to wonder if he had changed it since she left. They were alone in the house, yet he closed the door, making the space more intimate, their world exclusively.

He switched on the bedside lamp. The hunger in his eyes matched the gnawing ache in her belly. Shimmers of need tiptoed through her. He closed the narrow distance between them and gently rested his hands on her shoulders. He kissed her forehead, the tip of her nose, finally her mouth. His lips played over hers; his tongue slowly separated them. Carefully he began unbuttoning her blouse.

She shivered, not from cold, but from the sensation

his fingers generated as they fumbled between her breasts. She had to touch him. Biting her lower lip, she swept her hands across his chest and trembled with pleasure at the warm strength of massed sinew. He reached behind her and released her bra.

Desire, hot and desperate, swept through her as his tongue circled her hard nipples, one then the other. She threw back her head, leaned forward into his mouth, then let out a little yap when unexpectedly he bent and picked her up in his arms. He carried her to his bed, where, with crawling fingers, he finished undressing her. Shoes, socks. Shirt, bra. He tasted his way down her naked body. Neck. The shallow valley between her breasts. Belly button.

"I want to touch you," she whimpered as his lips dotted the sensitized flesh below her narrow waist. With fingers suddenly gone clumsy, she unbuttoned his shirt and watched the ripple of bunched muscles as he slipped out of it. Dark curls of hair accented the masculine contours of his chest. His skin was firm to the touch, hot against her palm, salty on her tongue.

When his hands unsnapped her jeans and started to slide them down, she lifted her hips to accommodate him. While his mouth continued its exploration along her exposed skin, she held her breath, aware only of Rolf and what he was making her feel. Sensations. Wild, amorphous images cascading through her mind. His touch became a part of her intimate world. The instant he stopped, withdrew, she felt bereft, alone, afraid. Her eyes flew open to behold him unbuckling his belt. The shadowy light from the lamp emphasized his manliness. He removed the last vestige of clothing. As he leaned over and took the sides of her panties, his touch sent shock waves thundering through her. A moment later, he stretched out beside her. Together they explored each other's nakedness.

Heat gathered in her belly and spread like sweet warm honey on a summer's night when he covered her with his body. She was liquid in his hands. She took the foil packet he groped out of the nightstand. With trembling fingers she cupped him, sheathed him, guided him. Her mind swam in a delirium of desperate need. He entered her.

"Together," he whispered in her ear. "Us. You and me."

The movement began, slow and teasing, building, faster and faster. Her breath caught when he paused, making her cry out. His eyes were shut, his mouth a straight line. Then he opened them, looked at her and smiled. "Together," he repeated, and drove them over the edge.

CHAPTER THIRTEEN

SUNDAY AFTERNOON, Rolf left for the lumberyard to catch up on the paperwork he'd been unable to do all week. Julie was taking out the trash when Bryn drove up to the detached garage behind her house.

"How are you enjoying your exercise classes?" Julie called over the honeysuckle growing on the three-foot-high cyclone fence that separated the two properties.

Daniella erupted from the passenger side of the car and slammed the door. "It stinks." Whether she was talking about perspiration or the idea of physical exercise wasn't exactly clear.

"Actually, it's going very well." Bryn stepped out of the vehicle and ran her hands down her hips, obviously pleased with herself. "I feel like a million bucks."

"I hear you," Julie told her. She didn't see much change in Bryn's form and wasn't likely to in a single week, but she knew a body could feel a lot different in that short time. "I'm glad you're enjoying it."

"*She* is," the girl snarled. "I hate it." She stomped toward the back door of the old two-story house.

Bryn gave Julie a knowing glance. "It hasn't clicked for her yet."

"When she begins to see and feel progress, maybe it will," Julie said encouragingly.

"I hope so." Bryn sighed at the sound of her daughter slamming the kitchen door. "She's miserable about her weight, but she's unwilling to do anything about it." Bryn shook her head. "It's my fault. I've been too easy on her, letting her eat whatever she wants, mostly junk food. But saying no to your kid is hard, even when you know it's good for her." She cringed at the sound of heavy metal throbbing through an open upstairs window. "I've modified her diet, you know. She hates that, too."

Fruits and vegetables didn't satisfy when a person was used to starch and fat. Time would change that if the girl gave it a chance. But Julie recognized that lack of discipline was the underlying problem. Bryn's inconsistency in enforcing rules made matters worse. She was doing the right thing now—the question was whether she'd stick to it. Julie wasn't sure the woman had the strength to follow through on her good intentions. Being regarded as the enemy by your own child wasn't easy to live with. Julie's father could attest to that.

"Have you considered counseling?" she asked. "Kids are often more receptive to strangers than parents." Julie lightened her tone. "After all, you're only her mother. What do you know? But a sympathetic stranger…now, there's someone who gets it."

Bryn chuckled softly. "I hadn't thought about it that way. Do you really think it would help?"

"It probably wouldn't hurt. There are times when kids just need space to work through things. And strangers are less threatening, so it's easier to open up to them."

"You may be right. Thanks. I'll consider it." She

noted the lid Julie was putting back on the garbage can. "My, aren't you the domestic one."

Julie wasn't certain if she heard sarcasm in the remark, maybe because she was so self-conscious about the new dimensions her relationship with Rolf had expanded to. Could the other woman detect the afterglow of a night of lovemaking?

"So how is it going with Rolf's brood? They can be a handful, can't they?"

"They're kids." Julie was relieved at the diversion. Actually, she hadn't found them all that difficult. Sure, they occasionally tested their limits. That was the nature of children, especially in their adolescence. In spite of the occasional grumbling, however, they were pleased when the boundaries were established.

Bryn glanced around. "Where are they, by the way?"

"Out at the Number One on a trail ride with my brother's kids and their friends."

A smirk from the neighbor told Julie she didn't have to mention the kids hadn't been home last night. "Looks like he's hit on a winning combination. A woman who likes playing baby-sitter—" she surveyed the yard, which was much neater than it had been a week earlier, and nodded approvingly "—and who obviously enjoys the domestic role. A lot different from Sheryl."

Julie didn't appreciate being compared with Rolf's ex-wife. She hadn't given Sheryl much thought since Rolf had talked about his divorce. The kids didn't mention her, either. It was almost as if she'd never been there, and from what Rolf had told her, that was largely true, at least in the last few years of the marriage.

"She wanted a career, you know, which he was adamantly opposed to. Insisted she be a sweet little housewife and homemaker for his kids. She finally rebelled. What smart, well-educated woman wouldn't?" Bryn examined her nails and frowned at one that was chipped. "I guess you suit him better. You can afford to stay home with her kids and make his babies. Did he tell you he'd like to have a dozen?"

"A dozen?" Julie was aghast. He said they'd agreed on two and that the twins had been unplanned.

"That's what he admitted to Sheryl when they were getting their divorce," Bryn crowed.

Julie screwed up her mouth. "I'm sure she was exaggerating." She laughed. "I hope she was."

Bryn chuckled. "Maybe about the dozen part. She could be dramatic at times. But believe me, what Rolf wants in a wife is a homebody, not a career woman. Not that you need to work, anyway."

"Mo-om," the girl called out from the back door. "Are we going to eat or what?"

"Gotta run," Bryn chirped. "When do the kids get back?"

"I'll pick them up in a little while."

"Yep. You fit the role. See ya." With a pleasant smile, she turned to her house and disappeared inside.

Deciding this was a good time to weed the flower-bed on the side of the garage, Julie grabbed her work gloves from the counter in the laundry room. Bryn's comments kept gnawing at her. Was the woman being catty, planting seeds of discontent as a means of running off her competition, or was what she said true? Did Rolf subscribe to the barefoot-and-pregnant phi-losophy of a woman's place?

She tried to remember if he'd ever mentioned anything that would give her a hint to the answer. He'd quizzed her about her professional ambitions. That had been early on, before they'd developed a relationship. She'd made no secret of wanting to advance in the educational system. He'd seemed impressed rather than disapproving of her goals. Knowing she was career-minded, why would he have continued their relationship if he disapproved? Or did he think he'd be able to change her mind later? Jerry had been supportive of her career ambitions, too. Until he proposed. Then he'd expected her to drop everything and serve him and his interests.

She was being silly even to listen to Bryn, and paranoid in taking the woman's remarks seriously. There was that word again. The one Rolf had called her when she'd first told him about the oath. Of course, she hadn't been paranoid, and he'd come to recognize the truth. Which was all that mattered.

At three o'clock, she drove to the Number One. The kids were still on highs of excitement, each interrupting the other to tell her about the things they'd done and seen. She loved listening to them, loved their exuberance.

"Mr. First let me drive the tractor," Derek announced. "It was awesome."

"We worked with a bunch of young colts," Jeff added. "They really like to run, but he put halters on them and had us lead them around, so they'd get used to being handled. They can't be ridden for like three more years, but—"

Julie smiled. She'd grown up in the ranching life, grown up with tractors and young horses, sheep, goats and cattle. For these city children they were a brand-new adventure.

"The polite thing for all of you to do," Julie told them, "is write personal notes to Mr. and Mrs. First, thanking them for their hospitality and telling them how much you enjoyed staying with them."

"If we do," Jeff asked, "do you think they'll invite us out again? The place is really neat."

"Moron," Leah huffed. "You're not supposed to thank them so they'll ask you out again."

"Why not?" Foster wanted to know.

Julie suppressed a smile. "I suspect they'll welcome you out again."

As the kids continued to talk and argue, Julie's mind kept wandering to her conversation with Bryn. Rolf expected his wife to stay at home and be a homemaker. Julie realized she'd been playing that role a lot lately—preparing their meals, helping the kids with their homework, weeding the garden.

She'd enjoyed it, too. But she hadn't earned her master's in education so she could run a car pool and bake brownies.

Not that there was anything wrong with cooking and cleaning and maintaining order, she reminded herself. Somebody had to do it. It was just that she had other skills, other qualifications. Other ambitions. A home and family were off in the future. Not here and now.

Isn't that what Michael had essentially said? That Rolf was too old for her, that he already had a family, that she deserved to start her own, not take over someone else's?

WHEN HE RETURNED from the closed lumberyard that afternoon, Rolf did his best to put on a smiley face for his kids. Reviewing numbers and assessing the full impact of lost business and his decision to cut himself off from profitable municipal contracts had been depressing. Unless he found a new source of high-volume sales, he was in serious trouble.

Fortunately, his children were so bubbling over with tales of their two days on the ranch they didn't notice the anxiety lurking behind his grins and enthusiasm. The glances he exchanged with Julie, though, made it pretty clear she did. Her eyes kept asking him questions that he didn't completely comprehend.

"Okay, time to clean up," she ordered. "Toss your dirty clothes in the laundry, put your camping stuff away and wash your hands. We eat in half an hour."

"You do that very well," Rolf noted, after the kids had darted from the room.

"Do what?" She set the table, putting out the place mats she'd found in a drawer of the china cabinet in the dining room. Eating in the big country kitchen was more homey, but that didn't mean it had to be plain.

"Get the kids doing what you want them to. I'm inclined to say it's because they love you—" he came up behind her, slipped his hands around her waist and nuzzled her ear "—but they love me, too, and they don't mind me nearly as well."

She lifted her shoulder, effectively curling her neck against his cheek. The softness of her skin, her gossamer hair brushing his face, the lingering scent of the shower they'd shared late that morning stirred images and desire.

He was about to add that his love for her was very different from theirs, too, when Leah pranced into the kitchen. She stopped short at the sight of her father with his hands around Julie's waist. Flustered, she stammered that they needed hand soap in the downstairs bathroom.

Keeping her eyes on her father as he sheepishly withdrew his hands, Leah slid over to the refrigerator and added the item to the shopping list Julie had posted on the door with a magnet.

Rolf removed glasses from an overhead cabinet. "Ask your brothers what they want to drink," he instructed his daughter.

"Julie already told me to check," she replied as she wrote on the shopping list. "They want cola."

"They're keyed up enough as it is. They don't need any more caffeine or sugar," Julie replied. "They can have water or iced tea. There's decaf in the fridge."

Leah giggled. "I told them you'd say that."

Suddenly aware of how easily she'd slipped into the maternal role, Julie glanced at Rolf.

He wanted to smile, but something in her expression warned him it wasn't a good idea. "Have y'all finished your homework for tomorrow?"

His daughter gave him one of her *duh* expressions. "We did all that on Friday, Dad."

Another thing Julie had been able to get them to do. Probably made it a condition for their going out to the ranch.

By the end of the meal, the kids were winding down. Jeff was so sleepy Rolf was afraid the boy's face would fall flat in his overfilled plate of enchilada pie. By nine-thirty, they'd been sent upstairs to take their showers and go to bed, and for once, they didn't object.

When the sound of running water finally stopped

and the last bedroom door clicked closed, Rolf settled on the couch beside Julie. He put his arm around her shoulder and drew her into his side.

"You look a bit tired, too, if you don't mind my saying so." He nuzzled her neck. "Didn't you sleep well last night?" he whispered in her ear.

She turned her head to smile at him. "What sleep I got was wonderful."

"And the waking moments?"

Her face broke into a grin. "Digging for compliments? Well, I have no trouble giving them. Last night was… Did I already use the word *wonderful?* How about *spectacular?*" She snuggled closer and planted her hand on his chest, feeling the steady beat of his heart.

He tilted her head at precisely the right angle and captured her mouth with his. She tasted so right, so perfect. He had the urge to take her there on the couch, to meld their bodies once more in last night's incredible passion.

"Can I ask you something?" She rested her cheek against the compact muscle of his chest once more.

He let out a little snort. "I'd say we know each other well enough for you to ask me anything you want."

"Why did you and Sheryl get divorced?"

Startled by the question, he shifted enough to gaze down at her, but she refused to look up. "I've already explained—"

"Tell me again."

He could hear the worry in her voice. What had happened to put it there? He felt her cheek against his heart and wondered if she realized she was the cause of its rhythmic chugging. He glanced down at the top of her head. "What's brought this up?"

She shifted enough this time to meet his eyes. "Please answer my question."

She was scaring him. It was the only word he could think of to describe the sensation rippling through him. He or somebody had made her...what? Doubt him? His capacity to love? Did she think last night was nothing more than fantastic sex?

"We divorced because she was tired of being a mother and my wife. Because she wanted a career instead of a family...because she fell in love with someone else."

"Couldn't she have had both? A career and a family, I mean?"

He'd been perfectly willing to let her have both. She'd taught at the university for years. But she wasn't satisfied with the classroom and occasional field trips. She wasn't satisfied with him. "Not the kind of career she wanted."

"Which was?"

"The all-consuming kind. The kind that left her free to explore different worlds."

Julie sat still, her arm slung across his belly. The intimacy of her touch stirred him, made him greedy for more of her.

"So you wanted Sheryl to give up her career," Julie suggested.

"Give it up? No," he assured her. "I had no objection to her having a career."

Julie looked up, her eyes hopeful. "You didn't?"

"Of course not. I knew she was frustrated when the kids were little. She hated staying at home, but we couldn't afford a maid at the time. Besides, we had very young children who needed a mother, not an anthropologist—a parent to be there to hold them when they cried. A nanny could help out, but a nanny wouldn't be their mother, the person who'd given them birth. So being a mom was Sheryl's primary job. When you think about it, isn't being a mother the most important job a woman can ever have? It shouldn't take second place to dry, dead bones. Then later...she found someone else."

Julie said nothing, and for a moment, he thought she might have fallen asleep. The day had been long and busy for her, as well.

"I have to go." She pulled away from his embrace.

"It's only a little after ten," he objected.

She sat up straight. "Tomorrow's a workday, and I still have a lot of things to do."

He didn't want her to leave. He wanted her in his bed...by his side...beneath him...over him.

"Of course." He held her hand and peered into her eyes. "I haven't been thinking. I've been too busy feeling good about having you in my arms." He kissed her lightly on the lips, not daring to go as far or as deep as he longed to. "I wish we could roll back the clock twenty-four hours."

"So do I," she agreed thoughtfully. "But time waits for no man—or woman."

She climbed to her feet and stretched luxuriantly. His mind flashed back to her sprawled out on his bed, naked.

"You've been a lifesaver. I hope you know that. The kids had a wonderful time." He winked at her. "I had an even better time. I'm sorry I couldn't spend more of today with you, but—"

"I understand." She started gathering up her things.

He couldn't let the day end this way. He pulled her into his arms and kissed her hard. "I wonder if you do."

JULIE SLEPT FITFULLY, in spite of the little rest she'd gotten the night before. She kept replaying Bryn's words, then Rolf's, trying to deny they were both saying the same thing. Rolf wanted a woman who would stay home with the kids, at least until they were old enough to be left alone. She didn't really have any argument with the concept, if it was what a woman wanted, except it could stifle interests that went beyond being a nursemaid.

Her alarm went off at six. She'd actually fallen asleep by then, and the harsh buzz of the digital clock was pure torment. After dragging herself out of bed, she went through her morning routine, dressed for work, hoping no one would notice—or at least comment on—the bags under her eyes.

Apparently, other people in the administrative building had had rough weekends, too, for most of the greetings she received were mumbled and distracted. She reached her office, to find a note taped to the computer screen: "Come see me. A."

She tucked her purse into the top right-hand drawer of her desk, then headed down the corridor to her boss's office. The practice test project wasn't completed, but she had enough compiled for the first list. She tapped on the door frame of Alyson's office.

Aside from the superintendent's suite, it was the biggest and most stylishly decorated private office in the building.

"Come on in, Julie, and close the door behind you."

Alyson remained seated behind her desk, rolling a pencil between her fingers. "Enjoyable weekend?"

"Fine, thanks."

"Good." She pursed her lips before proceeding. "We've decided to let you go, Julie."

Total silence encompassed her, even though she could hear the secretary's electric typewriter outside the door. "Let me go?" She was being summarily fired. Had they found out about her clandestine research? Had word of her sexual harassment affidavit reached Alyson or the superintendent? "What have I done wrong?" She sank into the visitor's chair.

"You're still on probation," Alyson stated without emotion. "We don't have to give you a reason."

That much was true. There was no appeal for a dismissal during the probationary period.

"I don't understand." She felt entitled to an explanation.

"In your probationary period, you can be released without cause, and that's what we're doing."

"Without cause," she repeated. That was absurd. There was a reason. But arguing the point would make her sound like a sore loser. She'd stepped on toes, challenged the establishment. Did they know she'd uncovered proof of test score tampering? Or was this a peremptory strike to make sure she didn't? They had plenty of legitimate reasons for firing her, but they didn't need one, and refusing an explanation left her in limbo, uncertain, off balance. It was a cruel use of arbitrary power.

"If you have any personal effects in the office—" Alyson didn't even say *your* office "—naturally, you can take them with you. If you need help carting them out, I'm sure the janitor will assist you. But I have to insist that you leave in the next hour. That's standard policy.''

Julie was still stunned. ''May I ask a question?''

Alyson nodded. ''I can't promise to answer it.''

''When was the last time you terminated someone on probation?''

Alyson shrugged. ''I have no idea.''

''So it's not very common?''

''Julie, if you think you can appeal this, I have to tell you, you can't. So don't waste your time—or mine.''

She wanted to rail, to shout and fight. ''An hour. I guess I'd better get busy.''

As Julie reached the door, she was automatically inclined to say thank you, except it would be a ridiculous comment under the circumstances. How would Alyson react if Julie told her she'd been seen with Dr. Picard in a very compromising situation? It might be worth it just to observe the stunned expression on her face, but Julie didn't want to waste that tidbit of information in spitefulness.

So at the door, she kept going and didn't look back.

INVOICES WERE COMING DUE, and sales were decidedly lagging. The lawyer had already sent a bill for their initial consultation. Seeing the hourly rate the attorney was charging, Rolf decided he'd better learn to talk faster. He transferred money from his savings account to checking. Undoubtedly, he'd need more cash in the months ahead. To weather the present crisis he'd have to borrow from the bank. He'd obtained short-term loans before to cover immediate accounts payable until accounts receivable came in. This one might have to be for a longer term than the others, but his credit rating was good.

His loan officer, Jerome Benton, seemed pleased to see him. Rolf accepted the proffered coffee and set it down on the edge of the desk as he explained how much he thought he'd require and for how long.

"I'll have to see your profit and loss statements for the last year," Benton informed him.

"P&Ls? You've never asked for them before."

Benton leaned back, his hands draped casually over the arms of his chair. "New bank policy."

This didn't feel right. Rolf was getting a sinking sensation in the pit of his stomach. "Sure. No problem. I'll run off copies this afternoon and bring them by on my way home."

"The amount you're asking for may be a bit of a problem." Benton tapped his fingers on the desktop.

The knot in Rolf's gut tightened. "How's that?"

"I understand the city and school district are suing your lumberyard over that construction failure at Tillman."

This was the first Rolf had heard of it. "If they are, they haven't informed me." He gave an amused chuckle. "I should think I'd be among the first to know."

Benton screwed up his mouth. "If it turns out to be true, I'm afraid we won't be able to extend your line of credit. Civil litigation can be a bottomless pit. There's no telling what size judgment might be brought against you."

"It's also possible I'll win the case," Rolf countered, trying to put a positive spin on it. "If there is one. Which we don't know yet. The awning installation passed city inspection a few days before the mishap."

"Nevertheless, we'd be taking a big chance. These things tend to drag out for a very long time."

"I still have a moneymaking business that's generating a reasonable profit," Rolf reminded him. At least that's what his current P&L statements would show.

"For the time being," Benton said ominously. "I understand you lost your contract with the city."

"Not lost," Rolf corrected him. "I terminated it because I didn't want my position on the school board to be misconstrued as a conflict of interest."

Benton shook his head sagely, not challenging his statement. "But it was, as I recall, a very lucrative contract. How do you expect to make up for the loss of income?"

"By expanding in other areas. I'm considering staying open later on Saturday and opening on Sunday. More and more people are doing their own repairs and renovations these days, mostly on weekends."

"Cash-'n'-Carry Builders Supply is already open on Sunday. Do you honestly think you can compete with them?"

The note of hostility creeping into the conversation wasn't encouraging. "I think there's enough of a market for both of us. I also offer goods and services Cash-'n'-Carry doesn't."

"Like tin shed kits and sheet metal installations."

Rolf wouldn't allow himself to be baited. But when he realized he had raised his boot heels and was poised on the balls of his feet, he consciously lowered them. That small measure of self-control released some of the tension.

"And garden supplies, gravel," he added evenly, "as well as landscaping rocks, paving stones and decorative bricks. A great many home owners spend their weekends gardening."

"Good points," Benton agreed quietly, and for a moment, Rolf felt a surge of hope. "But you also have a few things working against you. You're alienating people, including fellow school board members, by your opposition to Dr. Picard. Obviously, the lumberyard is doing poorly—otherwise you wouldn't be here. That's at least partly because you've given up—or been forced to give up—a money-generating contract with the city. Either way, it doesn't speak well for your business acumen. Now you're about to be sued. Doesn't add up to a very good risk."

At this point, Rolf realized he wouldn't be getting a loan, but he couldn't let Benton's statement pass without defending himself. "On the other hand, I have an excellent credit rating. I've never been delinquent on a single bill or payment due, and I own an enterprise that has a proven track record."

Benton conceded the points with a nod. "Bring in the P&L statements, Rolf. If the trend is up, as you claim, we'll certainly give your request serious consideration, though I doubt for the amount you're asking. We'll still need collateral."

"In other words," Rolf said, rising, "it's the old conundrum. You'll give me a loan if I don't need it." He forced himself to laugh at the absurdity of the situation. In a show of goodwill, he extended his hand. "Thanks for your time, Jerry."

Benton had already risen. They shook hands, but the loan officer's expression was smug rather than apologetic. "I hope you understand."

"Perfectly." Rolf turned and left the man's office.

CHAPTER FOURTEEN

JULIE PICKED UP the children at the lumberyard at the normal time on Monday afternoon, but Rolf immediately noticed there was something different about her. Not in anything she said or did, but in the way she looked at him. Her distracted glances set off alarms that made him uncomfortable. He didn't have time at the moment to delve into whatever was bothering her, but he vowed to talk to her about it after dinner that evening.

All day long, he'd been reflecting on her strange change in attitude the evening before after she'd asked about Sheryl. He couldn't imagine what he might have said to upset her. She certainly hadn't accused him of doing anything she disapproved of, yet the distinct impression she gave was that he'd failed her in some way. It was frustrating to feel guilty about a breach he couldn't even identify.

Maybe he was imagining it. With so much happening in their lives, maintaining objectivity about anything was difficult, but after a night spent making love to Julie, balance was impossible.

He loved her. There was no denying it. Sheryl had been right when she told him, ''Once love comes to you, you'll be glad you're free.'' He was glad. He was free to love Julie. He could conjure up all kinds of reasons for loving her. Beauty, grace, intelligence.

Her strength and determination. The way she fit in with his kids, and they with her. The way she gave herself to him in sexual pleasure.

They were all true, but he also knew they were rationalizations. The real reason he loved her was that she made him feel good, made him feel wanted and needed. When he was with her, his world was complete.

The letdown following the weekend of excitement had left the kids somber and cranky. No one, it seemed, was having a very good day.

While they were cleaning up the kitchen after dinner, Julie said she needed to talk to Rolf privately. He acceded with a wink, anticipating her coiling her arms around him until he kissed her. They went into the den. She closed the door. Smiling, he began to bracket his hands on her waist, but she pulled away.

"What's the matter?" he asked, taken aback by her rejection. He hadn't been imagining it. Something was definitely bothering her. "Tell me."

She took a deep breath. "I was fired today."

He stared at her, relieved that the problem wasn't *them*. Fired. No wonder she was upset. "Oh, sweetheart. I'm so sorry." He moved toward her, but she shied from his approach once more, her posture stiff, brittle, breakable. If only she would let him touch her. "Why? What reason did they give you?"

She shook her head. "I was still in my probationary period. They didn't have to give me a reason."

His hands tightened into fists and his pulse quickened. "The hell they—"

She shot him an impatient look. "They don't, Rolf. During the first sixty days, they can let an employee go without cause, and that's precisely what they did."

"Nothing is done without cause. They must have offered you some excuse."

"They don't have to and they didn't," she retorted, showing the first signs of real anger. "I was called into Alyson's office and informed I was being terminated."

"We'll appeal. We'll sue," he insisted.

"Don't be stupid," she flared. "It would be a waste of time and energy. Not to mention money."

Though he hated to admit it, she was right. But after all the things that had happened today, he needed to swing back at someone. Not Julie, though. He should be offering her solace and sympathy, not angry words and useless suggestions.

He held out his arms, inviting her into them. When she finally stepped forward, he encircled her and stroked her back. Quietly, he asked, "Why didn't you tell me earlier today when you were in the store?"

She squirmed out of his embrace. The resentment that had been so well suppressed in front of the children was spilling out now. "You had work to do. No point in your worrying about this."

Damn it, she was trying to spare him, when what he wanted was for them to share. "I thought we were in this together."

He extended his arms again, a plea for her to accept what comfort he had to offer. There was a hurt-little-girl quality about the way she finally came to him, trying to put up a brave front. But he could see she was close to tears, feel the vulnerability in the shimmering tension of her body pressed against his.

He dipped his head, laying his cheek against the top of her head. The warmth of her body clinging to his brought back sensations and desires that probably weren't appropriate in the circumstances, but he wouldn't have banished them, even if he could. Intimacy was a part of their relationship, a part of who they were and what they meant to each other.

"I received an official notice today, too," he confessed. "Right after you left this afternoon. Coyote Springs Independent School District and the City of Coyote Springs have joined in a suit against me, accusing me of gross negligence, fraud and a litany of other charges."

The legal war had been declared.

Julie snuggled against him. "Oh, Rolf, I'm so sorry. I've caused you so much trouble."

With the edge of his finger, he touched her chin, tipping her head up. "The only thing you've caused is for me to want you more than I ever thought I could want anyone."

"But if I hadn't started you asking questions—"

"Shh." He brushed his thumb across her lips. "What you did was right, and what I did was right. I have no regrets."

"I do."

The words hit him like a shock of cold water— until he realized she wasn't talking about them but that stupid damned oath. He tightened his hold on her and spoke over the top of her head. "Do you really? Would you have wanted things to continue on the way they were? Could you really have kept silent when you knew something wrong was going on?"

"No, I guess not," she muttered.

He stroked her back. "I know my timing on this is off..." He fell silent until she raised her eyes to him.

"What?" she asked.

His lips became a straight line very briefly, then curved up as his eyes softened. "Marry me, Julie."

She gazed at him, not sure she'd heard right. She'd just been fired from her job. His business was in trouble. He was probably going to be sued. And he was asking her to marry him. Then the light dawned. He was in serious financial trouble and she had money. Michael had been right.

"We have a lot of obstacles in the way of happily ever after," he acknowledged, "but together I know we can overcome them."

"Why?" She pulled away, fighting the conclusion she'd drawn. "Why now?"

His brows rose, as if to comprehend the question. "We fit, Julie." Why was her expression so reserved, almost sad? "We share the same interests, the same drives, the same passions."

Her lack of response confused him, compelled him to explain himself. "If you're worried about the kids, don't be. They adore you, and you'll be the perfect mother for them and for the children I hope we'll have together."

The blankness of her expression, instead of fleeing, intensified. Rolf's blood raced as panic began to worm its way into his confidence. "What is it, Julie? What's the matter?"

She separated herself from him, turned, then sank into a side chair. What he wanted, what he'd expected, was for her to throw her arms around him and kiss him with a passion that could test the tensile strength of his self-control.

"Marry you." She closed her eyes as if in unbearable pain. Bracing a hand on her knee, she levered herself to her feet. "I'm sorry, but I can't."

His mouth went dry. "But why? Is it because of the lawsuit, because there's a possibility I might go bankrupt?" Then it struck him. "I hope you don't think this is about money." He faced her squarely. "Because it isn't. I haven't asked you for financial support and I won't. I'm not going to fail. I was a management consultant before I bought the lumberyard. If I have to, I can do that again. If you don't believe…" He combed his fingers through his hair. "We'll wait until this blows over, till I'm back on my feet." His laugh was self-deprecating and without humor. "As I said, I knew my timing wasn't very good."

"It's not that," she said, referring to the issue of money.

He studied her somber face. At last realization dawned. "I see. You're telling me you don't love me." She tensed, but he continued. "I thought… Saturday night…I guess I misunderstood."

It had been that way with Sheryl, too, he reminded himself. Friendship had mingled with great sex. They'd confused the combination with love. He should be grateful to Julie for her honesty. He should be feeling a sense of relief that she'd helped him avoid yet another disaster.

What he felt was an emptiness. She didn't love him. She enjoyed his company, being around his kids, having sex with him, but she didn't love him.

He tried to read her thoughts, but the blankness he found in her eyes only confirmed that he truly didn't know her. She looked wounded and disappointed. Why? He was the one who'd just had his proposal rejected, who'd exposed himself and been humiliated. He was the one who should be incensed, not her. But it wasn't anger that had his pulse slowing and lethargy settling in. He loved her, but she didn't love him back.

"I've embarrassed you." He felt helpless. "I'm sorry."

Bewilderment softened her face. He had to control the urge to pull her into his arms and kiss her hard to see if she truly was rejecting him, if he could rekindle the passion she'd demonstrated the night before.

She hadn't uttered a word in a long time. He almost expected her to rail at him for spoiling what had been a very pleasant relationship. She turned to the window and gazed out at the fall garden she'd planted. The way her shoulders were drawn up, he suddenly wondered if she was crying. When she completed the shrug, he found himself almost relieved.

"I wish I could do something about your job," he said, hoping a change in subject might minimize, if not erase, his foolish blunder. "But you're right. They have the power, and I'm in no position at the moment to push my weight around."

"It would make matters worse for you."

Her voice was thick enough to confirm his earlier suspicion that she'd been at the point of tears. He'd made her unhappy when all he wanted was to love her. The realization cut like a sharp blade, swift and deep.

"This isn't about me." His words gushed out, blood from an open wound. He took a halting breath and softened his tone. "It's about doing what's right."

She didn't respond.

"Julie…" He wanted to beg, but for what? Imploring her to love him was futile and would further demean them both.

"Coyote Springs isn't the only place in the world," she finally said. She was fleeing from him, too. He wished his heart were stone so he wouldn't feel the ache. "I'll start sending out resumés, omitting the part about having been employed here so briefly. I doubt anyone will bother to check. I'll continue to pick up the kids after school." Her beautiful blue eyes were red-rimmed. "But I think it would be a good idea if you made other arrangements as soon as you can."

"If that's the way you want it. They'll miss you."

"I'll miss them, too, but it'll be best for all of us if I move on."

As she walked past him, he nearly put out his hand to grab her. "Do you have to do this?"

"Do what, Rolf?"

"Leave. What can I do to convince you you belong in this house, with my children? With me."

"Don't you see, Rolf? This would never work." It amazed her that she could keep her voice steady when her heart was shattering.

"Why?"

She heard in the single word the hope that maybe he could persuade her otherwise. But he couldn't. Her brother had been right. This wasn't the correct match.

"There are too many obstacles in the way."

"Nothing we can't overcome."

"Our age difference," she persisted.

"It's not that much."

"You have children who are old enough to be my kid brothers and sister," she pointed out. "They deserve a mother, not a baby-sitter."

"They respect you for the mature adult you are. They look up to you, Julie. They need you."

She liked being with them, too. But would their need turn to resentment? Would their being Rolf's first priority make her second in his life? Was he hiring another sitter for his children and partner for his bed? She didn't see any of those things in his eyes, but her track record in reading men wasn't very good.

"You're set in your ways," she persisted. "I'm still finding mine."

His hands hung at his sides, loose, limp, defeated. "I had hoped we might find a new way together." He shut his eyes, then refocused them on her. "I guess you're right. I've made a mistake." He turned his broad back on her. The gesture made her feel small.

Biting her lips, she went to the door, turned the knob and walked out.

JULIE WAS PHYSICALLY and emotionally drained by the time she reached home. Though it was now late, she filled her bathtub with hot water and tossed in fragrant bath salts. She didn't have to rise and shine in the morning. She could sit in the tub all night if she wanted to, let her mind wander, conjure up plans and schemes for making the world right again. Daydream. Night-dream.

She stripped off her clothes and dumped them in the empty hamper. She'd washed all her dirty laundry at Rolf's. Some sort of symbolism there, she was sure but she was too weary to examine it. Dismissing the errant thought, she eased into the tub and luxuriated in the caress of the warm soapy water.

Okay, so she had no options as far as the school

district was concerned. She'd enjoyed her short tenure as a curriculum writer and was sorry she wasn't able to complete the practice test project. Someone else would do it. She wasn't the only person capable of the feat, nor was she bringing unique insight into the never-ending quest for better grades.

Being summarily fired from her job was humiliating enough. Not being given the courtesy of an explanation was infuriating. She fed more hot water into the tub. Rolf's telling her he was being sued was the icing on the cake.

Then he'd proposed, and things had gone from bad to worse.

The man she'd fallen in love with had asked her to marry him. It should have been the happiest day of her life. In the back of her mind, in her heart, she'd fantasized about what it would be like for them to spend their lives together, to be committed to each other. He'd offered that opportunity but left out a crucial ingredient.

Did he intentionally not tell her he loved her? Of course he had. If she'd challenged him, he probably would have dismissed it as a mere oversight, that he thought she knew, that it was understood. But it wasn't. She didn't believe a man could love a woman, propose marriage to her and inadvertently leave out those vital words.

He hadn't even asked her if she loved him. Did that mean he was taking her love for granted, or that loving him wasn't important? He hadn't forgotten to mention his children. Bryn was right. What he wanted was a homemaker for his kids and a sex partner for his bed. They'd made love one night only. Apparently it was enough to satisfy him that they were physically compatible. She sighed. *Compatible* was too weak a word. That night had gone well beyond male and female bodies being in harmony. She grinned, even as tears slid down her cheeks. With Jerome, sex had been a rock-and-roll number. With Rolf, making love had been a symphony in multiple movements.

He was right about one thing—the timing was way off. His lumberyard was in trouble, and now she was out of work. Or was that part of his calculation? Being unemployed meant she could spend all her time as his housekeeper, cook and baby-sitter. He said he wasn't interested in her money, but how could she be sure?

She turned on the tap and released more hot water again. It sent up fresh billows of fluffy iridescent bubbles. She sank deeper into them, trying to lose herself in the fragrant cloud.

Another crossroads. What would she do now? Searching for work seemed a logical next step. But if she wanted to stay in education, she'd have to leave Coyote Springs, as she'd told Rolf. This was the place where she'd grown up, the place that made her feel comfortable, at home. A month could go by without seeing her brothers or father or stepmother, but she was always aware that they were close by. Moving to another town, another city didn't frighten her, but it left her feeling sad and alone.

What about Rolf? What about his children? Separation seemed the best solution for all of them.

ROLF DISCONTINUED his prefabricated metal building operation temporarily and laid off the two guys who worked it. Zack Oman was still out with his broken arm, but with sales down, being shorthanded wasn't a serious problem. Besides, Jake Tarns, his assistant, was willing to help out in any way he could, even though his mother's ill health didn't allow him much spare time.

Tuesday afternoon, Rolf was sitting at his desk, about to take his first bite of the deli sandwich he'd had delivered, when the phone rang. He'd grown to dread outside calls. Most of them were innocuous—people calling about opening and closing hours, product availability and prices, and occasionally asking advice on how to handle a repair or renovation project. But there had been crank calls, too, from people who lambasted him, occasionally in very colorful language, for his opposition to Dr. Picard. He wondered who was instigating these attacks, since he'd never made a single public statement against the man.

He picked up the phone.

"Mr. Murdock, this is Melinda Cruz, the principal at Great Oaks Middle School."

She sounded very formal and he wondered if, as part of the establishment, she was about to tear into him on behalf of the school superintendent. "Yes, Ms. Cruz, we met at the last PTA meeting."

"We've had an incident involving your son Derek."

"Is he hurt?"

"No, he's fine," she assured him. "But he has been in a fistfight with another student."

"A fight? Derek? Over what?" Rolf's eldest son was spirited, but Rolf had never known him to be violent.

"If you would come here as soon as possible, Mr. Murdock, we can straighten this matter out."

"I'll be there in fifteen minutes." He hung up the phone and stared at the sandwich on his desk, his appetite gone. What had prompted Derek to get into a fight? Another kid must have hit him first, and he was simply defending himself. Taking a deep breath, Rolf rewrapped the sandwich, tossed it on the pile of papers in his In basket and left the office.

After explaining to Jake where he was headed and that he didn't know how long he'd be away, he climbed into his van and drove across town to the school.

The principal's secretary escorted him into her office immediately.

Derek was sitting on a hard wooden chair in the far corner, his posture stiff, hands folded in his lap. Rolf noted the set of his jaw and the hard determination in his eyes. The boy didn't seem intimidated by his surroundings. If anything, he appeared defiant.

Melinda Cruz was immediately on her feet and moving toward Rolf by the time he was two steps inside the doorway. "Mr. Murdock—" she extended her hand "—thank you for coming so promptly."

He shook it. "What's going on?" He cast a side-long glance at his son, who had risen to his feet. For the first time, Rolf realized how tall the teenager was, not more than a couple of inches under six foot. At this rate he'd top out taller than Rolf's six-three. Might make a good basketball player, too.

"I'll let your son explain," the woman said, tearing him from his distracting thoughts.

Rolf turned his full attention on his son. "Well?"

"Pel Arens said it was your fault the awning at Tillman fell down, that crippled kids could have been injured or killed, that you cheat people, overcharge them for crap materials, that you're a fraud and an embezzler.'' The boy was almost out of breath and obviously still very angry.

Embezzler? Where had that accusation come from? He'd been called a cheapskate, a tightwad, a cheat and a crook, but not an embezzler.

Pel Arens. Pelham Arens III. His father, Pel Jr., owned a road-grading outfit on the north side of town. They did custom work for home owners and commercial enterprises. Another outfit that had a lucrative contract with the city and county.

''Go on.''

''So I hit him. Punched him in the nose.''

Rolf's brows rose of their own accord. He turned to Melinda.

''The other boy's fine,'' she assured him. ''He's in the nurse's office. A little bloody, but no serious damage done. His father's been called.''

Rolf turned back to his son. ''Are you telling me you took the first swing?''

Derek lowered his head at the tone of disapproval and nodded sheepishly.

The seconds of silence that followed lasted an eternity. Finally, Rolf removed his glare from his son and addressed the principal. ''What punishment will you impose?''

''A three-day suspension.''

It seemed a bit harsh for a first offense, but Rolf had to agree this wasn't a minor infraction. ''May I have a couple of minutes alone with my son?''

''I'll be right outside.'' She left the room, closing the glass-paneled door quietly behind her.

Rolf stood in front of Derek for an extended minute. At last, the boy broke the silence. ''I'm sorry,

Dad, but I couldn't let him keep running his mouth off about you like that. He was spouting things—''

Firmly, Rolf asked, ''Do you think punching him will keep him quiet now?''

Derek hung his head. ''I guess not. But you should have heard what he was saying. Ask Coach Salvati. He'll tell you.''

''The coach was there?'' Nate Salvati was one of the assistant football coaches.

''He heard the whole thing.''

Rolf wondered why he hadn't stopped it before it advanced to the violent stage.

''You will do two things,'' Rolf dictated. ''Apologize to Ms. Cruz for disrupting the school, then apologize to Pel and his father. After that, you take whatever punishment Ms. Cruz dishes out.''

Derek nodded unhappily.

Rolf went to the door and invited the principal to rejoin them. ''Derek has something he wants to say to you.''

Humbly, the teenager expressed his regrets for his actions and asked her forgiveness.

''Apology accepted,'' she said, and Rolf sensed genuine sympathy for the boy. ''But that won't be enough. I hope you understand that.''

''Yes, ma'am.''

Rolf told her they'd like to stay until Pel Jr. got there so Derek could apologize to them, as well. She agreed. Derek was told to wait in the outer office.

''I understand Coach Salvati was present during the exchange between the two boys.''

She nodded. ''He's standing by. Would you like to talk to him?''

''Please.''

She picked up the phone and hit a button. Five minutes later, the coach arrived. He was about Rolf's age, not very tall, but stocky and powerfully built. They shook hands.

Rolf asked the obvious question: why hadn't he intervened sooner?

"In retrospect, I should have. Several of the kids had been giving Derek a hard time. He'd been doing a good job of ignoring them for the most part, only occasionally giving a smart answer in return. He's never been any trouble, Mr. Murdock, and I figured he was handling it pretty well. I should have realized under the cool facade, his temper was rising and that inevitably he'd have to break. He's really a good kid, Mr. Murdock. Considering the provocation, I can't really blame him."

Rolf saw Melinda's mouth tighten in disapproval.

"I'm sorry I didn't interfere sooner."

Rolf shook his hand. "Thanks for your honesty."

"Don't be too hard on the boy, Mrs. Cruz," the coach advised the principal. "He was just defending his old man's name and reputation." He turned to Rolf. "He's lucky to have a dad he's willing to fight for."

After he left, Melinda gave Rolf a weak smile. The phone buzzed. She answered it. "Mr. Arens is here."

The three of them went down the hall to the nurse's office. Pel Arens III was sitting on the examining table. Rolf estimated him to be roughly the same height as Derek but considerably bigger in bone structure. His nickname on the football team was "Tank" for good reason. In spite of his bulk, he didn't seem especially intimidating at the moment. His right eye had already turned black-and-blue, and he visibly stiffened when he saw Derek.

The senior Arens appeared as belligerent as his son looked vulnerable. Hoping to defuse the situation, Rolf offered his hand. "Sorry about this, Pel."

Arens hesitated, but then shook his hand.

"Derek has something he wants to say to both of you," Rolf announced.

His son shuffled his feet, head bowed, jaw muscles working energetically. "I'm sorry."

"You'll have to do better than that, Son," Rolf prompted him.

"I'm sorry I punched you," he intoned to the victim, then turned to the father. "I'm sorry I hit your son."

Arens seemed a little surprised at the quick, unconditional apology. He gave his son a tight-lipped nod.

"Yeah, I'm sorry, too," Pel muttered, "for the things I said."

Melinda stepped up to the plate. "It would have been better for both of you if you'd considered the effects of your actions before you took them." She peered at Pel. "I expect you in class tomorrow."

"But this black eye..." he protested.

"Doesn't affect your ability to learn." She refocused her attention on Derek. "You are suspended for one day. Report to my office on Thursday morning before your first class. If there are any more incidents of this nature, you will receive a three-day suspension. Is that clear?"

Derek's eyes brightened with relief. "Yes, ma'am."

On the drive back to the lumberyard, Derek remained quiet until they pulled into the parking space behind the huge warehouse building.

"Dad."

"Yes, Son."

"I lied."

Rolf's hand froze on the door handle. He managed to relax it and swivel toward his son. "Lied about what?"

"I'm not sorry I punched Pel in the face. If I had to do it over again, I would."

The boldness of the statement took Rolf completely by surprise. He remembered Salvati's comment about the boy being lucky to have a father he was willing to fight for. What the coach didn't realize was how fortunate Rolf was to have a son willing to defend him in the face of public censure.

"I'm not supposed to say I'm glad," he told Derek, unable to suppress the smile creasing his face.

Derek's youthful expression glowed. "That's all right. I just thought you ought to know."

It had been a long time since he'd put his arms around his son. He did so now, and they both felt good about it.

CHAPTER FIFTEEN

JULIE SPENT most of Tuesday sipping cold coffee and
barely touching the pieces of toast she'd fixed. She'd
found a few bits of information she and Rolf needed
to discuss before the school bus dropped the kids off.
Her hands were sweaty, her insides queasy as she
approached the lumberyard earlier than usual. She and
Rolf were still friends, she reminded herself as she
got out of her truck.

Uneasiness melded into confusion when she found
Derek already in the store stacking precut two-by-four
studs. Judging from his coveralls, the dirt on his face
and the sweat on his brow, the teenager had already
been at it for some time.

Rolf was a few feet away, holding a clipboard,
checking off items.

"What's going on?" she asked. "Why's Derek already here? The school bus—"

"There was an incident at school," he told her.
"He's been suspended."

"Suspended?" She was shocked as much by the
announcement as by Rolf's strange casualness in de-
livering the news. She would have expected him to
be furious. If anything, she thought she detected a lilt
akin to pride in the comment.

He steered her down the electrical products aisle,
where he commenced to check the inventory of

switches, plates and plugs while he told her about the incident with Pel Arens. Derek fighting? Julie certainly didn't approve, yet oddly she understood Rolf's attitude and perversely agreed with it. But it also meant the situation was seriously deteriorating when children got into fights about what their parents were or weren't responsible for.

"I've done a little more research," she said, "and I found information you'll be interested in."

"About Picard?"

She nodded.

Rolf directed one of his workers to reposition a display so it didn't block the aisle. "More than circumstantial evidence this time, I hope."

She couldn't tell if he was censuring her or simply voicing a valid concern. She told herself it didn't make any difference. But she'd never been a very convincing liar. "Let's go back to your office."

Once there, Rolf closed the door. With plate glass windows on two sides, it didn't afford visual privacy. Maybe that was just as well. It made resisting the temptation to pull her into his arms and kiss her…easier? At least their conversation wouldn't be overheard.

"I checked Picard's record in Houston," she began. "He did essentially the same thing there as he's been doing here. By the time he left, three years after taking over, the school district was bankrupt, even though they supposedly received additional funding from a variety of outside sources."

"Isn't that one of the things he's credited with—finding cash cows? That's hardly an accusation."

Was the coolness of his reaction due to her rejection of his proposal or the recent trouble with his son? "The question is where'd the money go."

He leaned against the side of his desk, his hands curled over the edge. "I'm listening."

She crossed her arms to match his stance and faced him. "In Houston, the papers reported Picard received grants worth more than a million dollars from local, state and federal programs. After he left, no one could find the money."

"Didn't they investigate?"

"Yes, but they were unable to come up with an explanation for the missing funds."

"A million dollars doesn't simply disappear, Julie."

She sucked in her cheeks. "Aren't you the one who pointed out that large bureaucracies are perfect places for playing hide-and-seek with money?"

Rolf seemed lost in thought. Finally, he shook his head. "None of that proves anything, except an incompetent school comptroller. It doesn't mean Picard took it."

"No, it doesn't," she agreed shortly. "But there's more. Our school district gave Picard a cell phone last year. Right now, I can't tell you who he's called, but I can tell you how much he's spent."

Rolf moved behind his desk and sank into his squeaky chair. He folded his fingers across his flat stomach. "What does his phone bill have to do with anything?"

She grinned. "How easy do you think it would be to run up two thousand dollars' worth of charges in one month?"

His jaw dropped. "Two thousand dollars? Are you serious?"

"I have a friend who works for CellPhoneInc here in town, the carrier the school uses. I told him I was doing research on the cost of communications for the ISD. It's possible he didn't hear me when I commented I no longer work for them."

Rolf eyed her curiously, and for the first time she saw a hint of the old sparkle.

"He may have been talking to someone else in the office when I mentioned it. If they record conversations, though, it'll be very clear on the tape that I said it."

His grin was mischievous. "Will it also be clear he didn't hear it?"

"In a pinch a good lawyer could probably argue that if he didn't, it was his fault. He was after all talking to me on the line."

Rolf snickered approvingly and rocked in his chair. "I bet you know a good lawyer, too." But he dismissed the subject with a wave of his hand. "Were you able to get the phone record itself?"

"Good heavens, no." Appalled at the very idea, she plopped herself down on the hard wooden chair across from him. "It's confidential. The only people who would have direct access to that information are Dr. Picard and the comptroller, of course, since she pays the bills."

"You don't happen to know her, do you?"

"As a matter of fact, Vivian's youngest sister and I went to high school together. Naturally, she wouldn't release the information to me, though she did let slip that she really doesn't understand why he would be calling the Cayman Islands. She was very emphatic there was no prohibition against his using the phone for personal business. All he had to do was pay his share. She could only speculate that he must be planning a vacation there.''

Rolf's eyes twinkled. "Or he might be conferring with his banker.''

Julie's eyes widened. "Now, there's a thought.'' As if the notion hadn't even crossed her mind. "Oh, did I mention that she also said members of the school board are entitled to copies of the bills? And whatever other records the school district requires in executing their fiscal oversight responsibility.''

He cocked his head. "Why, no,'' he answered with a breezy grin. "I don't think you did.''

His smile still had the power to make her pulse skip. "Your next regularly scheduled board meeting is this Thursday evening, isn't it? Or has it been called off because of the special meeting you had last week?''

"No, that was an executive session. It had nothing to do with the regular public meetings.'' He pursed his lips. "I wonder if I'll have enough time.''

"For what?''

"To do all the research…'' He rose from his chair, sauntered pensively around the end of the desk and gazed at her. "You wouldn't happen to know anyone who might have time to act as my personal representative to various agencies, would you? The pay wouldn't be very good, I'm afraid.''

"Ah,'' Julie replied with a broad grin, "but the satisfaction of public service…'' She climbed to her feet.

Then he made a mistake. He reached out for her. When she pulled back, he told himself it was because of the setting. They were in a fishbowl. But he knew better. Her lips were slightly parted, as if she wanted to add a comment. To repulse him? To warn him? The sound of his children's voices calling for him relieved the moment of discomfort. The office door flew open.

"Is it true Derek's been kicked out of school?" Foster was nearly breathless.

"No, it's not true," the subject of discussion boomed from behind him. "I got suspended, that's all."

"For punching out Pel Arens's lights, right?" Jeff asked with undisguised admiration.

"I didn't punch him out exactly," Derek scoffed, though his chest was expanded. "I just gave him a black eye."

"Cool!" Foster hailed. "I wish I could've seen it. Was he all bloody? Did you knock him down?"

Rolf held up his hands. "That's enough. I can see I need to have a long discussion with you guys tonight about the use of violence."

Leah showed up a few minutes later, dragging her feet. She gave Julie a traitorous look.

"Did you hear about Derek?" Foster crowed. "He gave Pel Arens a bloody nose and a black eye."

She'd heard, and though she tried very hard to be less impressed with her big brother's prowess, Julie wasn't fooled. She remembered her own pride when her brothers demonstrated their manly valor.

"Okay, kids, let's go," she prompted. "Your father needs to get back to work."

"I'll bring Derek home with me," Rolf announced. "He has a lot more lumber to stack."

To Julie's amusement, the boy didn't seem to mind in the least.

"Dad said you're not going to stay with us anymore," Leah accused her, an unaccustomed closed expression on her face.

The others stopped and stared at her, then at Julie.

"I lost my job, Leah. I have to find another one."

"So?" the girl persisted. "What's that got to do with anything?"

"My schedule will be completely unpredictable," Julie offered, uncomfortable with an explanation that was at best a half-truth. She didn't like dissembling with youngsters who'd become an important part of her life.

"Did we do something?" Jeff asked, sounding hurt. "Are you mad at us?"

The unexpected feeling of reprieve and lightheartedness she'd shared with Rolf only a few minutes before now soured in her belly. "No," she tried to assure them. "It's just that…when I find a job it may not be around here. I may have to move away."

Foster dumped his books on the desk. "I guess you don't care about us, either."

Julie scanned the faces around her, knowing full well who the boy was referring to. Their mother had left them for a job, and now Julie was doing the same thing.

"Ah, honey, just because someone has to leave doesn't mean they don't care," she protested. "I care about you very much. I always will and I hope we'll always be friends."

Derek stood back, studying her balefully, but he didn't say anything, not with words, anyway. Leah had tears running down her cheeks.

Julie's heart broke. How had she managed to fall into this quagmire? The desolation she saw on the children's faces, in their eyes, matched the emptiness she felt in her heart. She shot a pleading glance at Rolf, but his silent expression was unreadable.

"It's not that I want to—"

They turned their backs on her.

She reeled at their rejection and closed her eyes, but that didn't keep the tears from spilling out. Numbly, she groped into a chair, raised her hands to her face and fought a sob.

Rolf stepped to her side, gripped her hand and pulled her to her feet. Without a word, he enclosed her in his arms. Rather than consoling her, the warmth and strength of his embrace made her all the more aware of how empty her life had suddenly become. He planted a tender kiss on her forehead, released her and offered her his handkerchief. She wiped her nose.

"Hey, you guys—" her voice was suddenly husky "—I'm not gone yet. Let's go home and fix supper, and we'll just wait and see how things work out. Okay?"

The four children left the office. Derek returned to stacking lumber; the other three moped toward the main entrance and the parking lot.

"I didn't know," she said to Rolf.

"That they love you?"

How could she not have? She loved them, as well. She loved Rolf, too, but he didn't love her. And now everyone's heart was broken.

OVER THE NEXT TWO DAYS, several local companies called Rolf to verify that the signed and notarized affidavit he'd given Julie First appointing her his agent was legit. Among them was the chief accountant at Coyote National Bank.

"Hey, Julie. How's the job treating you?" Jerry

asked, sticking his head in the door while his associate was on the phone to the lumberyard.

Julie realized before she arrived that she wasn't likely to escape without running into her former lover. Half the town knew she'd been fired from her job, so that detail wouldn't have escaped him, either.

"Fine. Working on a special project."

He gave her the unintended satisfaction of blinking. True to form, though, he recovered quickly.

"Saw your friend, Murdock, last week. Sorry I wasn't able to give him the money he asked for. Nasty situation, the Tillman mishap."

"What loan?" The question was out before she realized it. Rolf hadn't said anything about applying to the bank for a loan. "When was that?"

"Last Monday. He didn't tell you about asking for money to keep the lumberyard afloat? Oops. I figured he'd told you. Forget I even mentioned it. Hey, I've got to run." He held up his hand in a wave and backed out of the room. "Have a nice day."

Rolf had applied for a loan, been turned down, then asked her to marry him? Would he have proposed if the bank had given him the money he needed? It didn't really matter, she told herself. She'd rejected his proposal. The smug expression on Jerry's face indicated he'd taken a great deal of pleasure in refusing the loan request—and seeing her squirm.

"Everything's in order, Ms. First," the accountant told her. "Now, what can I do for you?"

THURSDAY EVENING, Rolf went into the Coyote Springs ISD board meeting with two thick folders in his attaché case.

He'd called Bill Marcus that afternoon and requested several items be added to the agenda. Predictably, Bill had balked, but Rolf had been very forceful, insisting he would demand a public explanation for not including the items if Marcus refused. Unhappily, the chairman had no choice but to comply.

Among the topics of old business was approval of budget items for the purchase of new computers for the administration building. In the past, such requests had been rubber-stamped, with little or no discussion.

"When were they last upgraded?" Rolf asked the table at large.

No one seemed to know, including the superintendent.

"Dr. Picard, these computers are for your offices. What software versions are you currently using?"

"My staff put this request together. I don't have time to keep up with that sort of detail."

"This sort of detail will cost our district more than ten thousand dollars," Rolf reminded him. The superintendent glared back. "By the way, Dr. Picard, can you tell us what computer resources are available in the classrooms?"

"The individual schools have hardware and software adequate to the needs of teaching the appropriate subject matter," he declared, his tone haughty and proud.

"So you don't know," Rolf concluded.

Picard's jaw tensed. When he did speak, his voice was calm and slightly patronizing. "We use a variety of suites, depending on the particular pedagogical requirements."

The room was very still as Rolf opened his briefcase. "I've done some research, Dr. Picard. According to my information, the computers in the administrative building were upgraded, at your personal request, a month after your arrival, although the old equipment was less than a year old. When I checked further, I learned that neither the equipment nor the software in any of the schools has been upgraded or replaced in over three years. That's a long time in the modern world of technology. Can you explain to us why the administrative offices need more modern computer systems than the students you're here to teach?''

"Mr. Murdock," Bill Marcus intervened before the superintendent had a chance to speak, "Now isn't the time—or place—for this discussion. We can take it up in executive session and report back at the next meeting."

"I respectfully disagree, Mr. Chairman. I believe this is exactly the right forum." Rolf peered out at the room full of people. Thanks to Julie, not only were parents present, so were several teachers. "These people have the right to know how their school tax money is being spent."

A male voice in the crowd called out, "Hear, hear."

Another voice shouted, "Answer the question, Doc."

The chairman banged his gavel. "This meeting will come to order or it will be terminated."

"That won't be necessary," Rolf stated, giving everyone the cue to remain silent. "But I respectfully remind the chairman this is a public meeting and the public has a right to be heard."

"Allow me to respond to Mr. Murdock's question," Picard said to Marcus. "Mr. Murdock, I am not aware that your information is correct."

"Are you calling me a liar, Dr. Picard?"

For the briefest moment, the superintendent looked taken aback. He clearly wasn't used to being so boldly challenged. But he quickly regained control.

"No, Mr. Murdock. What I'm saying is that I don't know where you got your information or how accurate it is, so it would be inappropriate for me to comment on it."

Rolf pursed his lips. "In other words, Doctor, you don't know how old the equipment in the district's classrooms is. Nor do you know how current the equipment in your administration building is. But you're asking us to upgrade your staff's technical capabilities nonetheless."

"As I said, Mr. Murdock, my staff put together this request. I'll check and get back to you." He flexed his jaw. "You realize, of course, that if your allegations are true and classroom systems are in dire need of upgrade, you're talking about millions of dollars, which will mean a new bond issue and higher taxes."

Grumbling could be heard from the audience.

"Not necessarily," Rolf informed him, loud enough to quiet the room. "You have been very successful in obtaining grant money for us from various sources. The funds already exist."

At the murmurs from both the people at the table and the audience, Rolf knew he had their full attention. He also saw the superintendent's eyes shift to the chairman and away again. "But we'll return to that later," Rolf added.

"The next item on the agenda—" Bill started.

"Hold on, Mr. Chairman. We're not finished with this one yet. I move that the upgrade of equipment for the administrative staff be tabled until we receive more definitive information from Dr. Picard.''

"I second,'' Herb Bellows said without hesitation.

Expanding his chest on a deep breath, the chairman had no recourse but to ask for a vote. The motion passed unanimously, the chairman abstaining.

Not a smart move on his part, Rolf thought, and judging from the muttering coming from the crowd, they didn't think so, either.

The next few items were not controversial and passed without fanfare. Then came new business and Rolf reached into his attaché for another folder of papers. The air of anticipation in the hall was palpable.

"Mr. Murdock, you asked that this next item, selected income and expense items, be placed on the agenda for tonight at the last minute. Since you weren't very clear on specifics, I'll turn it over to you."

"Thank you, Mr. Chairman." Rolf opened his file and addressed his colleagues. "As you know, last year the board approved a cell phone for the school superintendent's use. I believe it was at the same meeting where it approved his computer upgrades without verifying they were necessary. Let me state here and now that I have no objection to the superintendent having a cell phone to conduct school business at his convenience. I also acknowledge that at times personal matters may be inextricably involved. For example, calling his wife…or a friend to say he'll be late for dinner or even arranging for a car rental when his own breaks down. Essentially, the superintendent takes his office with him wherever he goes. I wouldn't refuse an employee the use of my office phone under those circumstances, and I don't believe the head of the school district should be treated with any less courtesy."

Several heads bobbed in agreement. The superintendent's wasn't one of them. In fact, he was peering at Rolf with undisguised animosity.

"There is a limit, however," Rolf went on to the assembly. "The board established a budget of two hundred dollars a month for cell phone use. I've checked the telephone records. I'm sure everyone here will be interested to know Dr. Picard's bill has averaged nearly a thousand dollars a month, and this past month, it was over two thousand dollars." The whispers in the room had risen to a babble.

The chairman rapped his gavel for silence.

"Can you explain that, Dr. Picard?" Rolf asked.

Picard's hands remained folded in front of him. "I don't have to respond to this. No restrictions were placed on my use of the phone. If the district selected an unreasonably expensive carrier, it's their problem, not mine."

"You're partially correct, Doctor," Rolf replied. "We are responsible for the calling plan. You are responsible for the use of the phone and for meeting budgetary ceilings. As I said, I am willing to give you leeway in its use, but not carte blanche. According to the telephone records..." He removed a stack of stapled copies and passed them down the table.

"Where did you get these?" the chairman demanded, his face growing red.

"I asked for them. As a member of this board, responsible for approving the allocation of funds, I'm entitled to a complete accounting of all expenditures."

"This is ridiculous," Marcus blustered. "We're not here to discuss telephone bills."

"Yes, we are, Mr. Chairman. It's on the agenda."

The chairman's scowl could have frozen the Tropics. There was fear there, too.

"I won't go through the entire list of calls, Dr. Picard. I'll only ask about a few. For example, why did you spend two hundred dollars on nighttime calls to the Cayman Islands?"

"That's none of your business," the superintendent retorted, his dark eyes black now with anger.

"Yes, it is, because we pay the bills. Did it involve educational matters?"

"Mr. Murdock," the superintendent countered coldly, "I repeat, that is none of your business."

"If it is about school issues," Rolf responded with the calm assurance of a man who held the long straw, "just furnish us the details and we can drop the subject. Or show us a receipt to prove you paid your portion of the bill. Before you answer, however, I should point out that I checked the numbers you called—actually only one number there. A bank, one known internationally for numbered accounts and being very closemouthed about them."

The audience let out a collective gasp, then fell silent.

"This is outrageous." Picard pounded on the table with white-knuckled fists. "You'll be hearing from my lawyer about this—this invasion of my privacy."

Rolf grinned and spoke slowly. "Not when it's on our nickel, it isn't."

To Picard's credit, he didn't continue to bluster. The spot he was in seemed to harden his resolve. He crossed his arms and glared at Rolf, and for a moment

Rolf knew how Derek must have felt with the principal staring him in the face.

"Let's move on," Rolf suggested. "You have been very successful, according to the newspapers, in getting our school district additional funds for various programs and projects. According to the *Coyote Gazette,* you successfully petitioned for a grant of $250,000 from the Hardesty Foundation. The money was to be used for classroom computers." His brows rose. "Yet, as we have seen, the equipment hasn't been upgraded in several years. I called the foundation this afternoon. According to their files, the money was transferred eight months ago. They were able to give me the number of the account to which it was sent. It isn't a school account. Would it be an account in the Caymans?"

"I'm not listening to any more of this slander." Picard rose to his feet with remarkable dignity and addressed the chairman. "I'm leaving and I recommend you end this meeting now before you and the rest of the board find yourselves defendants in court for slander and defamation of character."

"Dr. Picard, before you go," Rolf said, "I think it only fair to inform you that I've turned over the evidence I have gathered to the district attorney's office for further investigation. Since a number of your transactions, like your telephone calls, cross national and international borders, I believe they'll be contacting the FBI to assist them."

Pandemonium broke out, while the chairman pounded his gavel ineffectually.

AMONG THE PEOPLE who attended the meeting that evening were Julie's brother and sister-in-law. When it was finally over, the four of them went to the Coyote Café a few blocks from city hall.

"I can't believe the board let him get away with that stuff." Clare dipped her spoon into a dish of bread pudding with bourbon sauce. "I bet they card people before serving this dessert. Mmm, good." She savored another taste. "Whew. It's a good thing you're driving, dear," she told her husband.

"Why did they?" Michael asked. He'd selected an espresso.

"Picard did his homework," Rolf explained. "The two most influential personalities on the board had weaknesses he could exploit. Bill Marcus is having serious financial difficulties keeping his store open. Picard promised not to raise any objections when large contracts were awarded to his office supply without going through the normal competition process. Chase Milsap owns the town's biggest hardware store. It's not in trouble, but he's greedy."

"That's two. What about the other members?" Michael asked.

"Herb Bellows's focus is on order and discipline— one of Picard's strengths. Virginia Akers doesn't know a thing about accounting. Since they trusted Bill's judgment, they were willing to go along with whatever he recommended."

"And the loyalty oath kept other people from coming to them with information that might have aroused any suspicions," Julie explained.

Rolf nodded. "Exactly."

"Why did so many people accept the oath?" Clare wanted to know.

"For the same reason I did," Julie stated, none too

proudly. "I wanted the job. Others wanted to keep theirs."

"It's another indication of how smart—or slick— Picard is." Rolf sipped his iced latte thoughtfully. "Many of the older teachers and administrators are within a few years of retirement. They have a lot at stake in keeping their jobs. They saw what happened to Doris Berquist, the teacher who had the guts to voice her opposition. She was forced into early retirement at a significant cut in benefits. That one incident alone was enough to send shock waves through the system, letting people know they either kept their mouths shut or suffered the consequences."

"It also took one of the best history teachers in the system out of the classroom," Julie added.

"By letting her retire early rather than firing her," Rolf went on, "Picard could claim he was being charitable and considerate of the woman's age and past service."

"Even though the people on the inside knew differently," Clare muttered with a disgusted shake of her head.

"No one could call this guy stupid," said Michael.

"Then there were the believers," Rolf continued, "the people who actually thought the oath was a good thing. After all, why wouldn't employees want to be loyal to their boss?" He gazed at Julie with a smile. This was the argument he'd used with her.

"Nobody wouldn't," she responded. "But there are times when higher values take priority, when loyalty and ambition turn to conspiracy and collusion."

"I've dealt with Bill Marcus and Chase Milsap for years," Michael remarked, "and I never suspected them capable of this kind of corruption."

"I imagine they began honestly enough, but when Picard arrived, they were vulnerable. He offered them a safety line, and they bit hard."

Michael snorted in disgust. "The people who have to share moral responsibility for this mess are the ones who saw or should have seen what was happening and let it continue."

"That takes in a lot of people," Clare pointed out.

Rolf looked over at Julie. "But it only takes one courageous person with a strong sense of right and wrong to blow the whistle and make a house of cards fall down."

She bit on her lower lip and shook her head. "Don't make me out a hero," she insisted. "In a sense I had a tremendous advantage. I didn't have anything to lose. Mrs. Berquist forfeited a good deal of her retirement when she refused to cave in."

"You lost a job you loved and almost your reputation, which is even more valuable."

He gazed into her eyes with enough intensity to make her heart jump.

"Well, it's been an exciting evening." Michael climbed to his feet. "It's also been a long one, and I have work to do tomorrow." He held his wife's chair.

"Thanks for a very entertaining meeting." Clare gathered her handbag from the floor where she'd deposited it. "By the way, Rolf, thank your kids for their very nice letters."

"Do you think they'd like to come out to the ranch the weekend after next?" Michael asked. "We'll be moving cattle from summer to winter pastures. It won't be as big as the cattle drives they may have seen on TV—only a couple hundred head—"

Rolf had already gotten to his feet. Now his eyes gleamed. "Can I come, too?"

Clare smiled and Michael laughed. "I did sort of have that in mind," he said.

"We'll be there."

Julie kissed her brother and sister-in-law goodbye, then picked up her own purse.

"Come back to the house with me," Rolf invited her. "We can break the news to the kids together."

"They're already in bed," she reminded him.

He looked crestfallen. "Should we go out to the ranch on Friday evening or wait until Saturday morning? I didn't even think to ask Michael."

"Give him a call tomorrow. I hope you have a good time."

He grabbed her arm as she turned to leave. "You're joining us, aren't you?"

She stared at his hand. He removed it. "No, I'm not. I have other things to do."

"Julie, don't do this," he implored.

"Do what?" she asked innocently.

"Please, tell me what I've done wrong."

"You haven't done anything wrong, Rolf. Now, if you'll excuse me…" She turned and walked out the door.

CHAPTER SIXTEEN

THE DAYS THAT FOLLOWED took on the aspects of a comedy or perhaps a soap opera.

In a flamboyant press conference on Saturday morning, Picard announced he'd been offered the school superintendent position in his hometown in southern Louisiana. It was a wonderful opportunity, he declared, because the district had recently been recognized for having made the most progress in raising its academic standards.

Julie was skeptical, so she checked his claim out on the Internet and was amazed to discover the offer was legit.

On Monday morning, Alyson Shaddick submitted her resignation as district administrator, effective immediately, so she could follow Dr. Picard and "help him in his great work." Julie snickered. The best surprise, however, came later in the day when she received a call from Nancy. The clerk at the Ivory Tower, it seemed, had been spreading the word about Julie's affidavit. Now three other women were offering to come forward and recount similar experiences.

She met with the women the next day and persuaded them to visit her attorney, who took their statements for the record. An arrest warrant for sexual harassment was issued for Picard. The county probably wouldn't expend money to extradite him from

Louisiana, but it afforded Julie some satisfaction at least.

Wednesday's mail brought a letter from the Murdock residence. It was neatly written—she suspected by Leah—and signed by Rolf's four children, though not by him, thanking her for being such a good friend and expressing the hope that she'd come by and visit real often. It concluded with a renewed plea that she join them on the cattle drive. "It won't be the same without you."

For a second, she entertained the notion that Rolf had put them up to it, but quickly realized it wasn't his style. Which made her feel all the more guilty. Disgusted with herself, she did what every woman is entitled to do. She changed her mind. Digging out a blank greeting card with a horse on it, she dashed off a note saying she'd be going out to the ranch that weekend after all. So much for her resolve to keep her distance.

All week long, Julie had been searching the Web for employment in the field of education. She found plenty of opportunities to consider. Substitute-teaching jobs were always available, and with a master's degree she had little difficulty meeting qualifications. A few administrative positions were open, as well. As near as the next county. As far away as Alaska. She'd never been there and always wanted to go. What better way to explore it than as a state employee? She filled out forms for a dozen jobs, but never worked up the enthusiasm to hit the Send button. Procrastination wasn't like her, yet here she was not doing the simplest things necessary to move on. She hated being indecisive.

On Thursday, she received a letter from the school

board informing her the position of administrator, Alyson's old job, was vacant and inviting her to apply for it. It seemed a strange request, given she'd been fired by that very administration. Yet it was a kind of validation, too. Of course, only one person could be behind the request. Why would Rolf recommend her for so important a post if he wanted to marry her and have her stay home? The answer hit like a sucker punch. This was his farewell. He was giving his blessing for her choice of career over family. She fumed. She didn't need his approval to get on with her life. Still, she wanted this job every bit as much as she'd wanted the curriculum position. More. She called the number listed and made an appointment for the following week.

Restless and needing someone to talk to, Julie drove out to the Number One.

Clare was making sandwiches for Michael and the hired hands, who were mending fences in preparation for the upcoming cattle drive. Julie pitched in by depositing apples and oranges into a large cooler.

"I thought you and Rolf had something going there for a while," Clare commented. "What happened?"

"He asked me to marry him."

Clare's forehead rose at the same time her face broke into a smile, then as quickly, creased into a frown. "I gather you turned him down. Why? Oh, don't tell me Michael was right? He was after your money."

Julie shook her head. "I thought so for a while. He denied it, of course—"

"Of course."

"He even offered to put off the wedding until he gets back on his feet financially."

"Which has been pretty much resolved since that last board meeting."

It was true. "Most of his old customers have returned, and Pel Arens, the father of the kid Derek punched—"

"I remember who he is."

"Pel started an account with Rolf that promises to be even bigger than the old one with the city."

"That's great news. So why aren't you marrying Rolf?"

"He's just looking for a housekeeper—" Julie stuffed already cut celery into a plastic bag "—and a stand-in mother for his children."

"His kids obviously adore you." Clare glanced up from the block of jack cheese she was slicing with a wire cutter. "I gather you feel the same way about them." She regarded Julie under lowered brows. "What's the real problem, honey?"

Julie bit into a carrot stick before bagging the rest of them. "He doesn't love me. He expects me to stay at home, not work full-time. Just like Jerry."

"He's not like Jerry," Clare stated categorically. She'd never thought much of Jerome Benton, though she'd kept her opinion to herself until after the breakup. She folded smoked turkey on the bread. "Do you want to get pregnant?"

Caught completely by surprise, Julie nearly choked before swallowing. "What kind of a question is that?"

Clare regarded her patiently. "An important one. If you were to marry Rolf, would you want to have children of your own?"

"Of course." Julie stopped. "Yes, I would," she said firmly.

"And you'd still want to work full-time. How would you manage? A nanny?"

"No. I want to do that myself."

Clare sliced ripe tomatoes for the sandwiches and slipped them into a separate baggie. "It sounds to me like you're not ready to make a commitment yet." She gave a little hitch to her shoulder. "Well, that's all right. You're still young."

Julie huffed. Why did women always have to choose between being a parent and having a career? It wasn't fair. She stewed, then realized that if her father was here, he'd remind her life isn't always fair. Accept it. "The school board offered me the position of chief administrator for the district. Rolf had to be behind it."

Clare's brow narrowed as she pursed her lips. "That's wonderful. Congratulations." She studied her sister-in-law. "You don't seem very happy about it, though."

Julie pulled another plastic bag out from the box for the lettuce that would also go on the sandwiches later. "It's his way of saying goodbye."

Clare frowned. "That's quite a leap, don't you think?"

"What else can it be?"

Clare waited until Julie looked her way. "It could be his way of saying it's all right for you to work."

ROLF'S WEEK WAS equally chaotic. Following Picard's sudden resignation, the media started questioning Bill Marcus about the school superintendent's "alleged" misuse of his cell phone. They wanted to know why the chairman hadn't questioned the high bills, since the charges had grown for months. Under that kind of scrutiny, Marcus decided to resign from the board. So did Chase Milsap.

Rolf's big break came on Wednesday when the private investigator his lawyer had hired located Sam Dossard. The foreman who'd sabotaged the awning construction at Tillman was back in the bayous of Louisiana, not far from Picard's new post. Rolf's attorney was able to broker a deal whereby Dossard agreed to turn state's evidence in Texas in exchange for immunity from prosecution. Since no personal injuries had resulted from his reckless act, and he appeared to have information essential to a larger corruption and embezzlement case, the immunity was granted.

To Rolf's utter amazement, it wasn't Picard who'd intimidated Dossard into screwing up the work but Bill Marcus. He'd threatened to frame the ex-con for another car theft if he didn't cooperate. Marcus had then sweetened the deal by giving Dossard twenty thousand dollars in cash.

"Where'd he get that kind of money?" Rolf asked Nelson Spooner, his lawyer.

"The D.A. had the same question," Spooner announced. "Turns out Milsap gave it to him."

Rolf scratched his head. "Why were they so hellbent on destroying me? It seems like an awful lot of effort over a few contracts that might have been unethical but were probably not illegal."

"Turns out there was a lot more involved. Picard has been taking kickbacks from both of them and several other merchants in town, as well as pocketing funds intended for the school district. Marcus and Milsap were both afraid that if you delved too deeply, they'd be exposed."

The next day, Spooner approached the mayor on Rolf's behalf. There was no direct evidence that she profited financially from the city's shady contracts, but Marcus and Milsap had contributed heavily to her campaign for the largely ceremonial office of mayor. Weighing the appearance of impropriety on her part along with the district attorney's recommendation that the litigation against Coyote Lumber be dropped for lack of proof of criminal intent, she graciously withdrew the suit.

Rolf's kids were still angry with him since Mrs. Tremain started picking them up in the afternoon instead of Julie. Worst of all, he still didn't know why Julie was so upset with him. He'd gone over in his mind their conversations and his marriage proposal but couldn't figure out what he'd said or done wrong. Every attempt on his part to talk to her about it had failed. Women! They complained that men didn't express their feelings enough, then they clammed up when a man tried to find out theirs.

Maybe if he got her so riled she wouldn't be able to keep it locked up inside her…but she wouldn't even respond to his telephone messages. Perhaps he ought to go over to her apartment and tell her to go to hell and see how she reacted. Except in her current frame of mind, she'd probably slam the door in his face. Damn.

AS THE WEEKEND of the cattle drive approached, Julie found herself almost as jumpy as she imagined the kids would be. She'd be spending two days in the sun and wind, smelling pungent cattle, eating dust and listening to the bleating of fall calves as they trudged to lower ground, where winter grass and milder temperatures would keep them through the erratic weather of the winter months. And she'd pass a night at a campsite with Rolf nearby.

Leah called Thursday evening. "Can I ride to the ranch with you tomorrow night? Dad can take the boys."

Why not? "You're on."

Julie drove to the house Friday evening a full hour before Rolf was due to arrive home from the lumberyard. She kept telling herself she wasn't looking forward to seeing him. It would be unavoidable over the course of the weekend, but with so many people around, keeping their distance shouldn't be difficult.

"I have all my stuff ready," Leah announced. "Clare said to bring a couple of extra pairs of jeans and shirts. She said the trail ride is pretty dirty."

"With a capital *D*," Julie agreed.

Leah bounced onto the front seat of Julie's truck. "Will there be any boys in the ride?"

Julie smothered a smile. "A few. Some of the ranch families have teenage sons and daughters, so you shouldn't have any trouble finding kids to hang with."

"Great." The gleam in Leah's eyes suggested she wasn't interested in the girls. "Hannah at school thinks men in uniform are the handsomest, but I like cowboys even better."

"There is a certain quality about a man on a horse," Julie admitted. Rolf in the saddle. Back straight. Sitting tall. Long legs extended. One hand on the reins, the other on his thigh. Cowboy hat casting the strong lines of his face in mysterious shadow...

"I guess a cavalry soldier would be the ideal," she

mused, but the comment flew right over Leah's head. "So how have things been at school?"

"All right, I guess. The parents of a bunch of the kids are still mad at Dad for blowing the whistle on Picard, like Dad was the one who did something wrong. They keep bringing up the thing at Tillman."

"It's hard to admit you've made a mistake in judgment." Was she talking about Rolf's accusers, Rolf or herself? Clare said she was afraid to make a commitment. Was her sister-in-law right?

"That's stupid," Leah scoffed. "It just makes matters worse." From the mouths of babes...

They arrived at the Number One after sundown. Leah seemed disappointed that the place was so quiet, until the back door opened and a young man approached. "Who's he?" Her mouth was hanging open.

"My nephew, Brian Durgan." He was six feet tall now, with dark hair, a dark complexion and eyes that, even in the waning light, glinted with male self-confidence. He was also nineteen and unlikely to be interested in a twelve-year-old girl. But that didn't keep Leah from being mesmerized by him.

"He's cute."

He came to Julie's door and opened it for her. She made the introductions while he unloaded their things from the back of the vehicle. He barely gave Leah a nod.

Inside, Clare was directing the preparations of the rest of the family. "After supper. I want y'all to lay out your clothes for tomorrow. You can play one game of dominoes, then I want you to settle down for the night. Tomorrow'll be a long day. We get up at 4:00 a.m."

Julie mumbled "Ugh" at the thought of a predawn reveille. Leah chirped, "I'll be ready."

Clare slanted Julie an amused glance that said, *We'll see about that.*

"Your father called," she told the girl. "He's running a bit behind schedule." She turned to Julie. "I told him to go directly to the Home Place. Michael's over there helping your father load the panel truck for tomorrow. Sheila will be driving it. Michael can bring Rolf's boys over here when he's finished."

"What about Rolf?" Julie asked. She'd assumed he'd be spending the night at the Number One with his kids. The bunkhouse could easily accommodate twenty.

"He's staying in the guest house over there with you."

"With me?"

"Not just you." Clare grinned mischievously. "Kerry and Craig will be there, as well as Gideon and Lupe."

"They're back from San Antonio?" A secret part of Julie was disappointed, but she didn't dare show it.

"Got in this afternoon," Clare reported. "Lupe's as big as a house. Her doctor insists she's not carrying twins. I have to wonder, though."

Julie tried to imagine what it would be like to be pregnant, to have a new life growing inside her. To give it birth and nurse it. "I better get over to the Home Place then." She glanced at Leah, who was helping Elva, the family cook, set the table. "Don't let them keep you up too late," she told Clare, who undoubtedly wouldn't go to bed until well after midnight. She'd also be the first one up.

"You get a good night's rest, too."

With Rolf sleeping in the guest house with her? Not likely.

THE FIRST THING Rolf noticed when he pulled into the parking area behind the Home Place was that Julie's truck wasn't there. It could be parked elsewhere, he supposed, but was afraid she'd decided at the last minute not to stay. On the other hand, he hadn't passed her on the ranch road, so maybe she was still at Michael and Clare's with Leah.

The boys charged out of the van as if it were on fire and joined Michael's son, Dave, and his cousin, Miguelito. Within seconds they were talking animatedly about the coming weekend. Michael shook Rolf's hand, then called the boys to climb into his Suburban.

As they were pulling away, Adam and Sheila came to the ranch house door, greeted Rolf affably and welcomed him inside. There he met Julie's elder sister, Kerry, and her husband. Craig Robeson was a big man, six-four and broad-shouldered. Julie's brother, Gideon, who was himself over six feet, seemed dwarfed by him. Gideon's wife, Lupe, dark and Hispanic, was petite compared with the menfolk, except for her enormous belly. She was close to term and was probably miserable, but he saw only the joy of motherhood in her shiny black eyes. He pictured Julie with that maternal glow.

Gideon was about to escort him out to the guest house, when Julie pulled up in her white truck. Rolf's pulse quickened at the sight of her striding toward them in the harsh glare cast by the outdoor floodlights.

"Welcome back, lover." She placed her hands on her brother's shoulders and kissed him on the cheek. Rolf hungered for her touch, but she didn't even acknowledge his presence. "How was San Antonio?"

"Filling." Gideon patted his slim waist and grinned. "Lupe's sister and brother-in-law are very fond of eating."

"Sounds like you had a good time. Hello, Rolf." From the tone of her greeting, he might as well have been the mailman or a distant cousin.

"Hi." Now there was a novel salutation.

After shifting his glance between the two, Gideon relieved his sister of her overnight bag and led them into the guest house. Three two-bedroom suites, each separated by a bath, surrounded a large common room.

The married couples occupied two of the suites. Julie and Rolf shared the third.

"I'll see you both at dinner in a few minutes." Gideon dropped Julie's bag in front of her door and left. Rolf was standing at his, a few feet away.

They entered their rooms, then met in the common bath.

"We'll have to be careful not to lock each other out," she noted.

"I won't lock you out," he promised, his eyes dancing with hers.

Involuntarily, she smiled. "Thanks."

For a moment, he felt hope, but it passed. They went to their respective rooms and unpacked, then met again in the open central room and walked side by side to the ranch house. He wanted to take her hand in his, but out of the corner of his eye he could see she wouldn't be receptive. "Thanks for deciding to come with us."

"I'm glad you and the kids were able to make it."

He held the back door to the Home Place and followed her into the warmth of her family.

After dinner, Rolf gently clasped Julie's elbow and invited her for a walk in the cool night air. She declined, saying they both needed to hit the sack early.

"It ought to be in the same bed," he ventured.

"Rolf, don't," she pleaded.

"I love you, Julie. Isn't that enough?"

She stared at him, agape. He watched her eyes become glassy. Then she brushed past him and ran into her room. The door didn't slam, but the click of the latch sounded like a gunshot in his heart.

THE CATTLE DRIVE was remarkably like what Rolf had envisioned one would be. A huge herd of cattle bumbled across a wide expanse of prairie. Men—and women—on horseback moseyed alongside, keeping strays from wandering too far afield. There were the modern innovations, of course. Jeeps and off-road vehicles doing their part, and instead of a canvas-covered chuck wagon lumbering in their dust, a large van carrying hot and cold food and drink met them at strategic points. It wasn't until the evening that serious eating got under way, though. Then campfires were lit. Guitars, banjos and harmonicas appeared seemingly from nowhere, and melodies that went back to a simpler but more dangerous time were played and sung.

Rolf watched from the back of a hay truck as his children absorbed the pageantry of the scene. He couldn't help but chuckle.

"What's tickling your funny bone?"

He didn't have to turn to recognize the voice. It was so familiar, and it still did strange things to him.

"I was thinking," he reflected quietly, "the kids will probably take the memory of tonight with them through the rest of their lives. They'll tell their great-grandchildren about it, and that generation, as yet unborn, will either think the old ones are loonies or they'll envy their having been part of a golden age."

"A golden age." Didn't that imply contentment? Not a term she'd use to describe the way she felt at the moment. "Maybe in some respects it is. You think this way of life will be gone by then?"

Sadly, he nodded. "It's almost gone now."

"I'm afraid you're right."

He tapped the space on his left. "Join me."

She hesitated but then realized it was foolish pride keeping her from his side. She had, after all, sought him out. She could have stayed away. But last night he'd told her he loved her. Had he meant it? Her eyes had followed him throughout the day. Watched and waited, though she couldn't have said precisely what she expected to see. For him to come galloping up beside her, snatch her out of her saddle and charge off into the sunset? The image was absurd. What would they do on the other side of the hill? Make passionate love in the golden glow of an iridescent sky? Touch, stimulate, fulfill?

"Thanks." She hoisted herself on the cool metal tailgate. "Did you enjoy today?"

"Very much. It was very generous of your family to include us."

"They like kids." She added, "They like you."

"And you, Julie?" he asked into the night, then turned to gaze at her. "Do you like me?"

She kept her eyes trained on the campfire not far away, her nerves set to shimmering by his closeness. "Yes, Rolf. I like you. I respect you. I admire you."

"But you don't love me."

Rather than argue with him, she let silence be her response. The happy song the vaqueros were singing in Spanish had changed to a plaintive ballad in English, a lament to unrequited love.

"Why did you send me the invitation to interview for the chief administrator position?" she asked.

He continued to peer straight ahead. When he spoke, his voice was low and mild. "Because I think you'll do a good job. Because it requires a person with vision, energy and determination. Someone with the strength to put things right. I suspect you'll run into a lot of opposition along the way, but I also have confidence you'll overcome it."

"You make it sound as if I already have the job."

He glanced over, his smile rueful but reassuring. "It's yours if you want it."

She didn't respond immediately. "You said last night you love me."

"I don't understand why that comes as a shock or why you would doubt it." He covered her hand with his. When she didn't flinch, he turned to her. "I do love you, Julie, and I want to marry you."

"But you're offering me a full-time job. What about the family? What about staying home and taking care of them?"

He reached across with his other hand and cupped her chin, compelling her to face him. Her eyes were glassy. "Is that what this is all about?"

"Sheryl left you because you wouldn't let her work—"

"Whoa." He caressed the softness of her cheek. "Stop right there. I don't know where you got such an idea. Whoever told you that was wrong. My wife left me because she'd spent ten years putting her career on hold to raise four kids. When she felt it was time for us to be able to spend time with each other doing adult things—taking cruises, basking in sunny resorts, traveling and exploring, I immersed myself in *my* dream of owning my own business. It absorbed me twelve hours a day, six days a week. On the seventh, I barely had the energy to go to church and mow the lawn."

He peered off into the fire-lit night. Embers rose and died, the burned-out ash disappearing into the darkness.

"Just for a little while, I told her, but a little while was four long years. By then, she'd found someone else to love and share *her* dreams with." He heaved a deep breath and turned to her.

"I can promise you this, Julie. I will never take you for granted. I will never take your love for granted. I'll work every day to earn it, to prove to you that you're the most important person in my life."

Her voice shook when she finally spoke. "Then you wouldn't mind my having a job?"

A smile radiated across his face, brightening his eyes, curling his lips. "Of course not. The kids are old enough to handle living with busy parents. They can learn a lot from two people who work together to meet the challenges and circumstances fate throws at them. In fact, haven't we already proven we can balance our obligations to them and to ourselves over the past month? You've been working full-time, and so have I. We managed a schedule that was compatible for both of us. The kids were never neglected. In fact, they've never been happier.''

He leaned over and kissed her softly on the lips. ''When and if we have more children, priorities won't have changed, only the way we deal with them will. I'll still make every day an opportunity to prove to you that I love you.''

Pulling her with him, he scurried back onto the soft mattress of loose hay left from the bales that had been unloaded for the horses. Together, they lay on their backs, staring up at the night sky, their hands entwined.

''Will you marry me, Julie?'' he asked quietly.

''Yes,'' she murmured, ''I'll marry you.'' Her head rested in the crook of his shoulder. The air was cool, perfumed by the scent of hay. His body was warm. She could feel the steady drum of his heart beneath her hand.

He raised his arm and pointed to the black sky with its tiny pinpoints of light. ''All those stars I used to stare up at when I was a kid are still there. Except for one difference now.''

She lifted her head and gazed at him.

He brushed his fingertips along the silky texture of her cheek. ''I can touch them now.''

If you enjoyed what you just read,
then we've got an offer you can't resist!

Take 2 bestselling love stories FREE!
Plus get a FREE surprise gift!

Clip this page and mail it to Harlequin Reader Service®

IN U.S.A.
3010 Walden Ave.
P.O. Box 1867
Buffalo, N.Y. 14240-1867

IN CANADA
P.O. Box 609
Fort Erie, Ontario
L2A 5X3

YES! Please send me 2 free Harlequin Superromance® novels and my free surprise gift. After receiving them, if I don't wish to receive anymore, I can return the shipping statement marked cancel. If I don't cancel, I will receive 6 brand-new novels every month, before they're available in stores. In the U.S.A., bill me at the bargain price of $4.05 plus 25¢ shipping and handling per book and applicable sales tax, if any*. In Canada, bill me at the bargain price of $4.46 plus 25¢ shipping and handling per book and applicable taxes**. That's the complete price, and a saving of at least 10% off the cover prices—what a great deal! I understand that accepting the 2 free books and gift places me under no obligation ever to buy any books. I can always return a shipment and cancel at any time. Even if I never buy another book from Harlequin, the 2 free books and gift are mine to keep forever.

135 HEN DFNA
336 HEN DFNC

Name _____ (PLEASE PRINT) _____

Address _____ Apt.# _____

City _____ State/Prov. _____ Zip/Postal Code _____

* Terms and prices subject to change without notice. Sales tax applicable in N.Y.
** Canadian residents will be charged applicable provincial taxes and GST.
   All orders subject to approval. Offer limited to one per household and not valid to
   current Harlequin Superromance® subscribers.
   ® is a registered trademark of Harlequin Enterprises Limited.

SUP01   ©1998 Harlequin Enterprises Limited

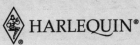

The Shannon Sisters

A Trilogy by C.J. Carmichael
The stories of three sisters from Alberta whose lives and loves are as rocky—and grand—as the mountains they grew up in.

A Second-Chance Proposal
A murder, a bride-to-be left at the altar, a reunion. Is Cathleen Shannon willing to take a second chance on the man involved in these?

A Convenient Proposal
Kelly Shannon feels guilty about what she's done, and Mick Mizzoni feels that he's his brother's keeper—a volatile situation, but maybe one with a convenient way out!

A Lasting Proposal
Maureen Shannon doesn't want risks in her life anymore. Not after everything she's lived through. But Jake Hartman might be proposing a sure thing....

On sale starting February 2002

Available wherever Harlequin books are sold.